Praise for Grace Greene's Books

Love the beach and Coastal Carolina? Consider reading the two series set in Emerald Isle, NC because ~ *It's always a good time for a love story and a trip to the beach!*

The Emerald Isle, NC Stories Series begins with the award-winning debut novel, *Beach Rental*, an RT Book Reviews TOP PICK. Here's what the reviewer wrote:

> "No author can come close to capturing the awe-inspiring essence of the North Carolina coast like Greene. Her debut novel seamlessly combines hope, love and faith, like the female equivalent of Nicholas Sparks. Her writing is meticulous and so finely detailed you'll hear the gulls overhead and the waves crashing onto shore. Grab a hanky, bury your toes in the sand and get ready to be swept away with this unforgettable beach read."

Or visit Emerald Isle, NC in the Barefoot Tides Series that begins with *A Barefoot Tide*, in which a woman from the rural town of Cub Creek, Virginia accepts a temporary job that takes her to the beach—and discovers it may not be so easy to go home again.

Regarding Cub Creek, Virginia—a rural area *in the heart of Virginia, where the forests hide secrets and the creeks run strong and deep*—where Libbie (in *Cub Creek*) goes to hide from a world where she doesn't fit in…and finds her life. Or where Hannah (in *The Memory of Butterflies*) keeps a devastating secret to protect her loved ones. Or where Kara (in *Wildflower Heart*) finds healing from old wounds and heartbreak. Or where Jaynie (in *A Light Last Seen*) finds that you can—and often *should*—go home again.

A Light Last Seen and A Reader's View of Cub Creek

From a reader about Cub Creek and A Light Last Seen: "'In the heart of Virginia, where the forests hide secrets and the creeks run strong and deep,' is a place called Cub Creek. A place that has meadows filled with colorful flowers and butterflies to chase, and dirt roads and Cub Creek to jump over and disappear into the woods. A living and rural place that draws the reader to the setting and the characters who have stories to tell. A place with light and darkness and as unique as the characters who live there. When I opened the beautiful cover of this book, I stepped into the Cub Creek world and met the main character, Jaynie Highsmith. This is her story."— *Reader/Reviewer Bambi Rathman, February 2020*

EMERALD HEART

BOOKS BY GRACE GREENE

Emerald Isle, North Carolina Series
Beach Rental *(Book 1)*
Beach Winds *(Book 2)*
Beach Wedding *(Book 3)*
Beach Walk *(Christmas Novella)*

Barefoot Tides Two-Book Series
A Barefoot Tide *(Book 1)*
A Dancing Tide *(Book 2)*

Emerald Isle, NC Single-Title Novels and Novellas
Beach Heart
Emerald Heart
"Beach Towel" (A Short Story)
Beach Christmas *(Christmas Novella)*
Clair *(Beach Brides Novella Series)*

Cub Creek Novels ~ Series and Single Titles
Cub Creek *(Cub Creek Series, Book 1)*
Leaving Cub Creek *(Cub Creek Series, Book 2)*
The Happiness In Between
The Memory of Butterflies
A Light Last Seen

The Wildflower House Novels
Wildflower Heart *(Book 1)*
Wildflower Hope *(Book 2)*
Wildflower Christmas *(A Wildflower House Novella) (Bk 3)*
Wildflower Wedding *(A Wildflower House Novella) (Bk 4)*

Virginia Country Roads
Kincaid's Hope
A Stranger in Wynnedower

www.GraceGreene.com

EMERALD HEART

BY

GRACE GREENE

KERSEY CREEK BOOKS

Published by Grace Greene and Kersey Creek Books
ISBN-13: 979-8-9862394-9-1 (eBook)
ISBN-13: 979-8-9862394-8-4 (Print)
ISBN-13: 979-8-9862394-7-7 (Large Print)
ISBN-13: 979-8-9862394-6-0 (Hardcover)

Cover design by Grace Greene
Printed in the United States of America

Dedication

Emerald Heart is dedicated to those we've lost, and to those who remain—who must find a new way forward without their loved ones. A special dedication to Robert and Carole who suffered a great loss as this book was being written, and to a dear friend, Michael Norbeck, who left us just as the book was being finished. You are missed.

Acknowledgments

My sincere thanks to everyone who contributed to making *Emerald Heart* the best story it could be. Thank you, Newsome, Pam, and Heather, for introducing me to Emerald Isle Woods Park and also for sharing your knowledge of the area—the park, Bogue Sound, wildlife and so much more. Thank you to the town of Emerald Isle for having such beautiful parks and natural resources for residents and visitors to enjoy. Special thanks to Jessica Fogleman for her editing expertise.

Extra special thanks to my grand dog, Kona, our own Sir Galahad, for allowing me to feature him in this story.

EMERALD HEART

Prologue

I am lost. It is only now, as I wake alone in my bed to face another day, that I realize how long I've been absent from my life—and how much I've missed.

I need a new way forward.

Each morning, when the weather is nice (which is almost every morning), I open the living room windows to welcome in the sweet breeze from the sound. Bogue Sound is the body of water that fills the low bottom between the island of Bogue Banks where Emerald Isle lies, and the North Carolina mainland. Within that body of water, saltwater marshes thrive. The sandbars and grasses make islands that the herons, ibis and egrets visit. The sound also hosts channels that the experienced boatmen and fishermen know how to navigate.

I've been told that if one's boat does get stuck or springs a leak, you can actually cross the sound on foot, essentially walking your way out of trouble. I wouldn't know about that personally. I don't plan to trudge through the muck on the bottom and ravage the oyster beds or risk the rare gator encounter. Nor do I want mullet, flounder or trout bumping into my legs and startling the heck out of me. It's enough for me to know that as the breeze skims the surface of the water and sweeps up the shore, it brings with it a certain energy and unmatched freshness. It fills the rooms of my home with a scent and a feeling that is like nothing humankind can create no matter how sincere the effort.

As I stand here this morning, only a short time past dawn, the breeze sets the soft blue curtains billowing in graceful swoops and swirls. The color echoes the sky above and complements the shifting shades of the dappled water below. These blues are the colors of my daughter Sebrina's eyes and of her favorite twirly dress.

Twirly. That had been Sebrina's word. A giggly word.

Mama, watch me twirl. Watch me spin.

Just thinking the words recalls her laughter to me.

Sebrina left us when she was six, so this memory is old, but I treasure it. Every so often I pull it out of the imaginary box in which I store such irreplaceable tokens of good things long gone—memory tokens I've saved for the days and nights when I need to feel their warmth, the energy of them, and their hugs again. This morning is one of those needy times.

Mornings are always the hardest.

Standing just out of reach of the curtains, I watch

as they curtsy in the breeze, and before me, like a faded version of the child I remember, Sebrina appears from behind the fabric. She spreads her arms wide and moves gracefully in and around the curtains, her laughter as bright and musical as that of the butterfly chimes that hang from the porch roof.

She isn't really here. I know that, of course. This is no more than a memory. But it feels so real. And then I hear Arthur's voice close to my ear. He speaks in a low mock-formal tone, saying, "My fair Mignon . . ." He takes my hand with a whisper-soft touch, inviting me to join them in their dance. For the space of a beat, my heart hurts as if dealt a mortal blow and I hesitate, but then my fingers respond greedily, eagerly seeking his.

I do not find his hand. Instead, my fingers touch Galahad's soft, silky cocoa-colored curls.

He looks up at me—the dog I never wanted, but don't know how I could manage without. His dark brown eyes are sad as if he is experiencing the memories along with me.

My cheek stings and I reach up to find a single, lonely tear.

We lost Sebrina long ago, yes, but my beloved husband, Arthur, is only two years gone. I still hear their voices but fainter now, as if the past itself is weary of waiting for me to catch up with the present and is choosing to move on without me.

You know you're in trouble when even the past is leaving you in the dust.

I am so tired this morning. I do not feel young.

Being fifty seems an odd place in which to find myself—barely out of my forties, but far from my sixties. Being widowed after a long, happy marriage makes it seem even stranger.

Mignon King, the widowed caretaker of a defunct hotel—*that's me*. I am embarrassed that I can't find my way forward. I have experience, resources, friends, but I'm stuck in this mire. I am disappointed in myself, yet unwilling to admit my weakness to anyone who might be able to help me.

This isn't healthy. I try to do one healthy thing every day to break this cycle of grief. At least one. But that's as far as the thought goes for this moment.

Because sometimes I'm not even sure I *want* to be helped.

Chapter One

The Emerald Heart Hotel was Arthur's dream. When we were dating in high school, we'd take his parents' flat-bottom skiff out into Bogue Sound. Arthur knew how the channels ran, and even though they might shift slightly, the main channel—the intracoastal waterway—didn't change much and dredging kept it open. When the old hotel came into view, he'd stop the motor and allow the skiff to drift with only the slow current moving us forward. The current was usually easy, unless you continued farther west, closer to Bogue Inlet. Rivers emptied from the landward side into the sound, but from the west, via the inlet, the ocean controlled the tides. When the tide was going out, the current picked up and could become dangerous for the unwary.

While the hotel was in view, Arthur was mostly silent, yet there was a certain light in his eyes, aligned with something akin to sorrow, especially over time as the old place grew shabby. His fascination mystified me. All I saw was an old house with a blocky two-story hotel awkwardly attached to its side. A broad swath of grass was in the foreground, the lawn broken only by the private road that delivered guests to the covered lobby entrance. The road couldn't be seen from the water, only a fringe of grass along the cliff's edge, but the building was flanked on the sides and from behind by dense woodland that framed the scene above. Below that, the rough cliff, covered in all sorts of wild, natural greenery, dropped down to a weird boxed-in sandy area that aligned with a dock and the tall marsh grasses. Arthur and I had laughingly called the sandy area the sandbox.

Arthur obviously saw more than I did in that scene on the promontory above. *Promontory* was Arthur's rather grand word for the cliff, and it did have a certain ring. But *what* did he see? I didn't know. Perhaps nothing more than mystery or unused potential.

Once he'd said to me, "They can't keep it up anymore." The words weren't spoken as if he expected a response, so I let them pass unanswered. I couldn't have cared less about the place. Arthur—as I would come to learn—was quite different from me in that respect. If he cared about something, he cared a lot.

At that time the hotel was still operational but had certainly seen better days. The owners were elderly. They occupied the residence up there. Occasionally we'd see them strolling through town or at the beach. Arthur had pointed the couple out to me when our path crossed theirs. We were in our teens back then and it was hard to imagine us ever getting that old, to believe that one day our youth, our energy, would bow to time. Yet, watching them walk arm in arm along Emerald Isle's bike path. . . I experienced a twist of envy, unexpected and fleeting.

Arthur and I married after college but found job opportunities elsewhere, and we didn't return to our hometown until three years later when Arthur's dad had a heart attack. He recovered well, but while we were visiting, Arthur and I took that boat ride again, and that outing took us on a path I'd never envisioned—not even once—since I'd first met Arthur in our freshman year in high school. As the time approached for us to end our visit, next thing I knew Arthur had finagled me into driving with him up that narrow private road through the woods to the hilltop where the Emerald Heart Hotel overlooked the sound and had looked down at us each time we'd boated past.

If hotels could think (and I'm not saying they can), this hotel surely had had no idea that one day Arthur and I would be married and that my husband of three years would be bringing me here in person to introduce me to the place up close and personal, as effusive as a matchmaker full of heart and hope—or as my mama would've said, *as charming as a con man trying to unload a lemon of a car onto an unsuspecting teenager.*

The former owners had moved out. One was deceased and the other had gone to live with family.

Arthur took my hand, saying, "Don't say no yet. You haven't seen it all."

"I've seen enough. Really." I smacked at a gnat that landed on my arm to dine.

"Please, Mignon."

I allowed him to walk me around the building to the back. *That* view snared me, and I almost said yes before my innate practicality shut the impulse down hard. Still . . .

It was a garden. A coastal garden with a grove of

live oaks. Beneath their arching and winding arms, the white, powdery earth was cool and silky-smooth. Huge, mature rhododendrons grew in a half arc ringing the oak grove. Beyond those stood the tall trees like a greenscape patchwork; the bark of their trunks varied by species, as did their leaves. This garden area was only one small part of an amazing forest that did, in fact, fill the many acres of this property. Best of all, capping off this natural beauty was reflection upon reflection of light and shadow spanning the back of the two-story hotel wing because the exterior wall was a massive wall of glass.

I *needed*, to see this view from the inside out.

Arthur whispered, "The rooms open onto a wide hallway with library nooks and sitting areas and, of course, garden views that rival the views of the water from the front." He squeezed my hand. "When Dominick gets here with the key, you'll see for yourself."

Our friend Dominick arrived on the scene, his real estate license still fresh from the printer, and full of reasons for why this was a great idea, and then Arthur's parents showed up looking excited, and I sensed a setup.

I said, "Oh, Arthur. You've pulled out all the stops to persuade me, haven't you?"

His face turned a tad pink. He shrugged. "It's meant for us, don't you see?"

"Do I see your vision for this place? No. Most certainly, I do not. What I see is that we aren't hotel managers. We know nothing about this kind of business."

"We both majored in business."

"*Not* the hospitality business."

"Look, there's a house for us to live in. We need that, right? And the size of the hotel? It's perfect. It's really no more than a large bed-and-breakfast, except the rooms have kitchenettes so we won't be serving meals."

I shook my head. Before I could say another word, he jumped in again.

"Dad wants to help fund this. I've got that severance from the layoff. We can do this, Mignon. We can. Won't it be fun to be back home again with our friends and our families?"

"What about your mom and your sister?"

"Mom wants this too." He grinned. "She and Dad are hoping for grandkids, and nearby, you know? As for Jeanette, she doesn't care. She's busy getting her master's degree and is talking marriage with the newest guy she's dating."

"Seriously?"

"When she left here after high school, I don't think she intended to return for more than a visit. Ever." He grinned. "When I told her what I was hoping to do here, she said her only request was that we give her special rates when she wants a getaway."

I sighed. The beach, the Outer Banks, the Crystal Coast—it was a beautiful place to live and to visit, but I'd wanted us to have these early years of our marriage away—away from here, away from family—only the two of us, together and depending on each other.

"Okay, I'll take a look at the inside, but I simply don't get this, Arthur."

"Trust me, Mignon."

We all toured the place together. The residence was sad and small. The lobby was huge. There were ten guest rooms—small suites, really—five up and five down, all with balconies on the sound side. And yes, the views were outstanding.

My husband's face positively glowed.

Being laid off from his first job had been a blow to Arthur. It had seemed to truly dent his ego, and so it had hurt me, too. I wanted to heal that hurt for both of us, and maybe because we were barely past our honeymoon phase, and also because I didn't yet realize I was pregnant, I agreed, thinking it was better to let him get this place, this crazy idea, out of his system so we could go back to our normal, pleasant life.

Our golden-haired daughter Sebrina was born soon after we moved in. She had her father's hair color and his beautiful blue eyes. I loved that because my own hair and eyes were so dark. I envied their bright curls.

While I had my hands full in the residence, Arthur went about *saving* the hotel, as he said. Because it was *special*, he'd said. And it was, but only because my husband Arthur King, a dreamer of dreams, a man who was also a doer, threw himself wholeheartedly into making those dreams come true. *He* made it special. I was his willing helper for more than twenty years, even during the grieving years after we lost our daughter.

Then he was gone too.

Without Arthur, this building was nothing more than an aging wood, concrete, and plaster structure with an exterior the color of old cream, filled with sadly dated, perhaps eccentric, probably corny, decor. Two years ago, I'd locked the door that separated the house from the lobby and the wing of guest rooms. I'd retreated to the house side to grieve and only visited the hotel wing every week or so to check for leaks in the ceiling and to make sure the plumbing and such still worked. Each room was kept locked. If someone broke in, locks would slow them down, and hopefully the alarm system would alert me before too much damage was done.

This morning, as I stood in the living room only a short distance from the window, the hem of the curtain finally reached me and brushed my face—and my phone rang.

I glanced down at the screen. It was early for a call, even from Dominick.

He meant well, but I let it go unanswered. I wasn't in the mood. In fact, I wasn't even fully here, torn as I was between the past and the present.

During that first year after losing Arthur, he'd still seemed nearby. Whether I was driving, walking, or doing all the ordinary things . . . he was there, near but just out of sight. In the night, I was aware of the weight of his body in the bed only inches from mine, or of him being in the next room ready to walk through the doorway at any moment. Sometimes the sensations were so strong that I held my breath, half expecting him to do exactly that.

Not surprisingly, as the sense of his presence had weakened over time and then had grown elusive, that my memories had become even *more* precious.

I cast one last glance across the way—at the water, the dock, the mainland on the far side of the sound—the entirety of my world for the past twenty-some years.

Once upon a time, I was a busy woman with a full life. No longer. Now I was caught in a bubble of waiting.

It was a strange realization that the memories I'd found so much solace in, that seemed comforting when they wrapped their arms around me—were empty and cold when real problems arrived and decisions needed to be made.

Arthur would never have wanted this nothing kind of existence for me.

I should sell Emerald Heart. Take the money and run—run anywhere and do anything that wasn't this non-life where my preferred, most constant companions were the memories of those who were no longer with me.

Yesterday evening I'd heard noises outside. They'd rattled my nerves.

Galahad was only mildly interested, perhaps keying in more on my stress than anything external. When you live in an old house on a cliff overlooking a body of water and subject to winds and other forces of nature, noises are to be expected. But then something triggered a motion detector light in the front of the house—perhaps no more than a blowing branch—and my nerves ticked up another notch. I'd told myself that one of the local semi-feral cats was on its nightly prowl or the opossums were looking for a late meal. Perhaps even a coyote had wandered by. I'd checked the security cameras and had seen nothing out of the ordinary. Still, it was hard to relax because after Arthur died strangers *had* shown up asking if I was selling the property. I'd notified the police, and per their advice, I put up No Trespassing signs and began keeping the big gate on the private road locked 24-7.

It had been a while since anyone had bothered me, but it was an ever-present possibility, so that was small comfort.

When viewed from the water, the hotel windows did look empty—vacant, yes, but not derelict. The huge trees flanking the sides and back of the building overshadowed it, contributing to the eerie feel. When the winds kicked up and the boughs brushed against each other, the forest seemed to be whispering secrets that felt directed at this place and me.

Last night, the noises had thrown me back into the days when my grief had been sharpest. I'd gone from window to window, worried, and distressing Galahad by my actions. When I looked out those windows, shadows were moving in the dark, but it was easy to see shadows on a breezy, moonlit night. That disturbance probably accounted for the disruption of my sleep and of Arthur and Sebrina being very much on my mind this morning.

A stronger gust blew the curtain aside, catching it with such *oomph* that the fabric flew up and wrapped itself around the drapery rod. In that instant, a man appeared at the cliff's edge as if out of nowhere—not via magic, no, but because he'd reached the top of the cliff stairs and thus had come suddenly into view.

He was a surprising sight on a sad morning. I stood there, amazed.

The man was wet. His hair was short, but sunlight sparkled in the droplets still captured there. His swim trunks were drenched. He looked fit. Age? I'd guess about mine. Maybe closer to sixty, but he was in good shape—better than me. Then again, I didn't swim in large bodies of water.

Before I could decide whether to go to the door or not, the man turned and ran off toward the private road. Good thing he was wearing water shoes fit for running.

I wasn't used to strangers coming up the steps unless they'd docked a boat, float, or kayak below—and that hadn't happened in a long time. For liability reasons, I kept the dock and cliff stairs in good repair, but there were No Trespassing signs down there, pointed directly at the sound.

It wasn't possible to run any real distance along the water here due to the realities of geography and private property. A runner or walker would pretty much be trespassing all along the way, so if someone did happen to wander past, I tended to turn a blind eye, preferring to accommodate neighbors or visitors so long as they didn't take advantage too often.

By now, I was standing out front and staring down the private road winding away into the woods and wondering about the man. He hadn't done any harm. In fact, his unexpected arrival kind of amused me—unless he was going to make these surprise appearances a regular occurrence. If so, we might have to have a conversation.

Galahad followed me outside. The morning sun lit up his glossy brown curls. His tail wagged briskly as he gave the area, his territory, a quick scan and then went about his business of sniffing and marking bushes and other such doggy duties while I crossed the road for a better view of the dock and the water.

There was no boat of any kind at the dock. It was a small dock. The original one was in poor shape by the time Arthur died. We'd stopped hosting guests long before that. I'd had the big dock pulled down and this small one built to replace it. Less inviting, yes. The kayaks and racks had also been hauled away. Emerald Heart had no need of them now. But Arthur's bench? I'd had that refinished and as long as it was in its place on the dock, it felt right to me.

The stranger had run toward the paved private road. Up here at the hotel, that road looped in front of the building under the canopied entrance, passed through the guest parking, and then wound down through the forest to the private gate—a big metal gate with the hotel name on it—until it passed Carolyn's house, which fronted on Coast Guard Road.

Public access ended at my property line which was beyond the gate and closer to the main road, but the gate was the official, unmistakable notice of private ownership. The sign on it, "The Emerald Heart Hotel", had been in place for years as a welcome to guests. The No Trespassing signs had been added much later. We didn't used to keep the gate locked all the time, but now it was just me, so I did. But the reality was that the gate only blocked vehicles. Pedestrians could easily step off the road and go around the large stone columns that supported the gate.

Did the stranger continue down the private road or veer off to follow the coastal paths through the forest? The main trail eventually came out at the newish subdivision of rather grand homes to our west.

A lot had changed since Arthur and I had moved here. Our acreage provided a substantial buffer from the changes. At the same time, it was that same large acreage that made it so desirable to those who thought I should sell. They all had ideas of how best to maximize the value of the property.

The Emerald Heart Hotel had been my husband's dream, and I'd been happy to join him in it. His dream had lasted twenty years. Good years. Years when the most frequent and favorite compliment from guests had been that the Emerald Heart had the conveniences of a modern hotel with the cozy charm of a family-run bed-and-breakfast. Those years and compliments had ended as his condition had worsened and we'd stopped accepting reservations and let our few employees go.

After his death, I told everyone there would be a short delay—a time of recovery for me before I reopened the business. But in the end, I couldn't. Of the two of us, Arthur was the dreamer and doer. I was the helper and facilitator. Without him . . . I sighed. I'd lost my direction and motivation.

A man swimming and running across my property, which happened to be in a beach community? So long as he kept moving, he was the least of my problems.

Mired in the past, I was running too—out of time and money. As Arthur's illness had progressed and we'd closed the hotel, we'd lived off our savings and retirement monies. And that hadn't changed since I'd been on my own. I must either reopen the hotel or let it go and take my life in a different direction.

About to return to my house, I noticed a crumpled paper caught in the shrubbery by the porch. A candy wrapper.

How on earth? It could hardly have gotten up here on its own. I remembered the noises and the sense of shadows moving last night. Someone roaming the property…and tossing the wrapper? The swimmer? Not likely, as far as the swimmer went. But trespassers in general? Always a possibility.

Chapter Two

Back in the house, I paced, unsettled. I fidgeted with the curtains, found a speck of dust on a table and a book I'd left out of place. Galahad was no better. Even though we'd just come back inside, he was already asking to go out again.

What a strange morning it had been. Not the curtains or remembering Sebrina and Arthur—that wasn't unusual. But the interruption of a mostly naked stranger appearing in an unexpected way, still dripping water and making himself quite at home in using my property? That was . . . yes, a different kind of start to my day.

Oddly, being interrupted and distracted seemed like it might almost qualify as the one healthy thing, daily, that I'd promised myself. Even if I hadn't initiated it. I had, at least, given in to an amusing distraction and curiosity for a few minutes. Maybe I owed the stranger a thank-you. One I'd never deliver, of course.

Galahad whined at the door.

He wanted out. *I* should want out.

Out shopping, out to dinner. I only went off the property when it was necessary, and it had been too long since my last errand run. I'd lost the knack of being easy with others, even with longtime friends. Having Galahad for companionship helped, but it wasn't the same.

Out.

Yes, I thought. That would be a good, healthy choice. A self-directed step forward. I could run errands in town that I'd put off and be around other people. Show people that I was not a hermit or in hiding—as many of them speculated or gossiped.

I called Dominick. "Sorry I missed your call earlier. Want to meet for lunch?"

After a brief pause, he asked, "Are you okay?"

He sounded surprised—which annoyed me.

"I'm fine."

"Sorry. It's just that I can't remember the last time you asked me to take you out."

I agreed. "Well, when it comes to that, I can't recall *ever* asking you to ask me out."

He cleared his throat, then said, "Let's start again." After a short pause, he spoke in a slightly formal yet more welcoming tone. "It's been ages since I've had the pleasure of your company. I'm delighted to hear your voice, Mignon. I would be even more delighted to meet you for lunch."

A soft laugh slipped from me, and my tone shifted to something softer. "I'm in the mood to get out and about, that's all. Are you free today?"

There was a moment of near silence, of clicking noises in the background. Perhaps a keyboard? Likely, Dominick was checking his schedule.

I imagined him, in that pause, looking at a clock or scanning an appointment book. I envisioned his thick dark hair and warm brown eyes. Kindness shone in them, as it always did, but also shrewdness when it came to business. I needed both.

He said, "It's your lucky day. I just had an appointment cancel. I'm all yours until about three o'clock."

"An *early* lunch, if you don't mind? Hopefully, we'll beat the crowd."

"No problem. The Beach Diner?" he suggested.

"That will be perfect. I haven't been there in . . .well, *ages*." I added the last in a joking tone.

We arranged our meeting time. Dominick said he'd get there ahead of me and save a table. I thanked him.

Dominick had been Arthur's friend first, and after Arthur had brought me into his circle of friends, he'd become mine. Dominick had said more than once that he'd known that very day—the day that Arthur and I had met—that we would marry. Dominick had been Arthur's best man. He'd offered unwavering support to both of us after we lost Sebrina.

Since Arthur's death, Dominick had encouraged me to get back into the world, even after most of our other friends had given up on me.

I trusted Dominick above anyone else in my life.

Since I was going to be seen in public with Dominick—someone known by most of the locals—I needed to ditch the old T-shirt and baggy shorts (everything was baggy on me now) for something a notch higher on the casual scale. I settled on a jeans skirt that I could wear with a belt, and then a blousy, cotton top. As for my hair—long, straight and untrimmed—I'd pin it up with a clip and that would have to do.

ößO

Dominick was seated at the back corner table next to the window. There was no true privacy in the Beach Diner, especially at mealtimes, and that table was about as close as one could get to achieving it. Though we were indeed ahead of the crowd, there were already diners here and it wouldn't be long before the seats filled up.

Paula, the owner, had chosen to follow tourist expectations of what a diner at the beach should look like and had decorated the walls with fishing nets, wood cuttings of shells and sea life, and even old building and traffic signs from the early days of Emerald Isle. Those signs were my favorite. Funny how the ambience looked touristy on the surface but also authentic. Arthur and I had eaten here many times, and it actually felt like home. Seeing it again after my general avoidance of coming into town made me regret staying away.

Several customers looked up when I walked in, but they were strangers and their interest seemed no more than a reflexive action. Behind the counter, an older waitress saw me and gave a second look before raising her hand in a half wave. I nodded, searching my brain for her name. Jane? Jen, maybe. Something like that. By then, Dominick was standing, gesturing for me to join him. He even came around and pulled the chair out for me. In a diner. But that was Dominick. He was wearing his usual slacks and a business shirt sans tie.

It was wonderful to see his friendly face. I offered a hug, which he received and returned.

He said, "I'm glad you called. We were overdue for a visit. You've turned into a hermit, Mignon."

"Not likely," I said. "But you do have a point, so I won't argue about it."

Sheila showed up beside the table with menus and utensils. "What would you like to drink?"

We both asked for iced tea. She nodded and said, "I'll be right back."

His dark hair and warm brown eyes seemed kindness personified, but he was also a businessman and a successful real estate agent. He'd have good information and advice, which I hoped I was finally ready to hear without blowing up or falling apart. With a bit of caution, I reminded myself that he also had a financial interest in my situation.

But I had to trust someone, and since I trusted Dominick, I let my defenses down.

"I'm too isolated. What you said is true."

"So are you thinking about . . ." His voice trailed off on the last word such that it was more imagined than spoken.

I appreciated his discretion. "About that . . ." I shrugged. "Maybe. Lots of thinking to do. Sharing lunch with an old friend seemed like a wonderful idea." I smiled. "And the fact of his expertise in . . . *his field* . . . is a plus."

Dominick grimaced slightly and glanced out the window before returning his gaze to me. He looked hesitant, even troubled.

"Is something wrong?" I asked.

"Not wrong, and I don't want to keep asking you this, but have you come closer to a decision?" He shrugged. "I don't want you to doubt my motives, but." He stopped there.

"Just say it, Dominick."

"Have you had uninvited visitors recently?"

"Do you mean people interested in the . . . you know?" I spoke barely above a whisper. "Why do you ask?"

He shook his head, looking irritated. He was probably as annoyed as I was with trying to communicate in cryptic tones and broken sentences. Finally, he said, "I'm getting queries again."

My back stiffened. "What did you tell them?"

"That you aren't planning any changes at this time."

I nodded.

He rested his forearms on the table and leaned toward me. "You *will* let me know, won't you, when you decide? Even if you want another agent to represent you." He shrugged, and his hands clenched, then released. "That's your right. No hard feelings or anything, but I'd like to hear it from you first."

I shook my head. "I don't want to work with another agent. Why would I when you're the best? You're also my friend. I trust you, Dominick. You'll be my first call, I promise." I thought of the noises yesterday evening. I asked, "If you've been getting inquiries again . . . then that's why you asked about the uninvited visitors? Do you think it will happen like before?"

"Possibly. Yes, let's say it's likely. The market's been hot, and developers are wanting acreage. Waterfront acreage? Highly desirable." He nodded. "That land where Emerald Heart sits on the cliff is prime for the right project. The market's hot now, but for how long?"

Sheila came for our orders. She took them and left.

Dominick leaned closer and lowered his voice to a whisper. "Selling—"

I grabbed his hand to stop him. "Not here. Let's eat and we'll take a walk." I whispered, "Away from all this." I waved my hand to indicate our fellow diners. "This cryptic chat nonsense is driving me crazy, necessary or not."

"We could go back to my office."

I groaned. "We *could,* but people would notice me *there* for sure. They'll start gossiping. In fact, us meeting here was probably a mistake."

"No, you're wrong about that. Staying secluded up at the hotel is what's causing the gossip. Live your life. No one will think that odd."

I nodded. "Eat, and then we'll take a walk down to the beach?"

He surprised me by deftly switching his hand from below mine to clasping it, and he gave my hand a gentle squeeze. "Whatever works best for you." He nodded,

"It's good to see you, Mignon."

He said more, but he'd turned his face away just as someone behind the counter dropped a dish and the word was lost in the clatter.

"Pardon?"

"What?"

"I missed that last bit?"

"Nothing important, I'm sure," he said, implying that he didn't recall.

I let it go and sat back as Sheila brought our food to the table, but I couldn't help watching his face, looking away before he caught me, because I was pretty sure he'd said, "Always."

ⵣ

Food eaten, check paid, Dominick held the door for me to exit ahead of him. We walked down the block, passing the shops and dancing around tourists who had vacation and distraction on their minds. No one was paying attention to us. Near the end of the block and the Bogue Inlet Fishing Pier, we took the steps down to the beach area.

Dominick tightened his arm around mine and said, "Selling . . . or even thinking about selling doesn't diminish how much you love the place, how much your memories mean to you—and will continue to mean into the future. But as much as you love the property, the part that truly matters to you *are* the memories. Am I right? I don't want to sound corny or bossy, but you'll take those memories with you no matter where you go."

"Of course."

He sighed.

We kicked off our shoes where the sand began and left them there. Dominick knelt to roll up the hems of his slacks. We walked barefoot to where the tide had rolled in and out again and the sand was firmer.

We felt the contrast between our clothing and the swimsuits and shorts around us. *So much for blending in. Oh well.* These folks were all strangers to me anyway and much more interested in the sand and sun and each other than in eavesdropping on my business.

"It's not as simple as memories." I stopped short. I couldn't tell him about the hold the memories had on me . . . the almost physical hold. That I was trapped. It was too pathetic to speak it aloud—like being caught in an embarrassing addiction. Instead, I did a quick pivot and shift. "Memories are one thing, but you know what a collector Arthur was."

He shrugged. "Yes, he was a collector. Keep what you want of his collection and sell the rest. Give away what doesn't sell. I can help you with that." He grinned. "I know people."

"I'm sure." I shook my head. His attitude bothered me. "You say that like . . . as if it's easy to . . ."

"It isn't always easy, true, but it's easier than you think once you get started. And it's necessary."

I went silent. He didn't understand. He'd never experienced loss as I had.

A rogue wavelet rushed ahead of the incoming tide and wet my toes. I yelped and stepped back just as two seagulls squawked loudly overhead. I looked up to watch them in flight, catching the wind with their wings and hunting for a meal. As they glided, I was stalling, seeking something light and trite to say that would end this conversation.

After a long quiet minute, Dominick said, "Maybe you're right. Maybe I don't have the full picture. I haven't been out to the Heart in a long time. Why don't I come by tomorrow? Probably late morning, if that works?" He tightened his arm again against my reflex movement. "Let me get a look at the property in case you decide to test the market. I'll get a better idea, an appreciation of what you're dealing with. As a matter of fact, I'd love to see Arthur's collection again."

"Okay. Sure. It's a date." I said it lightly, wanting to reset the mood.

Dominick said, "Regardless, Mignon, whatever you decide, I'm with you just as Arthur would be. Your friends want you to be happy, and no one wants that more than me."

I could've disagreed. I knew he cared, but in actual fact I cared more than anyone because I *desperately* wanted to be happy, to live my days fully, to look forward to new adventures and to laughter. I had to find a way past my fears, past the need to find comfort and safety in a world that no longer existed—to stop holding it close, keeping a death grip of sorts on the past.

But there were also practical issues that would

require big decisions that I didn't feel able to tackle. For instance, Arthur's mania, his gentle, sometimes expensive mania for all things Arthurian, and his collectables and décor—sword and grail and magic and whatever else his enthusiasm decided to include—graced the hotel wing. It had been part of Arthur and his persona.

At least one good, healthy thing a day, I reminded myself. *Be nice to a friend who means well.* As we walked back to the steps, I retook Dominick's arm and said, "Arthur and Galahad always enjoyed beach walks."

Dominick picked up the change of topic and ran with it. "It's a gorgeous day, Mignon. Take Galahad out to the bike path and enjoy a nice long walk out to The Point."

I drew in a sharp breath and then tried to cover my dismay. "You know how much Arthur loved that walk. He loved The Point. He'd stand there when the celestial cycles—as he called them—were right. He'd hold out his arms as the sun descended over Bear Island, while over his right hand, at about the same time, the moon would ascend on his left."

"I remember," Dominick said. My arm was still tucked into his and he gave it a quick squeeze. "It's okay, Meg. You're going to be fine. You're ready to step out."

Easy for him to say.

Chapter Three

Dominick walked me to the parking lot and to my car. After a thank-you hug for his time and his help, I headed back over to Coast Guard Road, turned onto Emerald Heart Drive, then drove past my neighbor Carolyn's house. Just past her place a road branched off to the right that went through the woods to the Holmans' house. But beyond that turnoff, straight ahead, was The Emerald Heart Hotel gate. The letters on the sign were faded and the gate was almost always kept locked in recent years, but anyone could walk around the stone pillars that supported the gate. It stopped vehicles, but not foot traffic.

I went through the usual unlock/lock/relock routine at the gate. After a short drive through the forest, I reached the hotel itself, passing the guest parking and lobby entrance and going to the far end to the private parking next to the residence.

At home, I found an envelope wedged into the tiny gap between my front door and the door frame. A note card type of envelope. I recognized Carolyn's writing. She had a key to the gate, and even to my house, but she'd probably walked through the woods to deliver this. Those of us who lived along this stretch of coast, with the trees and swamps thick around and between us, knew the paths well. In fact, Carolyn had had charge of her grandson back before Arthur got so sick, and more often than not, the boy, Nathan, had hung around Emerald Heart with us, or with Arthur, going fishing or kayaking, playing disc golf, and even earning a few dollars here and there helping me clean the garden and so on. That ended, but we were happy for him because his parents had reunited, and he moved back with them. So things did change, right? Sometimes for excellent reasons.

Carolyn was artistic. She handcrafted creative note cards and greeting cards that were like miniature works of art. Plus, she made the most amazing chocolate walnut candies I'd ever tasted. Delightful skills, yes, but her greatest gift was her kindness. Her children had grown up and left home except for those visits from her grandson, but she stayed busy with church, with projects, and sometimes I felt like I was one of those projects.

I carried the note inside with me. She was probably hoping to entice me to meet up with her book club friends again, or maybe this time she was planning a fundraiser or some such. I'd probably decline, and she'd be sweet about it, and I suppose that's why my defenses were down when I heard the doorbell ring. Still thinking of Carolyn, I hurried to the door with a smile on my face as I opened it wide.

And there she stood. But it wasn't Carolyn.

My smile died. I shut the door in my visitor's face and then collapsed back against the beveled wood.

Jeanette. After so long . . .

A strange day? No, this day had just morphed from

strange to unimaginable.

I pushed away from the door, vaguely noting that Galahad was crouched beside me, whining in a low tone. Worried again? I must be sending out weird vibes. After a deep, calming breath, I went to the kitchen and began preparing my tea, pretending that the interruption was not important, that it did not require a response from me. I would ignore Jeanette and she would go away.

Jeanette was good at leaving and shutting people out of her life. Even people who'd supposedly been important to her before they'd *stopped* being important.

Humph, I grunted, and dropped the used tea bags into the trash can.

Galahad was there beside me, giving me the *pul-lease* look, hoping for a treat. Not resisting, I took one from the treat bag and tossed it to him. He caught it midair, easily. He'd been Arthur's dog, attached to him from puppyhood onward. After Arthur's death, Galahad had been bereft and had transferred a slightly less adoring attachment to me.

I looked up and through the kitchen window and saw Jeanette in the garden.

The gardens had been beautiful before benign neglect had set in and nature had taken them over. I hadn't deliberately walked away. Or maybe I had.

The trees and bushes were still beautiful in their way. Just a bit more ragged and wilder now. I paid a local man to keep the grass mowed around the building, but I told him to leave the garden alone.

Funny how time passed. One day, you had a well-groomed landscape and a well-tended garden, and then life happened, and next thing you knew—*poof*—it had devolved into a messy place that begged for a rake and a weed puller.

And in the midst of my ruined garden sat my former sister-in-law on my favorite bench. The thick twisting trunk and branches of the live oaks framed her. She sat with her hands clasped on her lap, her legs crossed at the ankles.

She looked well enough. Only two years older than me, she was slim, and her brown hair was chin-length and held back on one side with a shiny hair clasp, leaving the other to fall forward, half shielding her face. She looked very different from Arthur. No family resemblance in the surface features, but the cadence of her voice and her facial expressions had so often mirrored his that their kinship was unmistakable. Frankly, I didn't want to be reminded of him by any meaningless gestures or expressions she might thoughtlessly throw my way.

I stared. Why was she here? Why now? I didn't care, and yet my increased heart rate said otherwise. Or was that the old anger? Maybe old anger never died, but just got quiet as it curled up and napped in a forgotten corner of one's brain until something shook it awake and it began to breathe and stretch again.

Willing myself to stay calm, I sipped my tea.

Galahad whined again.

He'd never been quite the same since Arthur died. He was more attuned to my moods and feelings since then. I tried to be mindful of it and not let my moods get the better of us.

I carried my cup of tea into the living room, sat by the window and my plants, and turned the TV on to fill the screen and my view with something mindless. My goal was to cocoon myself in mindlessness.

Galahad settled near the footstool where I propped up my feet.

Despite my efforts, it was impossible to keep Jeanette out of my brain.

Their differences notwithstanding, I'd expected to see Jeanette at Arthur's funeral. I'd worried about my temper and how I'd respond to her if she did come, but I never found out because she hadn't. It was beyond my understanding that someone could hold a grudge or nurse anger against a sibling even through losing them. As the weeks passed after the funeral, I half-expected to hear from her, or to see her on my doorstep, breathlessly explaining that she'd only just heard and how sorry she was, and so on and so on. With each passing day, my need to tell her how awful and selfish she was had hardened. I vowed that if she ever did show up, I would have my say and then forbid her to come anywhere near me or my home again.

I had stuff to get off my chest. Off my heart. But I never had a chance to vent it. I had an opportunity now. If she rang that doorbell again, she might just hear all the crap I'd stored up through the years, both before and after Arthur's passing.

Galahad stretched his neck to rest his muzzle on

top of my thigh, offering comfort. I pulled the throw pillow to my stomach. I held it close and hugged it.

This was a small living room. Cozy, Arthur and I had called it. The kitchen was through the doorway. Our bedroom was down the hall and we'd used the smaller room next to it as an office after Sebrina was gone. At the end of the hall, a door opened into the hotel lobby. Across the lobby was the wide hallway to the first-floor guest rooms. A staircase led from the lobby up to the second floor. An elevator was adjacent to the stairs.

Now it was like a mausoleum over on the far side of the door. Even though I kept an eye on it, the absence of life there was notable. Even the oxygen seemed thin. I never allowed Galahad to go into the hotel side with me because he . . . he sought Arthur. Relentlessly. Always expecting Arthur to come home.

Arthur wouldn't. And it broke my heart—all over again each time that truth slammed into me.

Arthur wouldn't come home, but . . ." I forced another deep breath into my lungs.

No, Arthur couldn't, but Jeanette had.

Chapter Four

Arthur had always been even-tempered and slow to judge, whereas Jeanette was impulsive and quick-tempered. Her divorce had changed her, but even before that she'd always acted with purpose, usually driven and self-focused, so unless she'd had a drastic change of personality, she wouldn't leave here until she'd accomplished whatever she'd come for.

The last words she'd spoken to me were said soon after their mother's funeral, at the gathering after. Her anger was still so strong, fresh from the latest argument with Arthur. She'd paused next to me, leaning toward me for privacy because there'd been many people around. I'd leaned toward her too, expecting to hear something conciliatory or reassuring, perhaps acknowledging that everyone was extra emotional right now and we could work out any issues together as a family. After all, this wasn't the first time she and her brother had had differences. But when she spoke, she said softly, "Tell your husband not to speak to me again." And then she walked away as if her words had been no more than a *"Have a lovely day"* remark. Her actions had stunned me. It had hurt me, and not just for Arthur's sake.

And yet, even then, I'd expected a coming together again—an opportunity to reconcile after the heightened emotion had subsided.

But no, it was not to be. Not then, and now it was too late.

This time, Jeanette skipped the doorbell and knocked. Then she knocked again, more loudly.

Squaring my shoulders, I went to the door. It was time to put an end to this unwelcome intrusion.

Galahad had been sleeping on his big pillow on the floor over by my chair. He glanced up at me, apprehension in his big eyes.

"Stay." I tried to sound firm, but inside I felt shaky.

I opened the door but didn't speak.

Jeanette met my eyes and pressed her lips together, as if unsure where to start. She was right to be cautious. What might her words touch off? Even I was wary of my temper these days.

But coming here? That had been her choice. As *not* coming had also been her choice. And now it was much too . . .

"You're late," I said. "Too late."

She nodded. "There were reasons. We had disagreements, of course, especially after what happened with Mom and—"

Interrupting her, I said, "Disagreements, you say? I don't care. Over your mother? No, it was a nothing thing—an argument that came out of worry and grief like a stupid pissing contest over who was her most distraught child and who was the most concerned for her care and who owed whom money for what. Everyone's feelings were running high. There is no satisfactory reason you can give me that could even begin to explain why you shut your brother—and me, too—out of your life. Even after I notified you he was sick, you stayed away. What was that about? Pride? Stubbornness?"

One of my hands was still firmly clamped around the doorknob. I waved the free one to stop her from speaking. "No, don't answer. I don't want to hear it. It's too late. Any reason or explanation you could offer lost its meaning long ago."

"Mignon."

"Go back to wherever it is you live now. Enjoy your life as you see fit—as you've done for the last several years. I don't have time for you, and with Arthur gone . . . What I might have forgiven before . . . well, the incentive to forgive is gone now too."

"It works both ways, Mignon. Not just—"

I interrupted again. "You lost the right to argue that point when you let him die with the break unresolved. Without the least bit of comfort from his only sibling whose heart was so hard that she put her pride or self-interest ahead of—" I broke off, shaking my head. "Go now. I'm glad to have had the chance to throw this at you—the truth as I see it. Beyond that—well, there's *nothing* beyond that. You stopped being Arthur's sister when you ignored him knowing he was dying. We have no connection now. Certainly none worth pursuing."

I shut the door. I didn't slam it but did close it very firmly. And behind the door, crouched Galahad.

Now that the door was closed, he was exposed, his tail twitching, but not wagging. His mouth hung slightly open, and his tongue was barely out. I heard his light, fast pants. This was a waiting stance.

"It's okay, boy." I smiled. "Would you like a treat?"

This time the *T word* didn't work its magic. His eyes looked lusterless.

I knelt and scratched under his muzzle and around his ears, finishing with a flourish on the back of his neck. "It'll be okay, Galahad. Good boy."

Having faced down Jeanette—and heard myself voice the words that had banged around in my brain for too long—now maybe it *was* time to sell the place. I'd opened the door to that consideration earlier when I had lunch with Dominick. Could I take it to the next step and cross that threshold?

My head and my heart were spinning, caught in a battle between thoughts and emotion. I waited as long as I could, and after peeking out of the windows and seeing no sign of Jeanette, I turned to Galahad who was still sad and uneasy looking. I put my hands on my hips, forcing a more upbeat tone into my voice, I asked, "Well, boy, where is your leash?" His ears perked up. I added, shaking my head, "How are we going to take a proper *walk* without it?"

଼ଓଞ୍ଚ

Galahad and I didn't always walk the same route, but whether we followed the private road or one of the paths that meandered through the forest, Galahad knew all the ways. However, I remembered what I'd said to Dominick. While I wasn't ready to tackle the walk to The Point, a quick drive back over to the beach side and a walk along the ocean was doable. Galahad had surely earned that.

While I was driving that way, I could also stop and check the gate too, just to make sure Jeanette hadn't left her car there and that she was truly gone.

No car. Yay. I unlocked the gate, drove through, and relocked it, and then we were off again.

Oh, Galahad knew. Yes indeed. The light was different nearer the ocean. The air smelled more strongly of salt and sea and sand. The pace was different too—more traffic, more tourists. Galahad crowded up close to the car window. I lowered the glass an inch so he could stick his nose partway out. By the time I'd pulled into a space in the pier parking lot, he was frantic with joy and jumping front seat to back and front again. It was chaotic. He wasn't huge, but he was a good-sized dog, so this was crazy. Next time, I'd be ready to help him control his excitement better. For now, I enjoyed his happiness, and as we exited the car, I held tight to the leash.

Pretending excitement, I encouraged Galahad to roll in the sand and nip at the fringes of the waves—all the good stuff—but when the effort began to weigh on me almost more than I could bear, I looked for a quiet spot and saw a set of crossover steps. They were mostly sand-covered, and no one was nearby. I sat. Galahad took my cue and leaned close to my legs. I scratched his head as he panted. "Good boy," I said.

Arthur had named him. Left to me, he probably would've been called Rover or Spot and that would've been a shame. I'd confessed as much to Arthur after Galahad's second birthday, telling him he'd chosen well.

"Of course, Mignon," he'd said. "Sir Galahad was the perfect knight. The *only* perfect knight—perfect in gentleness, in courtesy, courage and chivalry."

"He's a dog," I said.

"Exactly." And Arthur smiled. He went on to recite one of his many favorite bits of *Idylls of the King*—Tennyson's version of King Arthur's story in verse—in this case, verses associated with Sir Galahad. I was less taken with the poem because it was very long and wordy, but to hear it recited in Arthur's voice was itself like poetry because Arthur spoke it as if the words were drawn from his heart. Words that, spoken by him, touched me in so many ways—some with gentleness like a light caress of fingertips, while others called to me with a hoarse sigh of pain. I would close my eyes and listen to him, transported.

I closed my eyes now thinking of it, remembering his voice, feeling the sun on my body and the birdsong from the dune grasses behind me. Arthur would be identifying each bird species. "Listen to their music, Mignon," he'd say. He seemed to be just behind me. If I looked over my shoulder, I might see him.

Refusing to look back, I squeezed my eyes, closing them even more tightly.

The breeze had sprung up. It brushed my cheek like a warm breath, and I cried out. Galahad moved even closer. His silky fur caught between my fingers as I leaned down hugging him to me. His cold nose was pressed against my neck.

He licked my cheek.

Slowly, I opened my eyes. "It's okay, boy. We'll be all right." But my mood had plummeted, and really, all I wanted to do was cry.

"Are you okay?"

A man's voice.

I glanced up and Galahad gave a huffy little bark but didn't leave my side. The man was dressed in shorts and a T-shirt. His short sandy hair was peppered with gray. His eyes were light . . . maybe hazel.

My trespasser. The swimmer.

I forced a smile, hoping I didn't look teary. "I'm fine. Thanks."

He nodded. "Good to hear." He stepped away, clearly intending to resume his day, saying, "Sorry to have bothered you."

"Not a bother. Thanks for asking."

He nodded again and took off.

Seriously? What were the odds? Clearly, he hadn't recognized me.

It was midafternoon now. It had been only a few hours since he'd surprised me this morning. He was a busy guy. Or maybe a guy who wanted to be busy? He looked to me like a too-busy man in dire need of a tall glass of iced tea and a fishing trip.

Where had he come from? The Holmans lived on the bridge side of my property, so I'd have to guess he was coming from the subdivision, using the trails to cut through to Coast Guard Road and the Emerald Walk instead of running through his subdivision.

Unless he was pitching a tent out there on my acreage . . . Except now he was over here on the ocean side, so maybe he was just high energy and got around a lot.

Something about the idea of this man, this stranger who seemed only to move with purpose, pitching a tent in my woods tickled my barely functional sense of humor.

Well, anything was possible, certainly. People did walk in and follow the trails. Mostly, I turned a blind eye, like with the mostly young people who'd walk in to use the disc golf hoops that Arthur had installed a few years back. It was impossible to monitor all the activity on a property the size of Emerald Heart, so I'd put up the signs and kept the gate locked. If more was needed, I'd call the town police. They knew my situation.

Okay, I told myself. *Jeanette is gone and for good this time.* I wasn't going to worry about anything else just now.

"Come on, boy. Enough gloom." I stood, his leash in my hand. Clouds were gathering, some of them dark, and the air smelled like rain was in the offing. A low rumble of distant thunder confirmed my observation.

"Let's get home, Galahad."

Squalls rolled in quickly and unexpectedly at the

beach. The clouds would look ominous but safely distant, and then suddenly they were right on top of you, so Galahad and I cleared the gate as quickly as possible—locked it, as usual—and then drove up to the hotel and home.

Arthur had always kept objects in the yard battened down, and I did the same, but the porch needed to be cleared of loose objects. While I took care of that, Galahad performed his usual check of the area, refreshing the bushes and the few lawn ornaments, and when satisfied that his duty was done, he joined me on the porch. I took down the hanging pots of flowering plants and stashed them under the bench seat against the wall of the house. Good enough.

"Galahad, come." I opened the front door. "Let's close the windows, boy."

We went into the house to wait out the storm.

⊂⊃⊂⊃

The rain came with force, driving onto land at a slant for a few intense minutes. No hail. I always worried about hail because it could be so damaging and costly, not to mention inconvenient. The rain abated, the clouds blew out to the north of us, and I opened the door and stepped outside to enjoy the freshness that the storm left in its wake. There was even a faint rainbow arcing from the last fluff of clouds down to the far shore's horizon.

I retrieved the pots of flowers and was hanging

them back on their hooks when Galahad whined. I looked down at him and then in the direction in which he was staring.

She was walking up the road. Hobbling, really. Drenched. Her hair was wet, and her clothing clung to her. She was thin. She'd always been thin and stylish. Now she was thin like a wet, scrawny, bedraggled cat. And limping.

"No," I shouted. I pointed at her. "Stop. Don't come here." I meant it. Absolutely I did, even though I also shrank inside hearing the harsh, loud words coming from my lips.

Jeanette kept limping toward me. As she neared the porch, she said, "Sorry, Meg."

"Don't call me that."

"Sorry again." She pushed the dangling wet locks of mostly brown hair out of her face. Wet as it was, the gray strands were more noticeable. "I was climbing over the gate just as the rain started. It was slippery and I fell. My foot twisted when I landed." She touched her leg. "It hurt."

What hurt? The hard rain or the ankle? I made a rude, snorting noise. "I'll call you a cab." I frowned and asked, "Or did you leave your car at the gate and block me in? For that matter, if you weren't going to respect the gate, why didn't you just walk around the stone columns?"

She stood at the base of the porch steps. "Please Mignon, can't we talk? Just a little? You don't owe me anything. Not even the courtesy you'd give a stranger. I accept that. But I'd like to talk to you anyway."

She looked so pathetic.

"Someday maybe."

"Please."

"Please? *Please* go away, Jeanette."

"Could I have a drink of water?"

After a long pause, I said, "Wait here."

A glass of water. Just that and no more. I was back in a jiffy.

Silently, she accepted the glass and sipped the water. She glanced at me over the rim.

My impulse was to say that the drink wasn't poisoned. I kept those words inside, but I felt called upon to say *something*. Despite my reluctance to be civil, I asked, "Where are you staying?"

She didn't answer, but took another sip, seemed to savor it, then she shook her head, saying, "I wanted to speak with you before I leave." She clasped the drinking glass two-handed, holding it in front of her almost as if begging for spare change. "After . . . Well, I was about to leave but decided to make one last try."

"What is it that you want to say?"

"Can I sit for a few minutes? The porch, maybe?"

She was standing on one foot. Her other leg was bent with the toe of her shoe barely touching the ground, apparently to avoid putting weight on it.

I crossed my arms and stepped back. "You may think I'm rude and that I don't care," I said. "You're right. I don't. So don't bother playing for sympathy. Say whatever it is you want to say and make it fast."

Chapter Five

"Where should I start?" Jeanette asked, her hands tightly clasped and held close to her chest. "With guilt, maybe."

She sighed and shrugged. "Given everything that happened between us, I knew I wouldn't be welcome at Arthur's funeral. I told myself that it was more respectful of me not to . . . inject myself into your grief. But, yes, I should've come. Should've swallowed my pride. By the time I admitted that truth to myself, it was too late, and the guilt had grabbed hold of me. And then, well, I thought I could at least apologize to you. Perhaps that would release some of this . . . this awful feeling that's been weighing me down for so long."

"It's always about you, isn't it?"

"I presume the family dissension has been eating at you too." She squeezed her fingers together so tightly it looked painful. "I don't expect us to go back to the good old days—which were pretty good, weren't they? But if I can diminish this guilt in me and the anger in you, then it's worth whatever it takes."

She shivered from the damp clothes and wet hair.

"Would you like a towel?"

"I don't want to put you to any trouble. That's not my intention."

"Seven years, Jeanette. Seven." I paused for

emphasis and then added, "I'll be right back."

When I returned with the towel, I saw Galahad had come out to the porch. His spirit seemed weighed down, low-key, and he was intently watching Jeanette and then shifting his eyes back over to me. He settled next to my usual seat.

I offered the towel to my former sister-in-law.

Immediately, she buried her face in the soft terry and then rubbed it briskly in her hair. Arthur had also loved the feel and scent of freshly laundered towels. Somehow watching her perform that same action made me feel ashamed.

It wasn't *my* shame. I had every right to refuse to engage with her.

But there was a greater human right and responsibility—that of basic kindness.

"I'm not saying the past is forgiven," I said, "but I appreciate you trying. No, that's a lie. I don't appreciate you coming here, but maybe one day I will. For now, I hope that will be sufficient to ease your mind and you'll feel free to go back to wherever you've been living your life and leave me alone."

She pressed her lips together again. She nodded, folding the towel. As she moved to return it to me, she half-stood, apparently forgetting her ankle, but then she winced and moaned and sank back into the chair. There was almost a sense of fear, of desperation about her.

In a low, rough voice, I said, "Please just say it and be done with it."

"I'm in difficulty, Mignon. That's not why I came

here, but I had hoped . . . And now I have the ankle to deal with. I am out of whatever strength . . . whatever it takes to get up and do anything. Is there any possibility, the least flexibility in you, for putting me up for a night or two?" She shook her head. "Even if I can walk back down to the gate and my car, I'm not sure I should drive with the injured ankle, and I don't believe I can manage getting back on the road tonight."

"No."

"Please."

I jumped to my feet, nearly tripping over Galahad who scrambled out of the way. I said, "You're expecting hospitality from me? You can't be serious."

Jeanette turned to the side, covering her face as if I'd slapped her.

I stared at her, my palm burning, wanting to do exactly that, but what would Arthur have done? After all, she was his sister. His only sibling. He might have been less than welcoming when she first showed up— maybe—but would he refuse her a place to stay the night?

Forcing my fists to unclench, I sighed. Or maybe I groaned. Either way, it was a rough, ugly sound.

"One night only. The hotel wing is closed, but functional. I'll give you the key to the first room. 101. You'll find bedding and towels in the dresser drawers." I paused. "That's the best I can offer."

Was I really doing this? Being asked to do even this much seemed outrageous.

She nodded. "I am very tired. It's no fault of yours

and my situation is not your responsibility, but please know I appreciate your help." She limped across the porch to the door and worked her wet, messy shoes off to leave there.

I asked, "What about your car?"

She nodded again, then looked away from my eyes and said without inflection, "Down at the gate."

"Where are your car keys?"

She pulled them from her pants pocket, and I took them.

"I'll take you to your room and then bring the car up."

"I'm so sorry for all this, and for what happened back then too."

Feeling manipulated, and certainly resentful over being backed into a corner, I ignored her and went into the house to fetch my own substantial key ring from the cabinet drawer in our small office.

When I turned, I saw she'd followed me inside and was standing awkwardly, still bearing most of her weight on the uninjured ankle and foot.

"Do you need to get that looked at?"

"I'm sure it's only a mild sprain. If it's not better tomorrow, I'll go to a walk-in clinic on my way out of town."

Rather than respond, I turned away. I'd shown kindness, hadn't I? Reluctantly done, but yes. A *one more healthy thing* checked off. It was hard-earned, I might add…and now I had no more courtesy left in me. I gestured toward the door. "This way."

"I remember," she said, but very softly.

We headed to the interior door that connected my living quarters to the hotel lobby. Galahad kept close to me. I looked down at him and with a gesture, I said, "Stay."

He sat and didn't protest, which told me he was feeling the same reservations, the same cautious reluctance as I was. He'd been a puppy the last time Jeanette had been here. He'd liked her well enough as puppies did, but I wondered if he also associated her with the raised voices and the anger from those days. She'd left and the anger had ebbed to be replaced by sadness as we realized the break might be irreparable. I was angry on Arthur's behalf, and as he suffered through cancer treatment and then into hospice—and Jeanette still refused to interact with us—my anger grew beyond any bounds I'd ever known, and even now it was hard to put aside.

She followed me into the lobby. I closed the door securely behind us and continued across the lobby to the guest room hallway, but she wasn't following. She was standing there, staring.

"I'd forgotten . . . Or maybe it just looks different now because back then this place was in use and busy. It's something about the look . . . the air . . . now."

It was otherworldly. No lights were burning over here, so the only light in the lobby was either touched by water and sunshine or by the green of growing things, then filtered through the etched glass front doors or the garden doors. In between these natural light sources was rarified air, as if the two streams couldn't mix but one must try to overtake the other. The light caught on the gleaming mahogany bar, burnished the bronze objects in Arthur's displays, and glinted in the globes of the chandelier over our heads. The oxygen felt thin, but the air was heavy, as if the past itself was trapped in here and Arthur might indeed come wandering up the corridor. With a flash of surprise at seeing us here, he'd smile. His eyes would twinkle with a light unique to him as he moved forward to greet us.

"Wow," Jeannette breathed the word as her eyes roamed the room. "He really went overboard with that King Arthur thing, didn't he?"

Hoping to hide my jump of surprise when she spoke, and to do so quickly before I changed my mind and tossed her out, injured ankle and all, I said, "This way, Jeanette."

"Mignon," she began, but I ignored her, and her voice fell off to a whisper.

I unlocked the guest room door and ushered her in and flipped on the light.

"Do you have an overnight case in your car?"

Her look showed caution and more than a little surprise. She said, "Yes. A tote on the passenger seat, and the overnight case is in the trunk. Thank you."

When we walked into the room, she stopped just inside the door and stared at the large framed copy of a lithograph hanging on the wall over the bed. The Round Table. Arthur and his knights. I didn't know what was going through her mind as she stared at it, but to me, it felt like criticism or condescension, and it ticked me off. Everything about Jeanette *ticked me off*. I put the lobby door key on the dresser along with the room key—each attached to their old-fashioned oblong shapes of plastic.

"Don't use the lobby door until I disarm the alarm. I'll do that on my way out. I'll reset the alarm before dark and disable it again in the morning so you can leave as soon as it's convenient for you."

"This is a lot of trouble I'm putting you to. I'm sorry."

If she said *sorry* one more time, I was going to pass from being ticked off to blowing my stack. Before that could happen, I left to go fetch her car.

☙

I returned to my part of the building—my home. Galahad was sitting so close to the house side of the door that he'd practically melded with it. Gently, I pushed against the door to dislodge him enough for me to squeeze through the opening. He looked so relieved to see me that I stopped to give him some extra attention. He followed me to the alarm closet, where I disengaged the alarm for the lobby door. After a slight hesitation, I shut off the alarms for the rest of the building too, because Jeanette might decide to open a window or test the garden doors. So, that was done. Now I was off to fetch her car.

As I went to the front door, Jeanette's car keys

jingling in my hand, Galahad came after me with his leash in his mouth, the ends of it dragging on the floor after him.

"You can't come." Before leaving, I put some food into his dish. It was almost his suppertime. A small snack might ease his concern and distract him. He dropped his leash beside the dish. All the important things in one handy spot. I smiled. "Stay. I'll be right back."

My life would've been much sadder after Arthur's death without this dog that I hadn't wanted. But as Arthur had said when he introduced me to the goldendoodle puppy, "He's a mini," he said, "so he won't get too big."

"A dog? Really?"

"You think you don't want him, but you don't know him. You'll love him in no time. Trust me."

To the sound of his metal dish bumping along as Galahad pursued every last morsel of food, I scooted quietly out the front door.

I walked down the road toward the gate and Jeanette's car. The fresh air, post squall, was clean and energizing and my body responded. My attitude too. How strange this all was. How unexpected. Bizarre, even. In this space where the hotel was not visible because the road curved and the trees crowded close, yet that same geography kept the gate out of view, too, and I could almost bring myself to believe that this had been some strange dream. Maybe a product of an unplanned afternoon nap? Perhaps I'd sat in the chair to watch a mindless show and it had all interwoven in the way that dreams do. But as I rounded the curve, Jeanette's car was there on the other side of the gate.

So much for wishing unpleasant things away. Grimly, I unlocked the gate and swung it wide.

She could've walked around the stone pillars that held the gate erect. A few steps would've taken Jeanette past those columns and into the trees and right back onto the road. But she'd chosen to climb over the locked steel gate instead?

Humph. She wasn't stupid. It sounded fishy. Perhaps manipulative. And she'd gotten a night's stay out of it.

For what purpose?

Her car started easily. The car was older, but the interior was neat. She had an object hanging from her rearview mirror. I took a closer look. It was a Celtic medallion. I remembered when we'd gotten them many years ago from a booth at the St. Patrick's Festival in Emerald Isle. The town held it every year in March. I didn't know what had happened to mine, but Jeanette still had hers. It represented strength in the form of an oak tree—and Arthur had chosen a similar design for the lobby doors. I set the medallion to swinging and then turned my attention to completing my mission. I drove the car through the open gate, got out to relock the gate, and drove the rest of the way to the hotel. I parked in the space next to the lobby doors instead of going beyond to my residence.

It had been a long time since a guest's car was parked here.

Jeanette's small roller bag was in the trunk, and I retrieved it. I grabbed her tote bag from the passenger seat. There were more tote bags on the back seat, and a small plastic bag that might've had trash in it was on the front floorboard. There were items bagged and boxed in the trunk, but those weren't my business. Her tote bag, which clearly functioned as her purse, and the suitcase were all she needed for one night. I locked the car, pulling the suitcase along the flagstone walkway to the lobby entrance.

If Jeanette was watching from her window, she would've seen me. Deliberately, I hadn't looked that way. I went about my business, a reluctant, disgruntled hostess delivering luggage to an unexpected, unwanted guest.

I set the suitcase and purse next to the guest room door, rapped on the door with my knuckles, and called out, "Your suitcase and keys are out here. The lobby doors are disarmed in case you want to go back out to your car for anything." I was about to say more when the door opened.

Jeanette said, "Thank you."

"I'll leave the lobby doors disarmed until dark, but during the day keep the doors locked, otherwise you could end up with a curious stranger or two wandering in."

Her eyes widened a bit, but then she grimaced and nodded. "I understand."

I stepped away, and she closed the door.

ᘓᘏᘓ

Within a few strides, I was back in the lobby. It was darkish now, lit only by the fading afternoon light, and it seemed huge. I stood there remembering days long past when we'd had a good business, busy, with life, and voices and annoyances and laughter. It had begun as Arthur's dream and as he'd made it come true, I'd made it mine.

My appointment with Dominick Monahan was scheduled for tomorrow. Late morning, he'd said. By then Jeanette would be gone and, if I was being honest, and even if I didn't want Jeanette here, her intrusion had accomplished an important purpose in highlighting my loneliness. My isolation. I should sell and move on. Or demolish the hotel wing and live here like a regular person instead of as a caretaker.

From a distance, I heard Galahad whining—whining loudly, apparently, so that I *would* hear him. He knew I was here a few feet away, with only that one door between the hotel and the living quarters. Soon, he'd be full-out barking.

I called out, "Hush, Galahad. I'll be there in a moment, boy."

Was it time to list The Emerald Heart Hotel for sale? I wasn't sure, but yes, it was past time to discuss the options in real, concrete terms with the appropriate person—Dominick.

Chapter Six

Had I truly believed I could avoid offering Jeanette a meal? The kitchenettes weren't stocked with food or drink. There was water from the sink, of course, but . . . *Sigh.* As suppertime approached, and while thinking all this, I was standing at my own cozy kitchen counter dicing celery and carrots to add into the green salad mixings and wondering why I'd cut so much. I slowed down as I acknowledged that my subconscious had already figured it out and had the answer. Yes, I'd have to provide supper.

I could add serving supper to Jeanette as a good deed into my *one healthy thing a day* list. Maybe even get a little credit ahead or make up for the many days I'd missed.

The only question was where or how to serve the food. No neutral ground was available, but safe ground? Yes. I'd take her a tray. Simple.

She'd written her cell number down. I dialed and she answered.

"Would you like a salad for supper?"

"Yes." Her voice sounded surprised. Perhaps pleased. "That sounds—"

"I'll bring it over on a tray." I punctuated the sentence firmly with a short hard note in my voice so she'd know this offer held no invitation to chat about the menu.

I arranged the tray and hesitated only briefly before going to the storage closet where the last of the mini toiletries were aging well past any *best used by* date—but hey, it was soap and shampoo. Soap was soap. I put them in a bag, then added in a snack and a few other things.

The bag swayed against my hands as I carried the tray to the door to the lobby.

"Stay, Galahad," I said.

He did. I was able to shift my load well enough to snag the doorknob with a pinkie, and then I pulled the door closed behind me. Jeanette had the room door wide open. She'd showered and was dressed in a nightgown and robe.

"You should keep this door closed and locked."

Surprise lit her face. "The room door? I'm the only one in the hotel wing, right? And the main entrance is locked and alarmed."

"Yes, but there's always the possibility of someone getting in through a window. I keep all these doors locked, but it doesn't mean intruders can't force these doors open if they try hard enough."

Her surprise had changed to shock. "This is a real concern? No, I'm sorry, of course you are being sincere. We all see the news. But, Mignon . . . It's been how long since you stopped the business? Is this a regular routine for you? How can you live this way?"

I pushed past her and set the tray on the small table

by the window. "Not your business. Keep your door locked."

She'd followed me over to the table, still limping. She picked up the bag. "What's this?"

"Ibuprofen and pain cream for your ankle. There's several bottles of water and iced tea and soda. It's cold, at least for now. There's no fridge in here. I had them removed from the guest rooms. They are too hard to keep clean. They get stinky if you don't keep them cold." I shrugged. "Seemed like a waste of electricity."

"It's all great. Thanks."

I put a slip of paper on the table next to the tray. "My cell number, since you must've lost it." An open dig at how she'd never called or responded to my messages. "Use it if there's an emergency. I'll disarm the lobby doors in the morning when I get up to let Galahad out. If you need to leave before that, call or text me."

"Thank you for everything."

I gave my former sister-in-law a long look. Her eyes were dark. She seemed to be forcing herself to meet my eyes. I didn't see anything in her expression that made this feel worthwhile.

"Shove it," I said without an iota of elegance.

Pulling her door closed behind me, I left. As I walked through the lobby, I knew I should be embarrassed by my response to her, but no, letting it out had felt good. So good. Like a tiny shot for my dignity, or for my pride. I refused to feel guilty about my limited hospitality. I'd given her food and meds, not to mention clean linens and a good mattress for the night, right?

Enough. I'd done enough.

But this strange day wasn't done with me yet.

After my meal, and after the kitchen was clean, the sun was sinking low in the sky, but it wasn't fully dark yet, except in the wooded areas. I went to the alarm closet and turned on the hotel wing alarms.

I loved the colors of sunset, as well as the feel of night as the colors faded and dark crept in and settled itself into the nooks and crannies of the earth. Nights were hard when it was time to go to bed, to find sleep. But sunset? Sunset was nature's show and often felt like God's gift after a hard day.

This had been a very odd day indeed.

My house doors weren't armed yet. I walked out to the terrace to the Adirondack chairs, forgetting briefly that Jeanette was here. When I did remember, I was glad that the armed alarms would keep her inside. I smiled. She was sort of quarantined in that huge space over there. Unless she looked out her window, she'd never even know I was out here. So I gave myself permission to forget her and to simply relax.

Galahad had preceded me out into the yard and had immediately headed for the cliff stairs. I looked down there and saw him on the bottom steps, stopping just short of going onto the dock. He seemed to be staring, moving his head as if his nose was busy divining scents. Odd that he'd stopped there. And then I saw them too. The water spots on the dock. Much like footsteps.

Stop it, I told myself.

Small ones.

Don't go there, Mignon.

My heart was thrumming in my chest as Galahad crept down to the dock, approaching the first wet puddle ever so carefully, sniffing around it. Then the next one. Until he reached the handrail that a swimmer would use to climb from the water up onto the dock. I held my breath.

My hand was on the arm of the chair, but I could no longer see below because the rest of me was kneeling on the terrace. My knees were weak. I closed my eyes and put my head down, forcing myself to breathe.

Galahad loped up the cliff stairs back to where I waited, unable to do anything at all, and trying not to think. I was better. So much better. I couldn't go back to the worst days. Nor could I look down at the dock again. Those were just puddles. Maybe one of the larger birds had landed there after a catch. *Maybe, maybe, maybe.* I squeezed my eyes shut again.

The stranger? Might he have come back? The size of the puddles could easily be deceptive. Or Jeanette? Might she have gone down there while I was fetching the car or fixing the salad? No and no. Her ankle was injured. Or was it really? And how long would those wet steps have lasted anyway? Surely they were newly made.

I put my hands over my face, wishing I hadn't seen the wet steps, the puddles, whatever they were, and wishing I was healthier—brain wise and emotionally—such that seeing water on a dock didn't cause me to melt down.

As usual, it was Galahad who rescued me. My hero

dog. I was freaking him out and he deserved better. And yet, as I made it back up to my feet, and noted the color was already fading from the sky and the world around me was falling into night, and though I liked this time of day, I felt uneasy.

I stood absolutely still, feeling cut off, as if this building, particularly the hotel block, looked different. Colder, somehow. The woods, especially the evergreens, assumed shapes in the night. Shadows only. That's all. I was freaked out, whether it was justified or not, and I needed to calm down.

"Galahad?" I called his name. No response. I waited a few moments, then called again. "Galahad! Come!"

The forest seemed deathly still. Dark windows stared back at me from the hotel, even from the house. I drew in a deep breath. This was that feeling again—of time having moved on and left me behind. My body broke out in chills.

I could break this moment if I chose to. I could act.

"Galahad!" I shrieked.

Oh no. Even Jeanette must've heard that scream. Yes, she was in there. Even if the building *did* look empty and forgotten.

And then he was back, running from around the end of the residence, his tongue out which gave him that smiling, rakish look that said he was happy to see me. I walked across the grass and the road, straight to my front porch. I opened the door and stuck my hand inside to flip the light switches. *Yes. Thank God.* They worked.

One part of my brain said, *Of course they work. I pay the power bill every month*. The other part of my brain said, *Thank you for the light*, like a prayer. I didn't try to reconcile the two. They were both right. And that's just how things worked for me these days.

There'd been no wet steps on the dock. They were merely a trick of the fading light. I'd imagined them. Whatever. I didn't even need to go back and check. They'd be evaporated by now anyway, if they'd existed, which they hadn't. I turned my back to the terrace, slapped my thigh in a universal gesture that all dogs recognized, and together we entered the house. With the interior lights shining bright. I closed the door carefully and firmly and flipped the locks.

"Oh, Galahad. One step forward and two steps back." I sighed. "Who'd you go visit anyway, boy? Were you chasing after a rabbit or a squirrel?" I looked at him sternly. "If any of those coyotes are hanging around out there, you keep away, got that?"

Another breath and another sigh, and I was back. I was home, securely in present time and myself again. Galahad had earned a treat.

From the kitchen, I heard a noise, like knocking. I stepped into the living room, wondering, and then I heard my name called from a distance. From down the hallway. After a moment of shock—truly this day had overwhelmed me—I realized it was Jeanette.

I hurried down the hall and called through the adjoining door. "What's up?"

She yelled back. "That's what I want to know. Are

you okay? I heard you shout. You were outside? Are you okay?"

"I'm fine." I stepped back and unlocked and opened the door. "I'm good, as you can see. It's been a long day. Do you have what you need?"

"Yes." She eyed me carefully, as if trying to read my expression. "I'm good."

"Go to sleep, Jeanette."

She nodded. "Same to you. Sleep well."

Chapter Seven

Suddenly half-awake, I stared into the dim early-morning light. Had I heard a noise? Anything concerning enough to get me up? I listened.

Nope. Not a peep.

Satisfied, and before I could wake up all the way, I rolled over and hugged my pillow, my hand briefly straying beyond it to the sheets in that spot where Arthur had slept—a cool, smooth spot that should've been warm and rumpled—and pulled my hand back. Mornings—even the wee hours of the morning—were always the worst. A stab of grief, of loneliness, wanted to claim me, and then I remembered the day before. It had been awful. And Jeanette was here.

Now I was fully awake.

I groaned, not ready to engage with the day.

Galahad had heard me moving and came to the bedside, resting his chin on the mattress near my hip. At any moment, he'd start making his little noises urging me to get up and get going.

I took the phone from my nightstand and checked for missed calls or texts.

None. Okay then.

She might have already stowed her bags in the car and driven off, never to trouble me again. Except she didn't have a key to the gate. So . . . no.

Galahad was delighted when he saw the blanket shifting over my legs, and ecstatic to see me sitting up. He sat back on his haunches until my feet were solidly on the floor, and then he sprang up and dashed ahead of me to the door. I wasn't expecting Dominick until late morning. Jeanette would be gone long before that.

No decisions were needed today. This was just an opportunity for Dominick, an expert in the sales market, to get a look at the current state of the property, and for a discussion about options over coffee or tea with an old friend who'd known Arthur since they were kids. He'd been involved in our lives. He'd known us as a family before we'd lost Sebrina, and before all the losses that followed.

I let Galahad out solo to do his business. He'd return promptly for his breakfast, so no worries there. Then I disabled the lobby door alarm.

No breakfast was being served at The Emerald Heart Hotel this morning . . . except to the dog, of course, and maybe some toast and tea for me. First, I'd take a quick drive down to unlock the gate. Jeanette would be free to leave whenever.

No formal checkout was needed at this hotel. We offered easy-breezy departures—especially for former sisters-in-law who'd had the gall to show up uninvited.

⊂⊃

An hour or so later, Galahad asked to go back outside. It was a pretty day, so I didn't leash him, but I walked out to the porch and watched him do his usual run and sniff and walk and sniff. While he was doing his thing, I walked to the left, around to the front of the lobby, and saw her car still there.

Not all that surprising, I told myself. Jeanette was only concerned with Jeanette.

The curtains in her window were open. If not for that, I might've gone to her car to see whether she'd brought her suitcase back out, but since she would see me looking, I didn't. I walked back around to my porch. There was no sign of Galahad, not checking out the shrubbery or waiting for me on the porch. I called his name softly.

A rabbit or squirrel had probably caught his interest. Sometimes he'd run off on his own, chasing scents or taking longer runs along the trails, but that was usually in the afternoon when he'd be hoping that Carolyn or the Holmans would offer him a treat. If he didn't return shortly, I'd rattle the treat tin. Seemingly, he could hear that from almost any distance, and that rattle would bring him back in a flash. I walked inside, heading to the kitchen, and through the window I saw Jeanette in the garden.

She'd been there yesterday, and it gave me a jolt to see her out there again today. The bottle of iced tea I'd given her was on the bench seat beside her. Today, she was wearing light blue jeans and a plain jewel-neck silky-looking T-shirt. Her hair was brushed up and back and secured with a clip again on the side. From this distance, and in the filtered shade of live oaks, she looked almost ageless.

She had no right to be in my garden. She was supposed to be on her way back to her life elsewhere. This was my reward for trying to be nice. And the betrayal was doubly hurtful because Galahad was there at the bench sitting comfortably on the ground near her feet while she leaned over to scratch his ears and neck.

My eyes stung. My face . . . my lips . . . They felt odd. Was I pouting?

When I'd fussed about it with Arthur—how Jeanette had walked away from us as if we mattered less than an old pair of shoes she no longer had use for—he'd warned me about anger. Arthur often said he was the romantic in our marriage. That I was the warrior. But I wasn't a warrior. I was a human being, and I was hurt. And angry. Arthur said my anger was more destructive to me than to whatever the situation was or whoever had caused it.

I went out via the side door onto the back patio of the house. Galahad jumped up and ran toward me. Jeanette watched from the bench as I opened the door, shooed Galahad inside, then pulled the door closed and walked over to her.

My eyes fixed on her, I approached slowly and spoke very clearly. "You're ready to go." Not a question.

"Mignon. You're still angry. I can't leave with things like this."

"One night. That was all I agreed to, and only

because you were injured. You made it out to the garden on your own, so I assume you can walk and drive."

"My ankle isn't quite right, but it's better. I slept well, considering. But—and I know I'm going to make you angry . . . Well, you're already angry so I'll make you angrier." She shrugged. "I'll just say it. This is no way to live. You here alone? In this huge place? A business—what used to be a business—falling apart while you hide out here?" She gestured toward the residence, then shook her head. "You deserve better than this."

"It isn't for you to decide what I do or don't deserve. Don't you get that? You weren't part of our lives in those years when Arthur and I were grieving the loss of your mom. You weren't here when he got his own diagnosis and when we were grieving the imminent loss of *him*. You weren't here when it counted, and as far as I'm concerned, you aren't here now. You're just some woman who wandered in out of the rain yesterday and needed shelter for the night. Beyond that, you are nothing to me. *Nothing*."

Jeanette gasped, putting her hand over her mouth. Then, incongruously, the gasp turned to a light, casual laugh. She fixed her eyes on mine, then grasped my shoulders and pulled me into a quick hug before I could object. I was confused as she pushed me away, her amusement clear on her face as she said, "You are the best hostess ever." She spoke to someone beyond me, saying, "She never allows me to do anything to help. Even though it's been years since I've been here. She says I must relax and do nothing. Nothing." She took my arm and casually turned me around to face the newcomer, Dominick.

Dominick looked confused, then surprised and amused, as he said, "Jeanette."

She spread her arms wide. "It's me! I'm back. I surprised Mignon yesterday."

He came forward and Jeanette met him partway. They hugged as Dominick said, "Long time no see." He sounded a little off.

She laughed as if he were making a joke. "Just life, Dom. That's how it goes sometimes."

He moved toward me, and I said, "You're early. Thanks for coming over."

"Thank *you* for being willing to discuss possibilities." He gestured toward Jeanette. "It's nice to see old friends, right? Always good."

I forced a smile and grunted in a noncommittal way.

Jeanette asked him, "Do you still work as a real estate agent?"

Her voice—she sounded perky, and it annoyed me. Feeling a need to cut her out of the conversation, I jumped in. "He does. And he's the best agent in this area."

Dominick said, "High praise. Not sure I can claim the title of *best*, but I know the business and I do well enough, especially in the market we had this year, no question."

Jeanette shifted her gaze between us and said, "I'll

get out of your way so you two can talk business." She started walking away even as she said to me, "We can chat later." She smiled and pointed her finger at me. "And I *will* help out around here, I insist!"

I knew the sudden shift in our argument, along with those last words, had been offered as a ruse so Dominick would not realize that she and I had been working up to having an all-out no-holds-barred fight. Maybe I should appreciate her cover, but the truth was there would've been no reason to fight if she hadn't come here uninvited, without even a forewarning, and hadn't wormed her way into staying overnight. Plus, Dominick already knew quite well that I had no love or regard for Jeanette. She'd used up any good feelings I had for her long ago.

And her telling me we'd chat later? That meant she wasn't leaving yet.

I'd deal with Jeanette later. I had to focus on Dominick now, and my questions about Emerald Heart.

Dominick had come close. His expression was one of concern. "You okay, Mignon? You look . . . I don't know. Not yourself."

I patted his arm. "I'm fine. Just one of those moments."

"Worrying again, right? Instead, ask me anything. We can talk. I do that well, as you know. Let me be your sounding board. If you'd rather not deal with the sell-or-not-to-sell talk now, that's okay too. Just say the word. I'll settle for lunch together again. Here or in town."

Dominick was kind.

"I'm fine, and I'd like to discuss it now. I'm not sure if or when I'll make the decision, but it's time to understand my options." I gestured toward the hotel wing. "This can't go on indefinitely. It's already been too long. Empty doesn't go well with buildings. Buildings age and technologies change."

"You're considering renovation and reopening?"

I shook my head. "Not at this point in my life."

"Not without Arthur?"

Nodding, I glanced back at the old familiar building. "This was his dream. He accomplished it. We did it together. But that was then, and this is now. I must decide whether to stay, and if I stay, what to do about the hotel."

"Shall we start with a walk-through? It's been a while. I'd like to see it as it is now, the state of the building and so on."

I hooked my arm through his. "Allow me to give you a tour."

CRSO

"It's dated, yes, but the building has charm, a view, and potential. The overall structure looks sound. The views of the water and the wooded grounds—beautiful. Upkeep is challenging, I'm sure." He smiled at me. "You've done a good job."

Considering it's only you and you haven't done more than basic upkeep. He hadn't said those words out loud, but I heard them clearly.

We stood in the lobby, facing the lobby desk. The area was darkish except for the light coming in from the custom-made etched glass double doors.

The pattern was of the Celtic Tree of Life—I remembered the name now. It was the design chosen by Arthur—a much grander version of the medallions we'd purchased at the festival years ago. The details and textures in the glass were exquisite.

"But those." he pointed to both sets of doors. "Those are amazing."

Amazingly expensive. I kept those words in, instead saying, "Arthur insisted, and yes, they *are* beautiful."

Dominick must've heard the words I *wasn't* saying aloud because he gave me a look and nodded. Softly, he said, simply, "Arthur."

"Arthur." I sighed. With the least encouragement, my husband would unabashedly launch into tales and trivia about King Arthur and his knights and all the versions of that history—or historical mythology—with joy and relish to friends, to guests, to whoever cared to listen. He pored over archaeological journals whenever they mentioned King Arthur or Tintagel, or anything remotely connected to the subject. His mania—gentle but often expensive—was even responsible for our goldendoodle being named Galahad. "You know how he was," I added softly.

"And the rest of this?" Dominick asked. "There's more of it now, isn't there? Or was I not paying attention?"

I nodded. "It sneaks up on you, sort of. You were just used to it before. Not really seeing it all."

"Quite a collection."

He leaned closer to me and gave my shoulder a quick squeeze, then released me and walked the length of the lobby, pausing here and there, giving most of the décor—Arthur's collectibles—only a cursory glance. Near the front doors, he paused to examine the large, welcoming, heavy wooden chest on top of which a diorama of King Arthur with his Knights of the Round Table was displayed, then he quickly moved on to the painting hanging above of the promontory—the headlands overlooking the Celtic Sea with the broken stone profile of castle ruins.

While I waited, I stood patiently and scanned the room. Dominick hadn't seen this in a long time, and back then Arthur would've been here and this would all have made more sense. It always did with Arthur present. Over our heads a huge, intricate, antler-style chandelier was suspended from the ceiling. I hit the light switch and it blazed to life, the light reflecting in the reclaimed mahogany bar whose highly polished wood gleamed near the entrance. The bar served as the check-in desk. Everything around us testified to Arthur's eclectic tastes. Some might find the assemblage odd, and some might consider it dated—and they'd all be right. But Arthur had loved it and so had I, because it was part of who he was and of our life together.

This hodgepodge of eclectic collectibles would not long survive a sale, of that I was sure.

"He never got to go there, did he?"

I turned to see him pointing at a painting.

"To Tintagel? No, not even close, nor to any of the other locations associated with King Arthur," I whispered. "We were planning the trip to the UK. Scotland, Wales, England, Ireland . . . the works. He had this notion that he'd stand on the promontory and recite lines from *Le Morte d'Arthur*. The Death of Arthur." I laughed softly, having stumbled over the French pronunciation and warmed by the memory of my dear, occasionally goofball husband practicing. "He said he was going to wear a cape and feel the ocean wind blowing it back—like a heroic stance?" I shook my head. "Crazy, right?"

"Maybe."

"Crazy or not, I would've stood right there with him and cheered him on and taken his photo regardless of whether the other tourists laughed at us. Arthur knew how to live."

After a minute, I said, "I never quite understood why it was so important to him, but it was, and we were determined to make it happen." I shrugged to hide my shiver. "Then he got sick, and that was that."

Dominick nodded. "Funny how such an ordinary thing as calling attendance in kindergarten can spark a fascination that lasted many decades, and all because the last name was said first. King, Arthur."

"Kids teased him. There was some show or other about knights and King Arthur on TV at the time, so his classmates thought it was quite funny." I shook my head.

"Honestly, King isn't an unusual name, nor is Arthur. How many kids experienced the same thing in classroom roll calls?"

"Many," Dominick said. "And *our* Arthur embraced it."

"He did."

"Is the office still over here?" Dominick walked toward the garden side lobby doors and stopped in front of them.

"No," I said. "After we lost Sebrina, Arthur did more and more of his business in her old room. We started using the former office mostly for storage." I flipped through my big, old-fashioned key ring and unlocked the door. "Musty. No leaks, though. I check each room in the building every Wednesday." I added, "As well as after heavy rains. I hope to catch any leaks before they have the chance to grow. We've been very fortunate when it comes to hurricanes. I think it helps facing the sound instead of the ocean."

We bypassed Jeanette's room. I didn't open every room for him to see. They were all about the same, large with a sitting area and a kitchenette, and all overlooking the water on the sound side, and on the other side, each room opened onto a long, wide window hallway with a view of the gardens. Most of the rooms were decorated with some image or sculpture related to the legend of King Arthur. Seating was arranged in the hallway for readers or for dreaming. We'd once had an artist staying here who spent most of his visit set up in the second-floor hallway painting the garden. We'd taken bets between us on whether he'd ever sleep in the bed. He had, finally, but not until the last night. His paintings sold widely, and I liked to think the images of my garden were hanging in homes far and wide.

There was even a time back then when I'd sat in the garden and sketched the live oaks or relaxed in the Adirondack chairs out on the cliff terrace scribbling poetry and private thoughts in my journal and had felt at peace.

That was long ago now.

"No leaks anywhere thus far. We've been remarkably lucky." But in my head, I was saying, *How can I let this go on? Eventually, this situation will become untenable.* And the same voice inside my head responded, *How can I let all of this go? It's like letting Arthur die all over again.*

Dominick gave me a quick, sharp look. It was the use of WE, I knew.

I shrugged. "The royal *we*. Me, myself, and I."

"And now Jeanette, right? Nice to have a familiar face around, isn't it? Been a long time."

He'd known about the break. That was old news. He didn't need to know the details of the current state, I reminded myself. Without intonation, I simply said, "She's just passing through."

This time his smile seemed sad. He nodded, sighed, then said, "We should have an inspector come in to verify the condition. If we can certify the premises are in good condition, then that's a strong selling point. If there are underlying problems, buyers will want to know." He paused, then said, "Can we take a look at the residence?"

I blinked. "My home?"

"If you sell the property, that will be part of it."

"Of course."

He asked softly, "If you decide to keep the property . . . you've already said you won't reopen the hotel on your own. Are you interested in acquiring a partner?"

"A partner? No. I was thinking of demolishing the hotel wing and continuing to live here in the original residence as I do now."

"Wow. Well, I didn't know you were considering that as an option."

His tone implied concern. I asked, "And?"

"It's an expensive option. It will cost a lot just to have the hotel dismantled and even more to have it hauled out of here and disposed of. I don't recommend that. Your choice, of course."

My expression probably spoke for me.

Dominick said gently, "But it's good to have options. And..." He paused for effect. "If you do decide to list, you will have *many* options. In fact, Mignon, any hint that you might be willing to sell and interested parties will come knocking. You know this. Beware. Don't try to negotiate with them directly. Not all of them will be on the up and up, and they'll all be trying to score the best deal possible."

I considered what he was saying.

He said, "It's a valuable property. To you it represents family and memories. But to others? Most likely developers or hoteliers will want it. There's lots of room up here for expansion while retaining privacy. Appealing. Until you have someone else representing your interests, refer them to me—no strings from me— we've been friends too long for that. Directing them to me will give you a buffer."

I drew in a deep breath and let it out slowly. "I don't like the idea of those people inviting themselves onto the property to . . . I don't know . . . to examine what's left of my life."

"No, Mignon. Not that."

"They did the last time . . . back when I lost him."

"Not that. I mean, you talking about what's left of your life as if it's almost done. You have so much life ahead of you. You're young."

"I don't feel young." I was embarrassed at the *poor me* whine in my voice.

"Well, I'm the same age as you and I don't feel old, so this *age* you're feeling isn't due to years lived. It's the weight of what you're carrying around. Don't be tied to the past or to things."

"Says the real estate agent," I quipped and shook my head.

"Well, I do have a different speech for the ones who want to buy. Like, *Let's find the perfect place for your family to make a home and memories to last a lifetime.*"

"Right."

"And it's true too. Memories are the ultimate keepsakes when it comes to portability." He gave me a quick hug. "In the meantime, keep the gate locked and call me if you have a problem."

Forcing a smile, I said, "You'll put on your real estate secret agent cape and rush to rescue me?"

He smiled kindly. "You bet, Meg. Anytime."

⁓⁓⁓

Dominick was the only one who called me Meg. He hadn't called me that in a long time. Early on, he'd done it to aggravate Arthur—they'd been buddies for many years—and maybe his intent was also to aggravate me. I stopped telling him that *Meg* was not the diminutive for *Mignon* way back when because my chiding seemed only to encourage him.

Meg. Dominick had the right to call me that. It sounded right coming from him, but no one else.

Dominick left, and I sat on my porch. Galahad was glad to have me back, and he let me know it. I scratched his ears and neck.

When Dominick was getting into his car, I'd told him to leave the gate open for now. What I didn't tell him was that Jeanette would be using it very soon.

I would help her carry her stuff to her car, and I would gladly wave goodbye.

⁓⁓⁓

Soon after Dominick departed, Jeanette came

around the corner of the house as if on cue. "You're waiting for me to leave?"

"Yes."

"Are you going to sell Emerald Heart?"

"Maybe. Maybe not." I shook my head, refusing to soften my tone. "Not your business either way."

"No, it isn't. I don't want to argue about who did what, including the blame for what went wrong seven years ago and everyone's behavior since. Blame goes in more directions than just to me. And it goes back a whole lot farther than my argument with Arthur. You've never let it go, have you? You can't. You still blame me."

"Don't change the subject. You're deflecting. What happened was between you and Arthur, but the two of you not only hurt each other—I was the collateral damage to both of your stubbornness and pride." I stopped and waved my hand. "It doesn't matter. It's too late to change anything." I stood. When she didn't move, I added, "It's time, Jeanette."

Her shoulders slumped. "What if I told you that I've suffered a reversal of fortune. That . . ." She stopped and drew in a ragged breath. "That I need help?"

"You mean money? Are we back to your father's investment in the hotel? I warned Arthur that one day you'd be griping about the money your father invested in Emerald Heart, and I heard those very words when you fought with him. I heard *more* than enough. It was so horrible I couldn't even bring myself to tell Arthur *I told you so*. You should know that there isn't any money. In those last years, the hotel barely covered expenses, and it hasn't earned a dime since we stopped accepting guests, so you can forget about money from me."

"Money? No. I mean, I'm short of funds, but—"

"You want shelter? What?"

"Yes."

"Yes what?" My temper was short.

Jeanette seemed to grow a little smaller as she said, very softly, "Yes, I need your help, Mignon, to get back on my feet. A place to stay for a few days would help immensely."

I was so agitated that I clasped my hands together and squeezed hard to refrain from losing control totally. But she could see it—my agitation and distress—yet she stood and waited.

Coldly, I said, "You'll have to find help elsewhere."

"I will," she said. "I *will* find help elsewhere, but I need a place to stay for a few days while a friend of mine works things out, and then she'll be able to help me. A few days. No more."

When I didn't answer, she said, "Put me to work, Mignon. Cleaning, weeding, whatever. I'll do anything. Whether you stay or sell, this place . . ." She swept her arm around the visible property. "You've done an amazing job of keeping things together all on your own, but it's a big job. Anything I can do to help, I'm happy to take it on."

"I needed your help to heal what went wrong between you and Arthur. I needed your help when he was diagnosed with cancer. I needed your help when the treatments made him so sick. And I could've used your help when he was dying." I paused to breathe. "I don't need you now, and I have nothing to give you—not time or shelter or courtesy. Stay in 101 for a few days if you must, but keep away from me. Go to town for food. When you leave and return be sure to lock the gate." I turned away and went into the house to find a gate key for her.

With my back to the door, one hand gripping the doorknob and my eyes squeezed shut, I stood there and breathed. When my heart had slowed—not quite to a normal rhythm, but better—I opened my eyes. Galahad was sitting a few feet away staring at me. Just that, just sitting and staring. Was that disappointment in his eyes?

"You're a dog," I said. "Don't judge me."

CRSO

As evening bloomed in glorious sunset shades of lavender and gold, I looked outside and saw Jeanette's car, not quite parked as it had been before, so she must've driven into town for her meal as I'd suggested.

Suggested? Is that what I chose to call it?

I set the security alarms for the hotel wing, fed Galahad and let him out for the last trip of the day, then I went to my bedroom. My bedroom—I stopped in the doorway. I hadn't painted, redecorated, or moved a stick of furniture since before Arthur had gotten sick. I'd thought of it, but only in passing, certainly not seriously.

I knew I'd get a quick offer once I put Emerald Heart on the market. Yet the thought of packing it all up—boxing things to move, making decisions about what to keep and what not to keep, and ditching the unwanted—was almost insurmountable. What constituted unwanted, anyway?

I didn't want outsiders, even friendly ones, to see how sad this place—our home—had become. Old paint. Stale carpeting. Dusty blinds. People might laugh about Arthur's mania, but this had been a popular hotel full of laughter for many years. Kayaking. Fishing. Ocean charters. Even that daggone disc golf. What had I created alone and on my own? Only a life that was just marking time.

Doubts, regrets, grief—they often piled in on top of me as night approached.

Nights were always the worst.

Did I sleep that night? Not much. And I thought—*This can have no end but that of madness.* Something must change. Even if that meant giving up everything that had been my life for a quarter of a century.

But, I reminded myself, I'd done one good deed today, even if I'd done it poorly and grudgingly. I'd allowed Jeanette additional nights at The Emerald Heart Hotel . . . and free of charge. Maybe that qualified as *one healthy thing.*

Didn't feel that way, though. Not healthy or good.

Chapter Eight

I awoke trapped in tangled sheets and feeling hungover. Fleeting nausea twisted my stomach. The light was slanting in through the blinds, so I knew it was morning.

Where was Galahad? Why hadn't he awakened me with a cold nose on my hand or the chuffing noises he made when he felt neglected?

Pushing up to a half-seated position, I listened for the sound of his nails click-clicking on the wooden floor.

Nothing.

Gingerly, I pressed my bare feet to the floor, standing slowly as if I were eighty. The nausea had passed, but my heart was as heavy as it had ever been.

My eyes burned and ached as if I'd cried in my sleep. Fleeting remembrances of dreams—like vignettes from an ancient tragedy—came to me as I trudged out of my bedroom and down the hall. I'd dreamed of Arthur, of losing him. Of losing our daughter, Sebrina—but all over again in a nightmare land. No wonder my eyes ached and my tummy hurt.

I stopped in the office to disarm the system. If the alarm tripped this morning, its blaring might do me in altogether.

Galahad was in the living room, lying flat on the floor with his snout against the invisible opening between the front door and the threshold. When I walked over to him, he rose, but only to go to the window, to stand there on his hind legs with his paws braced on the sill. Watching. His ears up and back. His doggy lips quivered, even moving up a fraction to show his canines. His tail was not wagging, but doing an incredibly slow-motion swish that reminded me of cats when they were developing a battle plan.

He was watching. For something or someone.

My aches suddenly forgotten, I thought, *He hasn't done this since those days after Arthur passed.* And then I realized what might be disturbing him.

I joined him at the window. Seeing no one, I stepped quietly away, and went down the hallway to the door to the lobby. Dressed only in my pajamas, I considered stopping in the bedroom for my robe, but damage could be done in nothing flat. More than that, my temper was rising at the prospect of being forced to relive those awful days after losing Arthur. It drove me.

Very carefully, I unlocked and opened the door.

Despite the low light in the lobby, it was clearly empty of intruders. Stepping in and closing the door behind me, I paused again, staring at the double doors at the front entrance. No one was visible, so that was my next goal. I opened those doors and stepped out to stand under the awning . . . and that's when I spotted them.

Two men. One in khakis and one in jeans. Mr. Khaki was moving between the foundation bushes and the building, walking along the stretch of rooms and peeking in the windows. Mr. Jeans was about to walk around the far end of the hotel wing, presumably to investigate the back side of the building and the gardens—and so I yelled.

Mr. Khaki stopped peering through the windows and turned toward me. He looked more amused at my attitude than concerned about his trespassing. Mr. Jeans walked away from the building and began moving back toward the other man and to where I was standing by the lobby entrance. I patted my pajamas, realizing I had no phone on my person, nothing but wrinkled cotton nightclothes and a mass of long, mostly black hair styled only by a freakish night.

"Sorry, ma'am. Are you Mignon King?" He flashed me a smile. Too friendly. "I was hoping to speak to you about this property."

Shaken, I drew in a breath intending to demand that he leave, but instead of my own voice, it was Jeanette that I heard, her strong voice coming from behind me, shouting, "You are trespassing!"

The men stopped, maybe because there were two women now, both yelling at them.

"Call the police, Jeanette. Right now."

"Ma'am. Just wanted to talk, but—"

"Those are legally posted No Trespassing signs you ignored. That was a locked gate you walked around. Sniffing and spying about my property, uninvited." I pointed toward the eaves. "And that's a camera that's been recording you."

"Meant no harm, ma'am. I'll leave my card with you." He approached me with his hand extended.

"Get out of here."

"Okay." He knelt slowly and placed the card in the dirt, then rose and backed up. "Please contact me when you get the chance. I would greatly appreciate the opportunity to discuss your plans for this property."

"Charles," he called out to the other man. "Let's go." He cast a glance at me, then Jeanette, and then back at me. "My sincere apologies for any alarm or inconvenience my unannounced visit has caused. I am sorry."

They turned and walked away, heading down the road toward the gate, the men walked side by side silently at first, but as they got out of earshot, it was obvious they were talking to each other, and one of them cast a look back at us, at the hotel.

Jeanette came to stand beside me. She had a cane today and was leaving a trail of small holes poked into the earth in her wake. I hadn't seen it happen, but the image of her shaking that cane at the men as she yelled bloomed in my head and amused me. She saw me looking. Lifting the cane as if it were a show-and-tell event, she said, "Found this at the lobby desk. Probably don't need it—the ankle is much better—but it reminds me to be careful."

I let her explanation go unremarked.

In a smaller voice, she asked, "Did I overstep? I'm sure you could've handled the situation yourself. I acted impulsively. But what they did was. . . rude. Just rude."

I nodded. "Yes. Rude."

☙❧

My adrenaline must've still been up when I dialed Dominick. The card the trespasser had given me was in my hand, but I was so annoyed I could hardly read it. I waved it in the air, saying, "Did you tell anyone that I was considering selling? I didn't authorize that, Dominick. I never said—"

"Hold on, Meg. What's up? Did something happen? Are you okay?"

"Two men, Dominick. Practically at dawn. They were peeking in the windows even. I chased them off. One left his card." I squinted. "Owen Jones. Looks like a real estate agent. Do you know him?"

He groaned loudly.

"So you did tell someone!"

"No. I mean, *yes, I recognize the name*. Maybe someone saw us in the diner and overheard what we were saying."

"We were very discreet."

He groaned again. "How could I forget? Maybe that alone raised suspicions? All that hunching over and whispering and sidelong looks. Gee whiz. Who knows? But it wasn't me, Meg. I didn't say anything to anyone."

With my phone still pressed to my cheek, I sank into my favorite chair. Galahad was gone again. He'd been here and now he wasn't.

"I believe you. I thought maybe you'd contacted an inspector right after we spoke, that maybe word got out that way." I sighed. "It will sooner or later, I guess, regardless of what I decide to do." I shook my head, though no one was here to see my despair. "I don't feel up to dealing with all that, Dominick. Just being honest here."

After speaking with Dominick and feeling a bit calmer, I went looking for Galahad. He was in Sebrina's room. He hadn't come to us until many years after we'd lost her. Long before that, Arthur had changed her room into a small office. I remembered the day I'd discovered most of her bedroom furniture was gone. Only the small bureau remained, and when I yanked the top drawer open, I saw that Arthur had stored office supplies there. I was irate.

Arthur explained that he wanted to stay closer to me during the day, which struck me as odd, because the official office was just off the lobby with a clear view of it—as it should be. That realization sobered me. He was worried about me, and surely with reason.

But we'd made it through the loss of our child, hadn't we? Not all marriages did.

He didn't accuse me of being overwrought about the change in the office arrangements. Instead, he'd held me close and whispered that he'd kept her personal items, keepsakes, some of her clothing—and had boxed them up. That anytime I wanted to see them, to go through them, to let him know. He'd have them to me in a jiffy.

That had happened five years after Sebrina passed. Almost ten years before his death. I'd never asked for those boxes. Didn't even know where he'd put them. And I was okay with that. Even now, I didn't think I could bear handling her treasures.

If I started going through the closets and the attic for whatever reason, maybe to sell or move, I'd find them soon enough. My heart sank.

Maybe Arthur had been right to do what he did. For him, yes, but mostly for me.

I found Galahad lying beside Arthur's desk chair, half under the desk itself. Missing Arthur? Probably.

Kneeling beside him, I said, "Come on, sweet boy. Our day started wrong. Time to shake it off. We need a fresh start."

He showed more interest when I put his breakfast in his dish. Satisfied that he was okay, I started pulling out my own breakfast items. I'd feed Jeanette this morning. How could I not? I sent her a quick text saying as much, telling her to knock on the adjoining door at nine o'clock. But when I stood at the sink with the window in front of me, I saw movement. I assumed Jeanette was out there again, but a longer look told me no. Not Jeanette.

The woman was dressed professionally but with sensible shoes, showing she'd come prepared to walk up the road, so likely she was a developer or agent. And yet another trespasser.

Anger surged within me. I slammed the egg carton down on the counter, forgetting the contents. Galahad barked, echoing the noise.

"Stay, boy," I said, and I headed out my kitchen

door and onto the patio.

"Guess you chose to ignore the posted signs? Get off my property."

The woman grimaced. She came closer and extended her hand. "Thought the place was vacant. Sorry to have disturbed you." When I didn't respond in kind, she added, "Apparently this is the only way to get a look at this place. I apologize again, of course." She kept her extended, seeming certain that I'd accept it eventually. "If you *are* interested in selling this place, I have a very interested party." She offered her card. "Please give me a call."

Ignoring her outstretched hand, I said, "Dominick Monahan of Beach Heart Realty. Talk to him. If I see you here again, I'll take your photo and ask the police to arrest you for trespassing. Go."

❧

Jeanette had had my back that morning when the two men had shown up. As for this woman just now, it was pure chance that I'd seen her before she'd . . . what? Broken in? Maybe.

How grateful was I for Jeanette's assistance?

With strangers showing up uninvited, was there value in having someone else at the hotel with me? Did the value outweigh the annoyance and inconvenience? Given that the *someone else* in question was Jeanette, was it worth the emotional cost?

Staying a few nights—it's all she wanted, right? Another pair of eyes would be useful. I wasn't eager to go back to jumping at every noise, constantly on edge with only me to watch over things. Most of it had been nothing, but those times where it *was* something reinforced the hypervigilance. I'd found a balance as the trespassers had stopped coming, and I couldn't bear the idea of going back to that. Not alone.

When Jeanette knocked on the adjoining door, instead of handing her a tray of food I invited her into my house.

"Thanks, I appreciate it," she said.

Had there been an edge to her thank-you? I ignored any implied criticism. She'd earned whatever slights I might send her way. Even now, I could hardly believe I was doing this.

As we walked down the hallway to the living room, I asked, "Orange juice? Coffee? Tea?"

"Tea's good."

I left her checking out the mantel and went to the kitchen.

"Arthur's urn?" she asked, her voice clearly audible.

"On the mantel. Yes."

I returned and handed her the glass of tea. "Have a seat? I want to discuss something with you." I gestured toward the kitchen. "Might as well eat breakfast while we talk."

She looked momentarily confused by my change in manner.

"It might benefit us both to call a truce," I said. "If you're open to discussing it, have a seat in the kitchen and we can talk over breakfast."

Jeanette nodded, and we went into the kitchen.

While she was buttering her toast, I said, "Since you need a place to stay for a short while, I was thinking we could make that work for both of us. I'm not looking to be chummy or anything like that, but you'll have a safe place to stay while helping me watch out for intruders."

"Are you serious?"

"I am. As annoying as the real estate agents and developers can be, there's also ghost hunters, treasure hunters, even just bored people who get a thrill out of doing damage. You'd think people would have enough to deal with already, without . . ." I struggled for the right words and found them. "Without dredging up shadows and chaos from the dark corners of their brains."

"Are these people dangerous?"

I sighed. "No, not generally, but they can do a lot of damage to a building, as well as disrupt a person's life and peace of mind." I shook my head. "It's usually easy enough to run them off, but it drives Galahad bonkers." I smirked. "And me too. You need a place to stay for a few days, right?"

She hesitated, which made no sense to me.

"Stay here in room 101. Help me keep an eye out for trespassers. I've delayed doing anything about my situation here for too long. I'll have this figured out soon. By then your friend will be ready for you to move in."

CRISO

I'd always had a soft spot in my heart for Dominick. He'd been Arthur's friend first, and then mine after I met Arthur. It would have been all too easy to depend on Dominick after my husband's death, so during that hardest time, I'd kept him at a bit of a distance. But this was about business, or the potential for business—not just about me being needy—so I called him to discuss the intruder problem again.

"There's interest. I've had a few messages. I'm telling everyone that you are undecided at this point, but marketwise, now is an excellent time to list it."

My silence told him a lot.

"So, okay, let's talk about something else."

"Like?"

"Like that you are alone too much."

"And you are a broken record." I ended that with a little laugh. "But you should know that I've invited Jeanette to stay on for a few days. With people showing up unexpectedly, I feel better having someone else around. Isn't there a law against such behavior?"

"Trespassing? Sure," he said. "But when money and opportunity is involved, the more the money, the less consideration and respect it drives." He said, "As a matter of fact, I'm free right now. Why don't I drop by?"

"Two days in a row? I'm sure you have other things that need your attention."

"Mignon, I'm your friend. You wanted some

distance and I gave you that, but things have changed. I'm not too busy to be your friend."

"Dominick—" I wanted to say that there was no need, but the truth was, I wanted to see him and talk to him.

After we disconnected, I walked out to the garden and sat on the bench.

Money. Only developers would pay the kind of money that would drive this much interest. The faded cream-colored and stucco-textured walls of Emerald Heart seemed to stare at me, but innocently. Unsuspecting.

I felt like a traitor.

Telling Dominick, *Yes, I'm ready to sell*, would be tantamount to condemning those walls. Not only the walls would be knocked down, but what of the trees? Most of the garden would probably be plowed under for a tennis court or a pool or a larger parking lot. Flashy condos with lots of amenities that required even more trees to be felled would probably yield the best return for a developer's money.

Dominick found me there in the garden. He knelt and touched Galahad's head. "Hey, fella." He looked at me. "Doubts?"

I shook my head. "Of course." I sighed. "It's not likely that someone would buy this location for the view and the privacy and all that, and keep this small, old hotel here. Taxes, insurance, upkeep—in those last years before we closed it down, this place was barely break-even. As it is, even without the operating expenses, I feel like I'm bleeding money to keep it intact while time takes its own toll. And time is winning. One big, damaging storm and I won't have a choice."

Dominick had moved from greeting Galahad to sitting beside me on the bench. He leaned toward me, speaking softly. "I can't dispute what you're saying. While there's a lot to be said for still being in that space where you have options, if an adverse weather event happens, or if the economy takes a downturn, those options change. But is that what this is really about?"

He was trying to help me think this through. I took a moment to gather my response.

"Dominick, it's about all that and more. I'm juggling too many moving parts and trying to do that while handicapped by emotion. If I do sell, I'll need to start all over again. My only work experience is hotel management, and I don't want to manage a hotel, especially not someone else's. I only did it here to help Arthur.

"But how do I afford a fresh start? I don't want to miss the opportunity of a good market. On the other hand, if I simply demolish the hotel but stay in my home, I'll reduce my costs and insurance and all that. I could stay here at Emerald Heart... well, the house part surrounded by acreage and... just me. I could afford that, but there wouldn't be much extra. Maybe *no* extra if the cost to pull the hotel wing down and haul it away is too high."

"You could sell off some acreage to cover the expense of clearing the grounds." He shook his head.

"But demolition and disposal will be costly." He paused, then asked, "Mignon, expenses and financial considerations aside, can you handle this emotionally?"

"Yes." I gulped. "No."

"Mignon."

I sighed. "There are bound to be second thoughts and regrets, right?"

"What would you like to do next, if you do make a change?"

"Find a small place with a view."

"Staying local?"

"Probably."

He smiled. "Good."

"Maybe travel a little."

"Let me know if you'd like company."

He said it, but sort of lightly. I decided to take it equally lightly.

"Ah, but I was counting on you to take care of the pooch sleeping here at my feet while I see the sights."

He grinned and moved back ever so slightly. "Happy to help in any way. Just let me know when and how."

"I'm sorry I need so much handholding. The choice to sell seems the most obvious. But it is so very hard."

He took my hand. "I think you already know what you need to do."

"Mind telling me? It would save me a lot of angst."

He said, "I repeat, I think you already know what you need to do. You just don't want to tackle what must be done first."

I smacked his hand and shook it off.

"Ouch," he said. "That's what I get for giving you the benefit of my experience and expertise?" He shook his hand in mock pain.

Smiling, I said, "Being right can be painful. Still, I appreciate it."

"Start simply. Begin with the items no one cares about. Attic, closets . . . you know, the stuff that gets shoved to the back of the cabinets that no one even remembers. Begin there."

Chapter Nine

I had a good night's sleep, which I credited to my chat with Dominick. It was true that talking to trusted friends about problems really could be helpful. And healthy. I was going to retroactively mark that chat as another healthy thing done yesterday.

This morning, when I'd opened the windows, I hadn't lingered, afraid I'd be caught up in memories again. I'd made a list of to-dos the day before and was determined to focus on them. No more mornings that started in the past and ended with me wondering how a whole day could've slipped by without me accomplishing anything real. One wasted day might be considered a gift—an opportunity to rest and refresh. More than a day here and there without the excuse of sickness or injury was simply a squandering of one's life.

I could give myself a pass for the first year after losing Arthur. But the second year? Nope. The temptation to lose myself in those memories, to find comfort in the time before things went so wrong, was incredibly compelling when the future was so uncertain.

The idea of doing one healthy thing each day? I wasn't hitting 100 percent with that, but hey, I was doing better in my interactions with Jeanette, right? And I'd resisted the lure to raid the imaginary memory box.

I would continue that progress. Today would be one more day of moving forward. I would *make* it different. I could start going through things. Not the items that triggered my anxiety or the past. Those would be saved for when I was stronger and more confident.

It was hard to know where to begin, but I thought the office would be best. We had a lot of stuff stored in there and in the closet too, so it seemed a natural place to begin. Yet I stood there with my fingertips pressed against the closet door, not quite able to push it aside. How long did I stand there? A while, I thought. And I shivered. Luckily, Galahad came in just then and started nudging my calf with his nose.

"You want out, sweet boy?"

He did that little curtsy-like jump with his front paws to confirm the question.

"Gladly, Sir Galahad. I am at your service."

Grateful, I turned my back on the closet and went to let him out the front door.

The air out here was different. It was fresh. The sky was blue. Still feeling a little shaky, I walked across to the terrace and stopped at the low rock wall Arthur had had built to stop folks from inadvertently stepping off, or driving over, the edge of the cliff. The view was amazing.

The view? I squinted. Was someone swimming to my dock again? The same someone?

I blinked. Yes indeed. Not a boat in sight. This was not some hapless vacationer stuck on a tube or in a kayak sans paddle and unable to steer. A body—one I'd seen before—was moving strongly through the water with sure, elegant strokes and was just reaching my dock. Short hair, bare shoulders, and his back were breaking the surface, then his hands gripped the ladder railing, and the rest of him emerged from the water, dripping as he raked his hand across his face and his scalp. Swim trunks or shorts? Couldn't tell which, but not the same ones he'd worn before. This was clearly a habit or routine. All I could think of was Mr. Darcy emerging from the pond to the surprise of Miss Bennet. Bravo, Miss Austen.

This time I moved decisively. I'd be at the top of the stairs when he arrived there.

I crossed the distance between my terrace and the cliff stairs. He hadn't noticed me up above, nor did he come to the stairs. I wanted to be annoyed, and I was a little, but his style was a novel, more energetic approach to trespass than I'd encountered before.

Galahad came into view below. He'd gone straight down to the dock. My dog made himself known to the man, and the man acknowledged him with a word and a pat on the head before moving to stand on the side of the dock, his back to me and his bare feet hanging a toe's length over the edge. He posed to dive as he stared forward at the next dock, actually quite a distance away in that neighboring subdivision. I started to call out, but again was too late as with a quick, easy move he dove into the water. No deep dive, thank goodness. That would be a good way to break one's neck in this shallow water. I released my held breath. He'd hit the water smoothly, lithely, more as if he were treading the surface and making scarcely a ripple. With strong strokes, he soon moved beyond the promontory and out of easy view.

Wow.

I needed another sign down there—*Shallow Water, No Diving.*

Galahad had been quite a welcome party. Clearly, he remembered the stranger too.

Huh. Further, it occurred to me, that seeing someone jump from the dock of Emerald Heart had not distressed me. I hadn't even thought of Sebrina. . . until now that I had, of course. That was progress, right?

Maybe I could add this to my list of healthy things? No. But it was fun to feel somewhat entertained by the show.

And here came Galahad—my loyal, trusty companion and protector—who hadn't issued a single bark at the intruder and was now coming back up the stairs to me and looking illogically pleased with himself.

I knelt and gave him a hug and scratch. It pleased me to see him looking perky and, yes, that was a healthy thing and *would* make the list.

〇⟊〇

"Let's get your leash, Galahad."

Anything to avoid what I was supposed to be doing? Yes.

I carried the leash instead of fixing it to the

harness. We weren't likely to need it staying on the trails.

The woodland trails skirted the low, dark swamps and climbed the steeper paths to views of the sound below. Today we followed the trail down that crossed the narrow wooden footbridge with its up-close-and-personal view of minnows and other tiny creatures in a water source flowing from the swamp toward the sound—a personal favorite of Galahad's. He always paused, his nose just short of a wetting, and peered at the small but fast swimmers.

When he was satisfied that he'd seen enough, we climbed to the ridge above the swamp where the trees overhanging the path were draped in Spanish moss. The fine white dirt was soft and cool to his paws, and the shade was kind to us both. The trails avoided the larger tree falls, some with massive trunks scoured by the weather and bleached gray with the passing of years.

We stopped at our favorite bench at the top of a hill. The woodland scene went abruptly down—much like Arthur's promontory, but untamed—and between the mature trees and the saplings, the view was of marsh grasses at the edge of the water, a small boat out by the sandbar, and houses on the far side of the sound.

This was one of the many views that were dear to me. Arthur and I had spent many hours hiking these trails and sitting on this bench. He'd spent even more playing disc golf with Carolyn's grandson. Disc golf was not my thing. Sometimes I tagged along to cheer and advise.

But this view. This was my thing. And it was only a small part of what I was facing the loss of.

This wasn't something I could pack up in a box.

As I sat there, I noticed scuff marks in the dirt. The white, soft, dusty ground was actually hard-packed and not inclined to show footsteps, but here before me, were shoe marks, as if someone had sat on the bench kicking at it, digging their shoes into it.

Who would that be? Well, I couldn't keep everyone out. That would be impossible. Even undesirable. But this seemed different. Not a casual trail walker. Rather someone who'd stayed awhile.

Yet another reminder that I had big choices to make, easy or not.

Chapter Ten

For the next few days, Jeanette and I fell into a routine that mostly involved avoiding each other. I disarmed the alarm in the morning, rearmed it before dark, and we kept the foyer doors locked around the clock. We came together at mealtimes. While the food wasn't fancy, it was better than what she could cook using only the guest room microwave. We didn't share long, congenial meals, but neither did we throw food or plates at each other, so I counted that as acceptable and healthy.

Jeanette's limp had vanished and there'd been no more intruders traipsing around the property. No other incidents worth noting. It was a huge relief. At breakfast, Jeanette said, "I'm driving into town to run some errands. Need anything?"

After a pause to think, I gave her a short list.

"Lock the gate behind you, please. I know it's a pain to stop and do that, but it's best that way."

"Of course, Mignon. I understand. I'll be gone awhile. Maybe a few hours."

We watched her drive away. I looked forward to having the place to myself again for a little while. Galahad may or may not have agreed with me. I think he enjoyed her being here. It was my ambivalence that confused him.

After that awkward stalemate at the closet a few days ago, I'd returned to the office but steadfastly ignored the closet itself. For the past couple of days, I'd been going through old binders of promotional materials and activities pamphlets, and other assorted stuff that should've been ditched a long time ago. It was still difficult because memories of Arthur and I planning these together kept surfacing, but I did okay. I was now down to focusing on an old box of receipts and papers— not business-related because the accountant handled those. These were the kind of odds and ends one tossed into a pile in case a purchase might need to be returned or you were cleaning out your purse and didn't want to pause to take a closer look.

It was tedious for me, and Galahad looked bored and restless. When that particular box was empty, I said, "We need a stick." I said it in an exaggerated way that Galahad loved.

Galahad jumped to his feet and all but danced. In that moment, he seemed to shed at least a few of his almost eight years.

He dashed out into the grassy lawn ahead of me.

Arthur had insisted on widening the green swath of lawn that faced the sound when he'd had the rock wall built. At that time, he'd also had the stone terrace put in to abut the wall and added colorful Adirondack chairs, so there was plenty of room for games of fetch. If the thrower's arm was strong enough, there was always the guest parking lot beyond to accommodate the reach.

"Okay, boy," I said. "Where's that stick?"

Off he raced across the grass, heading straight toward the woods and passing any number of perfectly fine sticks along the way. Galahad was a stick connoisseur. I waited, and soon he was loping back to me with his stick of choice carried between his teeth like a prize.

The stick was maybe a foot long and perfect for throwing games.

I reared back dramatically, waving the stick in the air to get full mileage out of Galahad's excitement. He jumped and pawed the sand, thoroughly engaged and excited. I let that stick fly. It sailed as far as my puny biceps could throw it. Which is to say, it wasn't all that far. Galahad was back in no time for the next throw. I was quickly bored, so after a few tosses I waved the stick out to my side and ran a few steps before throwing just to switch it up for him. I soon lost count. One more time, I told myself, and as Galahad eagerly watched to see what tricks I might have in store for him, anticipating that the stick would ultimately soar through the air for him to chase and capture—a voice came from behind me.

"I'm sorry to interrupt. I saw you out here and was hoping to have a word."

Instead of putting the stick into flight, I pulled my arms back and grasped the piece of wood two-handed like a weapon. It was the man. The swimmer. The stranger.

Hands to his side, palms out, he shook his head slowly and repeated his apology, this time adding, "We met, sort of, the other day over on the beach."

I stared at him, trying to gauge his intent. He was better dressed today. Jeans and a shirt. Though *better* depended on one's perspective. He wasn't barefoot today but was wearing sneakers, untied as if he'd hurried here.

Loose shoestrings always bothered me. I frowned at them. At him.

"I have seen you before, yes, at the beach and on this very property . . . which is odd, considering that this is private property and I have no idea who you are."

He frowned. "I promise that I'm not spying or stalking you." He scratched his cheek, but in a thoughtful way. "I like to exercise . . . running, swimming. That kind of thing. There's not a lot of other options here. Sorry about the trespassing. Hope I didn't disturb you."

He was polite. I had to give him that.

I shifted the stick between my fingers, which caught Galahad's attention and he looked hopeful.

"Shall I?" the man asked, and he deftly acquired the stick from my hand and held it up.

"Be our guest."

He tossed it much farther than I'd managed, and Galahad, my erstwhile protector, took off after it like a shot.

The stranger said, "That's a beautiful dog." He smiled. "I'm staying at the Holmans' house?" He gestured toward the bridge.

I looked in reflex, but of course I knew the Holman family. Their house was across the ravine on the next promontory. A distance beyond their property was the bridge.

"We've been neighbors for years, so yes, I know them," I said. "Are you visiting them?"

"Renting."

"Oh." My resistance was ebbing, and I was feeling a bit foolish, thinking he might have been watching me. Was I being overly suspicious about people stalking me for the property?

"I'll be staying there for another month."

His frequent appearance was now making more sense.

This time when Galahad returned, he offered the stick to the stranger.

The man accepted the stick but then held it out for me to take. I shook my head, and much to Galahad's delight he threw it again.

"Are the Holmans okay?" I'd been so reclusive for so long. Had something happened to them?

"As far as I know." He shrugged. "The management company said something about them going south for the winter. Maybe Florida? Not sure, but I guess they got a head start on the snowbird thing. I live in the city but wanted something different for a while. I've been here almost a month now. I noticed the hotel, so I asked around. You're the owner, right? It's quite a sight overlooking the water, and the forest is amazing. I apologize for trespassing. Didn't realize so much of it was privately owned."

"Despite the No Trespassing and Private Property signs?"

He shrugged. "I could say I wasn't sure which

parts of the property they applied to, but mostly, in my defense, I just wanted to exercise and wasn't planning on disturbing anyone. I should've asked first."

I said, "I did see you, and no, I didn't really mind, but yes, you should've checked with me."

"I stand corrected."

"That's a big house you're renting. You must have family with you?"

"No. Just me. I'm between jobs. Not a sad story but due to a noncompete clause when I sold my business."

I grinned. "And you're already bored out of your mind?"

He returned my grin, realized Galahad was butting his leg with a new stick, and gave it a throw. "Somewhat. Beautiful place. No mistake about that. It's peaceful. Real peaceful."

He drew the r-e-a-l p-e-a-c-e-f-u-l out as if it wasn't as desirable as he'd expected.

I smiled again. "We love the peace and quiet."

"And your hotel guests love it too?"

My smile, perhaps even my grudging goodwill, was wiped from my face. His question seemed unnecessarily spiteful. The parking lots were obviously empty except for the two cars. I faced him squarely and said, "They used to. The hotel is closed. Hence the signs. Hence there's no reason for anyone to be using this property without my consent."

He ignored my warning tone and continued with what was on his mind. "I was curious but not enough to ask about it because I hadn't planned to stay. Another month alone here? No. But then I heard in town that you might be selling. Speculation only, of course."

"Yes."

"I asked at the realty in town. Mr. Monahan said he isn't representing you officially—not yet, anyway—and that you aren't sure about selling at this point."

This time, when Galahad returned, I reached down and grabbed the stick before my visitor could. "All done, boy. Time to go inside."

"Are you okay? Have I offended you? If so, I apologize."

I suspected he was an excellent negotiator and that the use of the words *offended* and *apologize* were chosen deliberately to mollify me. It was beyond me why he'd want my hotel and property, but I didn't care. It wasn't for sale. *Not yet, anyway,* as he'd said. Besides that, he wasn't staying. Yet he was asking about the hotel? *Bah.* Well, his business was none of my business—and vice versa. Altogether, he was much too calculating, too slick and devious for my taste.

I said, "If I do decide to sell, Dominick is the person who'll handle it." But I wasn't done. I added, "You didn't need to be nice to my dog to make a pitch for the property. My answer's the same either way."

He started to respond, and I cut him off and changed the subject without apology—*my specialty.*

"Have you even been to The Point?" I asked.

"The Point?"

I nodded. "I know you've found the beach. What about fishing? Boat or shore? How about kayaking?"

"I scheduled an ocean charter but haven't gone yet."

"What about Beaufort? Shopping, restaurants, and a fascinating old cemetery. Have you taken a boat over to Shackleford Banks? World-class shelling, you know."

He looked aside, seeming frustrated, then shook his head, his movement morphing into a nod as he grinned. "I see your point. Sorry, no pun intended."

I ignored his pathetic joke.

"Also, that super nice asphalt pathway out there on the main road? The thing most folks call the bike path? That's officially called the Emerald Path. It's also good for runners. Eleven miles from the Indian Beach town limits to The Point at Bogue Inlet. Bonus is that there's all sorts of eateries along the way, including ice cream shops and a stroll on the pier to see what the fishermen are catching." I held up one finger crooked to the side like a turn signal. "Just remember to stay on the right and pass on the left. On the Emerald Path, that is." I returned his grin and gestured at Galahad, "Come boy. Inside."

As we walked toward the house, my stranger-neighbor called out behind me, "My name is Blake."

I waved without turning around. A casual wave-off would remind him that we weren't friends, or even acquaintances. Even if he *had* offered me a kind word at the beach and had thrown a stick for my dog just now, a trespasser was still a trespasser, and this one also seemed to be a conniver. Be it a pleasant stranger or an ex-sister-in-law, a conniver was not to be trusted.

But daggone, hadn't I had my moment of triumph

by promoting local sites and opportunities for a vacationer who didn't properly appreciate what the area had to offer? Dissing my hometown indeed. I'd earned a bit of swagger, and it felt good. It felt both good and healthy.

I could check that off my to-do list for today. Maybe with a gold star added.

☙❧

Jeanette's car was still gone. It was past noon. She'd probably be gone awhile longer, taking care of her errands.

As I was shifting laundry from the washer to the dryer, I was thinking I was due for another trip to town myself. I'd enjoyed it the other day, and the encounter this morning had gotten me a bit riled up. Instead of calling Dominick this time and arranging a meetup, I might surprise him with a drop-in visit. Maybe entice him into a late lunch or early supper. Glancing over at Galahad, I confirmed he was still on his pillow, where he'd collapsed after a long drink of water. He was sleeping now, and judging by a twitch here and there, he was dreaming.

He woke just enough to give me a disinterested glance as I picked up my purse.

"Stay, boy. I'll be back soon."

I had to stop at the gate to unlock it and pull it wide, then drive my car through and then stop again to close the gate and relock it. Annoying, but necessary. At various times, I'd been tempted to upgrade to something electronic, but that was costly. Besides, I'd been doing this same action for so long that it was almost second nature now.

Dominick's real estate office was on the corner a block from the Beach Diner. I'd suggested the diner before because even though it was public, I thought it less likely to attract attention than me walking into the real estate office. Dominick and I were friends, after all. Even so, look what had happened. People had drawn conclusions and had, apparently, spoken out of turn because other people had shown up uninvited on my doorstep.

So today I'd go directly to the office and try to be low-key and discreet without looking odd or secretive.

I parked in the public lot, then walked around to the office via the sidewalk. The weather was lovely, and the sun was shining.

What would I do if I sold the hotel? Dominick had asked me that and I'd had an answer of sorts, but truly, I did not know.

Here was Dominick's office space—Beach Heart Realty. I pushed against the door, and it swung open.

The reception desk was unattended, but through the large glass window in Dominick's private office, I could see he wasn't alone. A woman—likely a client—was there with him. A woman with short brown hair. Her back was to me.

She had her elbows on the desk and was leaning

forward, facing Dominick. Dominick's posture indicated he was likewise engaged, smiling and very friendly as he nodded at the woman.

I wasn't smiling. I was stunned.

She'd said she had errands to run.

Had she been here the whole time? Or was this visit just a stop along the way? They looked comfy. Chatty. What the heck was going on?

Dominick hadn't noticed me because he was busy laughing with Jeanette.

I was frozen in place. My shoes were stuck to the cheap carpet. I forced myself to unstick them and turned back to the door. As I pulled it open to step outside, Marion, the receptionist, was returning. She had a bag of wrapped sandwiches in her hand. From the diner. Three of them.

Sort of like a party, huh? And I wasn't invited. That much was clear.

Marion said, "Are you okay?"

"I'm fine. Gotta run."

"Oh, okay," she said as we switched places, and she took over the door management by pushing her hip against it to slide inside.

And I—like a hurt puppy—tucked my tail between my legs and slinked away.

I was embarrassed by my retreat and felt utterly betrayed.

Chapter Eleven

Dominick called just as I arrived home.

"Where'd you vanish to?" he asked. "Marion said she saw you, that you were leaving just as she returned with the sandwiches. You should've joined us. We had plenty. I tried to catch you, but you were gone too quick."

I sat in the living room staring at my phone as I listened to Dominick over the speaker. His easy manner sounded so very innocent of anything untoward and was almost seductive. It would be so much simpler to accept that I'd misread what I'd seen, and that I'd overreacted. But I couldn't. The only words I could think to say resisted being spoken. Finally, I forced three of them out. "You were busy."

"Mignon? You sound . . . upset, maybe?"

"I'm fine."

"No, you aren't fine." He paused, then asked, "Is it because Jeanette was here?"

I didn't answer. I stood, needing to move.

"Oh." He added, "Ouch. Okay, so I'm feeling that icy silence all the way over here. I thought you were good with Jeanette now. She's staying with you, right?" He paused again, perhaps thinking I might contribute to the conversation. When I didn't speak, he resumed with,

"I'm sorry. I was pleased that you two had worked things out. In fact, judging by her manner, I think *she* believes that you two are well on the way to mending the break."

"Sorry to disappoint you, Dominick, but what's between Jeanette and me isn't your concern. There's nothing to make up or fix. She owes her apologies to Arthur, and that can't happen this side of heaven." I lowered my voice. "Jeanette is more a stranger to me than family or friend, but guess what? Even I can be helpful to a stranger who needs a place to stay for a few days."

I'd been pacing as I spoke, and when I stopped, I found myself face-to-face with the fireplace mantel. I reached out to touch the framed photo of Arthur and Sebrina. Sebrina was sitting on his shoulders. They were dressed in costumes Arthur had thought appropriate for the medieval fair we were attending.

Never in a million years would I have expected to attend such an event. My upbringing had been more practical, grounded in the present. Arthur brought that gift to me—that of imagination without any expectation of benefit except to simply enjoy our lives.

Dominick had finished speaking and I hadn't heard a word.

I said, "Sorry. I'll have to call you later. I'm done with this subject for now."

I hung up but continued to hold the phone close, thinking.

I'd stopped at Dominick's office because I wanted to get his thoughts about the man renting the Holmans' house and delve again into the possibility of selling. I was checking for pain points—asking questions and discussing possibilities and maybe even answers—and checking to see what hurt and what didn't hurt quite so much. But I couldn't do that with Jeanette there. I had to ask myself whether it was fair to Dominick? I hadn't gone there to *be* a friend, but rather to get his help. To lean on him yet again.

And then I'd subjected him to my hurt and bad temper.

I had to figure out how to think for myself. I seemed to have lost the knack.

Ditching the phone and hugging the framed photo to me, I sat in my chair. Galahad came and lay across my feet. The gloom that settled over the both of us was solely my fault.

I was going to give myself a few minutes to sort out my emotions, and then I would find my to-do list and focus on next steps. I would consider the tasks, imagine myself performing them, and if I kept trying, I could do this.

"I can do this, Galahad."

Jeanette was still gone. While I could move about the hotel without her underfoot, I would. I put a movie on TV that had dogs in it, told Galahad to nap, and then went through the adjoining door into the lobby.

CR80

I moved a lamp and a couple of small, framed prints into the storage room and then decided to go through and rearrange what was already in there. Seemed like it should be simple. It wasn't. Arthur had stored an assortment of stuff in the back part of the room. The old hotel holiday displays were too outdated and too info specific to be useful to anyone. Trash. But there were other things. I moved some old Christmas wreaths and found a photo album beneath them, left on a pile of dusty garland. Why was it here? I would've loved to ask Arthur and then to yell at him, but I couldn't, and when the hanging wire on the back of one of the wreaths snagged on the garland and dislodged the album, it all began to slide, heading for a fall.

I hadn't seen this album in several years, but perhaps I should've. I'd been in this room many times. I could've spied this album peeking out on any of those visits. Was that what was meant by willful blindness?

Today it was still there, lying in wait for me. Today I *saw* it. I shouldn't have touched those wreaths. I shouldn't have touched the album, even to break its fall. It was too much like inviting the memories, the sensations, the longings, actively back into my days, taking over my life. This was not how chains were loosened, much less shaken free of.

And I did shake. I caught the album before it hit the floor, and some items slipped out, but then I fled. I locked the storage room and made it back through the adjoining door and into my living room. Collapsing in my chair, I pulled the throw pillow from beside me and hugged it closely, refusing to look at the front windows, tightly closing my eyes so I wouldn't see the gentle, barely-there rippling movement of the curtains.

Pathetic, that's what I was.

Galahad brought his leash to me as if it might offer a solution. Sometimes when I felt the losses most keenly fresh air and exercise *did* distract me. But not today, because in my hand was a photo. It had fallen from the album. I didn't remember picking it up from the floor, but I must've. A photograph from Sebrina's fourth birthday. The candle on the cake was a big number four, trimmed in green with green and pink dots on it. Arthur and I were grinning behind her. Someone else had snapped the photo. I didn't recall who.

I thought I should leave the photo on the side table, but instead I continued to hold it.

Galahad made a weird little noise. The metal clasp at the end of the leash bumped my bare shin. I gave him a look. It was a firm *no* on the suggestion of a walk.

"The porch, boy. It's the best I can do. I'll sit outside and you can run around for a while."

I left the photo inside. Or thought I had. But as I stood on the porch, I saw it was still in my hand. I crossed the grass and the drive to the terrace overlook. The clear blue sky arched high above. Thirty feet below was the sandbox, the dock and then the water. I breathed it all in as deeply as I could and when I was able to hold that breath and its slow release, I allowed myself to sit in one of the colorful Adirondack chairs that Arthur had adored. I slid back into it, letting my head rest against the smooth boards of the back.

Galahad checked out his territory but with less than his usual enthusiasm. I saw him casting worried glances my way.

Numb—that's how I felt. From energized to empty in nothing flat.

No wonder I felt numb. Much like that strange day very recently when I'd first seen the swimming stranger, Blake—and then Jeanette had arrived—and then wet areas on the dock that had taken on a level of horror in my mind—but this day . . . this day had eclipsed that one. Blake had used my dog to cajole me into discussing the possible sale of my property, and then I'd stumbled on Dominick and Jeanette in a very cozy little meetup. And now this.

The photo.

I looked at it again, wishing I could simply see it for what it was and enjoy the memory, and if not that, then I wished I'd never found it, when suddenly a gust of wind snatched what I couldn't release on my own. The photograph fluttered from between my fingers and took flight.

It blew straight up and over the rock wall, twirled and dipped like a kite and then took a dive, catching in the twiggy bushy greenery on the steeper slope of the cliff.

I stared down at it. I couldn't breathe. I wished it would blow free and vanish into the sound—and was equally terrified that it might. That fear gave me the impetus to move. I needed that memory back before the wind caught it again and it was lost in Bogue Sound.

It was out of reach from an anchored position where I could cling to something, but as I put one leg over the stone wall, my hands holding onto the edge, I judged that if I moved carefully, I could make up just enough of the distance to be able to stretch and reach the photo. With one hand on the wall, I continued to inch down the slope, increasingly dismayed at how deceptively sharp the groundcover was, and how deceptively loose the top layer of fine white earth was.

There had been a moment as I went over the stone wall that my innate practicality kicked in and I'd noted my footwear—sandals—and questioned whether I should go back, but it was too late. I was committed.

Meanwhile, above me, Galahad was in full whine mode. I began to worry that in *his* worry he'd come over that stone wall too, and then I'd truly be sunk. And I was. Where the soft sandy spots mixed in with the harder, rockier turf, I lost my balance and slipped, but flailed and in my flailing I got lucky. I grabbed just enough of an old root sticking out of the cliff that it kept me from falling, but I was stuck. Totally. I couldn't move down, and I couldn't move up, and that stone wall was at least a foot beyond any hope of my fingers reaching it.

Still clinging to the side of the bluff, I saw Galahad on the cliff stairs seeking footholds to join me.

"Stay, boy. Stay," I heard someone call from below. From down by the sandbox? I recognized the voice. The man. Blake. Here again?

"Don't move," he called out to me. "I'll come up

and help."

I didn't want his help, even if I needed it. "I'm good. I can handle it. I just have to figure out how to—" My right foot, in its impractical sandal, slid down about an inch. The thin scrabbling sound of tiny bits of earth trickling down below me was alarming.

"Wait," he said. "Stay where you are."

Dirt continued to make little avalanche noises as it cascaded down from around my feet.

"Not as easy as it sounds." There was an edge to my voice. The fall wasn't far enough to kill me, but with the brambly bushes I'd be plenty scratched up, and I might sprain something. Plus, there were the timbers framing the sandbox and large rocks at the base for erosion control.

But I'd probably be fine. Just a little scratched up. I did have the photo back in my hand and was still hanging on to it. With my free hand, I slid the photo inside the neck of my shirt and lodged it in my bra. It might end up slightly the worse for wear, but if I went down the hard way, the photo would be with me.

Blake was running up the stairs and nearing the top. "Hang on. I can reach you from above."

Galahad was happy to see help coming. He did the Lassie thing, raising his muzzle into the air and woofing at the stranger—Blake, that is.

The earth shifted again beneath my sandals. I should have had better sense than to have worn sandals in this situation, which in itself was a stupid thought since I'd hardly had time to make a conscious decision before going over the low wall—but those thoughts were interrupted as Blake appeared above me.

He stepped over the wall, testing the ground before trusting it.

Keeping one hand on the stones, he eased himself—his feet clad in sturdy dock shoes—a foot or so down toward me and stretched his free arm my way, and all the while Galahad woofed instructions and encouragement at us.

Trying not to move unnecessarily, I reached toward his hand. My fingertips touched his. He lunged a few inches closer to grip my hand—then gripped it more firmly, and then he said, "Okay, come up as I steady you."

The strength of his grip reassured me. Fear had a paralyzing effect that had tightened my muscles making them less responsive. I felt the opposite happening now, the release of tension, as I prepared to move.

"Ready."

Even as I spoke, the loose earth continued to move. Blake held on to the edge of the stone wall with one hand, as he pulled my hand with his free one. I leaned forward, trying to make my feet work with the plan. The joint motion was smooth and seemed to be working perfectly until my sandal caught the edge of the wall and I lost it, became unbalanced and fought to get a better hold on Blake as the dirt cascaded down the side of the cliff and into the sandbox.

"Hold on, Mignon. Steady."

Only Blake's quick movement, his hand releasing

mine and his arm moving swiftly around my waist, stopped me from tipping backward and tumbling down the slope over sticks and brambles and whatnot. In fact, he not only stopped that from happening but in one slick motion, he swept me up and onto that wall. Suddenly I was sitting there, gasping, with him half-kneeling and leaning back against the stones, asking, "You okay?" before he pulled himself up and joined me on top of the wall.

"Yes. Thank you," I said.

Galahad joined us too, putting his dirty paws on my thighs, my sandal firmly gripped between his teeth—which gave him an insanely odd-looking grin, as if he'd arranged the whole rescue.

Chapter Twelve

Blake retrieved my sandal from Galahad who relinquished it with a lot of saliva. Blake offered the sandal to me.

Again, I said, "Thank you." I accepted the sandal, though gingerly, as I asked, "What's your name?"

He looked surprised. "Blake."

"I know that. I mean your full name."

"Blake Stuart."

I nodded. "Pleased to meet you, Blake Stuart." I looked at the sandal. Instead of sliding it back on my foot, I removed the other one and tossed them both onto the terrace. At least my feet would match. My poor sandal needed some TLC. Blake and I both swung our legs over to the landward side of the low wall, and he offered me a hand up as if we were in a fine-dining establishment. I couldn't help feeling . . . cared for, maybe? The cool part of my brain warned me to keep my distance. But I liked his short, sandy-gray hair and gray eyes. And his smile. And for coming to my assistance and saving me from a nasty fall.

"Blake, how is it that you're here again? Twice in one day?"

"I was on the Holmans' deck. I heard your dog barking and saw someone clinging to the cliff. Thought it might be you."

"Seriously?"

"Cross my heart." And he indeed made the *X* across his shirt as he said it.

"Then tell me this, Blake Stuart. What *is* your interest in my property?" I held up my hand for a long moment, adding, "This is an unofficial discussion, you understand. Any actual discussions must go through my agent."

"Dominick Monahan."

"For now," I said.

Interest sparked in his eyes.

I rephrased. "I mean, yes. Dominick. He's the guy."

He smiled more broadly, then shrugged. "Actually, I appreciate the chance to explain my interest again. I didn't do a good job of it before. This is the thing—if I hadn't been living one hill over and sharing the same stretch of water, I wouldn't have known about Emerald Heart and wouldn't have heard about its mysterious, reclusive owner and become aware of the speculation about whether she might sell and who might be interested."

"You sound a little too happy about it."

"Almost a month here, remember. Alone."

"Seriously? Not that again."

"No, I mean that I'm used to being engaged in business. Entrepreneurial type, right? The mystery grabbed me." He shrugged. "I have no business of my own just now to stick my nose into, so I barged in uninvited—trespassed into yours.”

“Mysterious? No. As for reclusive, clearly I’m not reclusive enough to deter the idle curious.” I shook my head. “The interest died down long ago, but it didn’t take much to get it sparked up again.”

“If you don’t mind me asking, why did you close the hotel?”

“Losses.” It was all I could say.

“Financial pressures? I imagine it would be difficult to make a small hotel pay.”

“No.” I touched my chest and flinched when I felt the edge of the photograph. I kept my hand there for a long moment. “*Serious* losses. Those of the heart.”

He said, very softly, “I lost my wife a few years ago.”

I waited, but he stopped there, and somehow that impressed me more than if he’d launched into sharing the details. We hardly knew each other, after all. A whispery voice in my head agreed, reminding me to direct him to Dominick.

“Sorry if I seem cautious and belabor the trespassing issue and speaking to Dominick. It was very difficult after my husband died, with people wanting the property. I don’t want it to be like that again.”

“It will help if you firmly—no nonsense—direct anyone expressing interest to your real estate agent. If you seem even remotely receptive to a conversation, they’ll show up here. They’ll try to talk to you either to get in ahead of a competitor or because they think you’re more . . . vulnerable without your representative. These folks—whether they call themselves agents or representatives or interested parties or developers or whatever—are basically here with a purpose and most are, at heart, salespeople, and they're good at it. Tell them to talk to your agent and slam the door."

Yes, the voice in my head said. He probably knew all that because that's how he was himself. Was he trying to warn me? Or was this a way past my defenses? Out loud, I asked, "And I should take the same approach with you? Unless you've changed your mind and are no longer interested?"

"Touché," he said. He stood and offered a hand. "Shall I escort you to your house?"

"Pretty sure there are no other cliffs for me to climb between here and my porch. I think I can manage it. I offer my thanks, though, for the rescue."

He nodded. "I think I'll take the forest path back to the Holman house. Do you mind? I ask with respect because part of the trail is on your property."

"Oh, well, that makes rewarding you for your help easy. I give you leave, sir, to use the path at your convenience." Without thinking, I'd lapsed into the playful, semi-archaic phrasing that Arthur and I had used. *Give you leave . . .* I smiled, but it felt more like a grimace to my face, and I looked away, but before I did I caught a flash of something in his eyes.

Odd eyes. Gray, but like with layers or depth. I wondered if he was wearing some of those special contacts that altered eye color. But that was neither here nor there. *Focus, Mignon,* I told myself. However pleasant this was, it really was still about business.

I walked with him around the house. "By the way, I'm aware that you sidestepped the question of your plans for the property."

He stopped and gave me a look. "Did I? If I'm correct, I believe you asked why I was interested in the Emerald Heart property, not about my plans for it if a sale were to happen and involve me." His gaze swept the garden and the back view of the hotel and landed back on me. "It was a pleasure to meet you, Ms. King."

"Mignon."

He nodded. "I hope we can continue the chat soon?"

He left without an answer, walking away into that space between the live oaks and the outer arc made up of the rhododendron. Galahad wanted to go with him. He chased after Blake—my temporary neighbor, perhaps the next owner of our home—big maybe, there—before running back to me and pawing the ground—as if to say, *Hurry, Mom, we're supposed to be going that way too.*

I followed his lead. Blake was waiting just beyond the start of the path.

"I guess we'll walk part of the way with you? Do you mind?"

"Not at all. I'm glad." He knelt to pick up a stick and tossed it ahead of us. Galahad took off after it. "So is he." He grinned. "He's training me well."

As we walked along, I said, "We used to walk here all the time. Mostly he was still a puppy back then, but he remembers, I suppose."

"I've seen him near the Holmans' house. I didn't know about the path until he started showing up there."

"Margaret Holman usually kept treats for him."

"Guess I let him down on that score." He shrugged. "He would never come close anyway, but always stopped at the entrance to the path, watching me on the deck. He looked healthy, but I admit I was curious, and I followed him back one day. I was surprised . . . not sure why, though. I'd seen the building and house from the water and even on my runs, but coming out of the woods . . . the bushes were in bloom and the sunlight . . . the light hits the live oaks in a crazy way that I can't quite describe but it looks like a place set apart, surrounded as it is by the rest of the garden. It's like in a panoramic or 360-degree view. It was striking. I realized then where the path had led me, that I was indeed trespassing, and the dog was okay, so I left quietly."

For some reason, my eyes burned. I was afraid I might cry. But why? His words had touched me. Again, why? Galahad loved the water and the woods. It was not unexpected in the least that among his other forays he might take the path. Except in my heart, I knew he was looking for Arthur. Always seeking Arthur.

I stumbled. I'd been looking down but not really seeing. Blake reached out reflexively.

He said, surprised, "You're barefoot. I forgot about the sandals."

"I'm fine," I said, shaking off his hand gently. The ravine where my property ended and the Holmans' land began was ahead. "Galahad and I will turn back here."

"Are you sure? You're welcome to join me for a cup of coffee or tea or chocolate. Mrs. Holman left the kitchen well-stocked."

I was surprised he'd offered. Maybe I'd given off friendly signals despite myself. I pulled those back now, calling out, "Galahad. Come. We're going home." I turned to Blake. "Thank you so much for helping me on the cliff, and for being neighborly. If you want to pursue your interest in the property, keep in touch with Dominick. He'll represent me when—if—I put it on the market."

His face changed. The gray eyes cooled (was that possible?), and he moved an almost imperceptible step away from me. "Will do."

I almost called the words back but this time when that voice in my head said, *Move on*, I listened. Even so, after Galahad and I followed the path back, when we reached the garden benches, I sat. Galahad plopped down on his side in the cool, shady dirt.

Blake was right in what he'd said about the garden. I was pleased that, despite the neglect, it could still catch his eye and his interest.

I retrieved the photograph, safe from being tucked away and only a little bent. I touched my fingertip to Sebrina's face and then to Arthur's.

Adding a formal garden area had been part of Arthur's original plan, but other than a statue here and there and a couple of benches, the details had fallen to me. Arthur had more of a historian's interest, certainly a collector's eye. He was a people-person. Plant life that changed with the seasons and required more care, new plantings and such, hadn't been within his area of interest. To complicate the task, the live oaks had to be accounted for and worked around. When Arthur hinted at removing one or two, he saw my reaction and backed off immediately.

"It's all yours, Mignon." He took my hands in his and gently kissed them. "Whatever you need me for, let me know. Your wish is my command." He added a courtly bow.

How I loved him.

Even as I built the garden—formed the beds and plots and altered the walkways—Arthur had kept muttering that we'd get a regular gardener on staff to manage the care of it—because he didn't understand. For Arthur, if he wasn't interested in something, it was confusing to him that someone else might find the nurturing of it fascinating and satisfying. Over time, though, he became a believer—that I *did* love it—and he stepped back and happily left the garden management to me, and I left the day-to-day hotel decisions to him— mostly.

During the years that the hotel had been in operation, I'd hired extra help with the garden as needed. Otherwise, I'd done the bulk of the work alone and it had been a joy. I understood what I was good at. Arthur's skills were different and mine supported his well. But I'd made the garden my primary focus. Compared to how it had thrived during our busy years, it was looking pretty sketchy now.

I felt eyes on me and saw that Galahad was watching my face. I leaned forward and down to scratch his head, saying, "What would I do without you, my friend?"

Little things, right? They said you had to appreciate the little things, the small moments, before you could embrace the larger ones.

The bench faced the window wall of the hotel extension. The hallway behind the glass wasn't lit, and the shadow combined with the soft, filtered light of the garden, made it difficult to see clearly from the outside in—only vague shapes and suggestions of movement.

Thinking of the artist who'd spent a month here painting from the second-floor vantage point, I thought—just for the briefest of moments—that my imagination had brought the artist back. Then I thought perhaps it was Arthur. Perhaps his spirit was here and observing his kingdom. But to still be here, stuck in this place? No, that would be too sad. I felt that pain again and touched my heart, and I blinked. Blinking cleared my vision, and I saw that the figure was truly there and was moving.

Jeanette. It must be her. Who else?

She'd seen us, Galahad and I, emerge from the path. Had she seen us going into the woods with Blake Stuart?

None of her business, I reminded myself.

I stood, calling out to Galahad that it was time for his treat. He joined me eagerly and we went inside. A short time later, I made a special trip to the hotel wing and double-checked each door just to be sure I'd locked everything up tight, especially the storage room door, skipping only the door to the room Jeanette was using.

Nothing seemed amiss.

Maybe she'd noticed the movement in the garden and was no more than curious. But from upstairs? Perhaps she'd gone up there for a better angle of view? Curious or not, all the rooms were locked. Jeanette could only access the hallway and the lobby.

☙❧

Jeanette showed up at my front door soon after I returned to the house. She knocked on the front door, and when I opened it, she handed me a grocery bag.

"The items you asked for," she said. In her other hand was a larger bag. "I picked this up too. Precooked. We can warm it for supper, if you like." Without asking, she walked past me into the house and to the kitchen where she set the package on the counter. "In fact," she said, "why don't you let me fix the meal tonight? I can mix a salad to go along with the manicotti. What do you think? You've had all the work on you. I'm here to help, right?"

"Are you?"

A frown came and went before she said, "I thought that's what you wanted."

"With regard to trespassers."

She stuck her chin forward and frowned. "Well, as a matter of fact—"

I interrupted. "Doesn't matter."

"As *a matter of fact,* when I saw people in the garden, I *did* take a closer look, just in case it was trespassers."

"I saw you upstairs."

"Yes. You were with a man. Was he on the property with permission? Because if he was trespassing, then it could've been risky for you to be out there where it's so secluded."

"He did me a favor."

"Oh? What?"

I smiled, but not nicely.

She said, "Not my business."

"I'll text you when the meal is ready," I said. "About six o'clock."

She accepted my rude interruptions with better grace than I would've. Instead of responding in kind or leaving in a huff, she walked back into the living room. She paused at the bookcase. It was a custom built-in case of shelves and cabinets. Arthur's own hands had crafted this our third winter here. Arthur had been a man of many interests and when he was interested, he was, if not obsessed, then he was absorbed.

Jeanette wasn't admiring her brother's handiwork, but rather his collection of books, many of them very old. She ran her fingertips along their spines. Most of them referenced King Arthur and medieval England and even more ancient history. Dividing one type of books from another, used like bookends, were small metal sculptures related mostly to King Arthur, but also to other literary fiction like *The Canterbury Tales*.

"He was certainly single-minded, was he not?" She spoke almost wistfully, as if speaking only to herself, but then she turned to me, asking, "Who was that man with you in the garden? Was he asking about buying the property?"

I stared at her and refused to answer.

Her expression showed displeasure. She said, in a clipped, brusque tone, "Remember, direct all inquiries to Dominick. These people will take advantage of you." She walked to the front door. "I'll see you about six, then."

"I'll text."

She pursed her lips. I waited.

"Of course," she said, but instead of leaving, she added, "I've been keeping the lobby and garden doors locked, as you asked. Mind if I walk back through the connecting door? Thought I'd read a little, put my foot up and rest my ankle. It's much better, but I've been walking a lot today." She touched the books. "Mind if I take something to read?"

"Just don't turn down the page corners."

"Thanks." She slipped several books from the shelf. I wasn't looking too closely because all I wanted was for her to return to her room.

She hadn't mentioned Dominick or her visit with him. I refused to ask. Since Dominick had called me, they'd surely discussed it between them. Discussed me behind my back. Even if innocent or well-intentioned, it felt like a betrayal.

I walked down the hallway, unlocked the door to the lobby, and opened it wide to allow her to pass.

She said something low that might have been *thank you*, then passed by me, and I pulled the door closed and flipped the lock back into the engaged position.

And she knocked.

I opened the door again. She was standing there looking disgruntled. I asked, "Is there a problem?"

"You could've asked about me visiting Dominick today. I could practically hear it churning in your brain. It might not be *your* business, but I wouldn't have minded you asking. Since you didn't bring it up, I will. I know you don't like that I had lunch with him, and that you didn't know about it or approve it beforehand."

"Not my job to approve anything you do."

She ignored me, saying, "You forget that I've known him most of my life. Longer than you, in fact. I'm allowed to visit old friends without getting your permission."

"Okay." What was I supposed to say? I added, "That's true."

She shook her head. "Good. Just wanted to be clear about it."

With that, she turned and walked across the lobby and down the hall. I was still standing there when she reached her room door and gave me a look back before she walked in and closed *her* door.

Seemed to me that Jeanette might get her supper on a tray tonight. Might be better for both our digestions.

Chapter Thirteen

The next morning, I settled myself at the computer on Arthur's desk to search for contact information for the nearest storage facilities and moving companies. Having made good sorting progress in here, I felt confident enough to call around to check unit sizes, pricing, and availability. I called a local mover to ask if they took on small jobs like transporting unneeded items from a residence to the storage place, being careful how I phrased the questions, not wanting to start up speculation again in case they recognized the name or location.

Jeanette's car was parked out front, though there were no signs of life coming from her room thus far.

I'd been pretty hard on her yesterday. In the end, we'd shared supper, but it had been quiet and rather grim atmosphere-wise. The tray route might have been the better choice after all. This one-upsmanship joust was wearing thin for me.

After I had gathered basic information about storage and local moves, I left Galahad alone in the house and went to the lobby, heading to the storage room.

The lobby was darkish with only the light from the foyer doors and the garden doors easing the gloom of it.

I unlocked the door to the storage room. How

much *could* I manage to move to a storage facility myself? I hadn't even gone through the upstairs rooms yet. I didn't fool myself that I could do the physical part alone. But it had to be done. At the very least, I would put Emerald Heart on the market to see what kind of offers came in, but not with Arthur's collection on view. To allow the world in to see Arthur's quirkiness without his presence—his presence that made it all make sense— it would be . . . disrespectful.

Some people might make jokes. Plus, some of his collection of King Arthur-related items and other things might be worth something. Not big bucks, but still . . .

Whether selling or demolishing, these items served no purpose hanging on the walls or standing in corners. Now would be a good time to pick and choose what to keep and what to get rid of—or at least make a start with that task. Truly, it seemed herculean.

Baby steps, I reminded myself.

My choices. My decision. I reminded myself of that too.

And it would be my screw-up, if it came to that, but considering my present stalled circumstance, making a change would likely be worth the risk.

I paused to listen to the silence. I was glad of the quiet and the privacy, yes, but I kept thinking Jeanette was going to walk in any minute—after all, her car was here. She'd show up and start butting into what I was trying to accomplish.

By the time afternoon hit, worry was gnawing at

me. I didn't know what had kept her away from here for seven years and felt sure there must be more to it than a family disagreement. What had she been doing? Was she stable? Emotionally or mentally? I hadn't really considered that. Suppose she was sick now? Stuck in her room and unable to summon help?

I left the storage room and knocked on her room door. There was no answer. I tried again, and finally I called through the door, "Jeanette, answer me or I'm coming in."

She didn't, so I did. I inserted the master key into the door lock and pushed the door open gently in case the chain lock was engaged. It wasn't.

"Jeanette?" I called out.

No answer. The bed was half-made, like an afterthought, and some clothing and personal items were scattered around the room, but in a logical, orderly way that wouldn't indicate anything was amiss. I crossed the room and checked the bathroom.

She wasn't here.

Her roller case was in the corner, standing upright and zipped. No tote bag that I could see, so she must've taken that with her. My fingers itched. I considered going through the roller case or better yet, taking a quick peek in the drawers.

No. I wouldn't invade her privacy to that extent. Unless it truly seemed necessary.

Instead, I looked out her window at the parking lot. Her car didn't appear to have been moved but I couldn't be sure, so she might've been gone since last night or she might've left early this morning. She wasn't answering her phone or responding to texts. It could be something or nothing. She might just be on a super long morning stroll.

This self-focused behavior was just like the Jeanette I'd always known. First, she'd invited herself back into my life, and then thought only of herself, showing no consideration for anyone else.

So be it, Jeanette. You do you. I have my own life to figure out.

I closed the room door and relocked it. Instead of returning to the lobby, I decided to do a visual inventory of the guest rooms. The activity would feel good. Perhaps I'd even grab some of the small items to get a feel for how this process would go. Good timing for the task, too, with Jeanette gone who-knew-where.

Master keys in hand, I went room by room. I wouldn't keep or try to sell the mattresses. The mattresses and box springs were old but had use left in them. Was it possible to donate them? What were the health codes for that? I could sell or donate the furniture—bed frames, bureaus, etc. A big yard sale? Satisfy or arouse more community curiosity. A cringeworthy thought. No, better to donate.

The TVs were mostly too old now, I guessed. Televisions had changed a lot over the years. These TVs were probably not *Smart* enough to be worth anything. The curtains could be donated somewhere. The bedding too. I'd keep the framed prints and paintings on the walls, along with some small decorative items like the sculptures in the lobby. Arthur had chosen those personally. A few of the lamps might be worth keeping too.

Actually, it suddenly seemed to me that 99 percent of the task might be easier than I'd dreaded. Could it be that easy to disassemble a life well-lived? The realization made me sad.

Our lives, at least this earthly one, was the *only* life I had firsthand experience with. Lives and history had come before me and would come after me, but this was the life in which I'd felt loved, had also felt great despair, and had even been lost. It was almost incomprehensible to me that after I was gone, time and events would scarcely ripple as they filled in the momentary, miniscule gap left by my departure.

The darkness that so often seemed to wait nearby got heavy. I dropped the figurine I was holding onto the bed. Enough for now.

By now, Galahad would surely want *out*. Which was as good an excuse as any for me to get out of here.

I didn't run from the room, but I wanted to.

Galahad was glad to see me return from the rooms of yesterday to where he was confined—alone—in the present. I gave him a treat. He'd gobbled it down before I reached the front door to let him out, and he went outside eagerly without waiting to see if I'd follow.

Sometimes being alone was more about context than actuality.

I walked over to the Adirondack chairs and sat, sliding down the seat until I hit the back and then rested my eyes while Sir Galahad did his business, made a nosy survey of the area, then did his business again. I was lost in my own musings about what my future would look like. Different. Yeah. My anxiety was rising—so much for calming down—so I closed my eyes again, focusing only on the sough of the water, thinking how the rhythm matched my own sighs, even the beat of my heart, how even when the rhythm altered as a boat went by or the tide changed, it always resumed it natural rhythm soon enough. Within time . . . within its own time.

Baby steps, right? And how easily the water would close over us when we stopped being part of this world. It kind of made everything seem . . . empty.

If Arthur were here, he'd tell me I was looking in the wrong direction. He would say to stop, to clear my mind and look deep inside myself. He would tell me to breathe slowly and then pray.

I couldn't get past the *clearing my mind* part. As for looking deep inside myself—I feared I might not like what I found.

Chapter Fourteen

A new day arrived, but not Jeanette.

Her car hadn't moved.

Why did I care? Why wasn't I celebrating her absence? Because it didn't feel right. Something could be wrong.

As far as I knew, the only local people who'd recently been in contact with her were me, Dominick, and whoever the friend was. She'd mentioned the friend's place was over on the mainland. I should've asked her more questions.

I called Dominick, thinking he might know more. "Have you heard from Jeanette?"

Dominick said, "What's this about, Meg?"

"She's not here. She hasn't left word, not a note or text or anything, to indicate she's okay." I added, "Her car is here, but she isn't."

In his silence I read his question. He was asking himself why did I care? Was my concern sincere or just some sort of tantrum? It was legit that he might wonder.

I said, "She's been gone, at least I think she has, since early yesterday. You may well ask, why do I care? And I don't care, except that since she's staying here. I feel, reasonably or not, somewhat responsible for . . . whatever. No different than if I had a hotel guest who suddenly went missing."

"She's an adult."

"She's so thoughtless."

"What's the big deal?"

"Big deal? *She isn't a guest*. I agreed to let her stay one night to help her out. Then allowed a few more. But she *doesn't live here*. She doesn't get to come and go without notice as it pleases her."

"Did you try calling her?"

I went silent.

"So why ask me? I don't get it, Meg." He paused, then added, "Or maybe I do."

"Don't go there, Dominick."

"It's the same old grudge, isn't it?"

"No, it's the same old Jeanette."

"I'm on my way over. You and I are gonna talk again."

"Not now, please. I'm not in the mood for a *chat*."

He said, "You hear me better in person."

I bit my lip.

"I'm leaving the office now. I have the gate key. I'll see you in about twenty minutes."

He hung up.

It was closer to thirty minutes before he arrived, but then Dominick was, at heart, an optimist. Optimism was probably a prerequisite for real estate agents.

I opened the door. "Come in. Would you like some tea? I have instant coffee too."

Dominick walked inside and followed me into the kitchen, but when I put the glasses of iced tea on the table, instead of sitting, he stopped in the doorway, facing me.

"When is the right time, Mignon? If not now, when?"

"To chat?" I was confused.

He stared, his eyes fixed on mine. I stared back. He broke first.

"When is it, Mignon? When it's too late and is therefore a moot question because it no longer matters to anyone? But it isn't moot in the heart, is it?" He pointed at me. "You know that for sure. When pain and anger—the habit of having been hurt or offended and then nourishing that hurt until it all but has a life of its own? Those are poor substitutes for the lost relationships with family . . . and even with friends."

"I have relationships."

"Do you?" He shook his head. "You miss her. Admit it. Or rather, maybe you miss having someone around, even if it's Jeanette."

He came close to me and put his hands on my arms. He stared me in the eyes and said calmly, "You aren't obligated to keep people in your life who are toxic to you, but, Mignon, you have insulated yourself so well, to protect yourself, your feelings, that you've cheated yourself and others of what might've been . . . of what could've been good." He lowered his voice almost to a whisper. "There is peace in knowing you tried and that when you do finally walk away, you will do so knowing you've done all that you could to mend the break."

"When did *you* become the peacemaker?"

I meant for the words to sound harsh, even mocking, but they didn't come out that way. I heard my voice, the pathetic whine of it that neither of us could miss. My lower lip trembled. I turned away.

Gently, he said, "You are the most stubborn person I know—that I have *ever* known."

"I never claimed to be perfect."

"Please take a deep breath. Remember I'm a friend and someone who'd do just about anything for you . . . because I'm about to tell you something that's gonna piss you off in a big way." He shook his head, then ran his fingers back through his hair. He groaned, then nodded.

"Okay, here it is." He tapped his chest with his fingers. "It was me. I called Jeanette." He shook his head. "No, I didn't know where she was living or what she was up to, but I saw her name come up in a real estate transaction and wondered if it was her—the girl I'd known back in the day. I thought of you, and of Arthur.

"You can say it wasn't my business to interfere, but Mignon, you don't get to decide that. Arthur, Jeanette, and I grew up together. We have history, practically since diapers. You can cut me out of your life too, if that's what you want to do. I'm not promising I'd accept that decision, but you can try. But what you don't get to do? You aren't allowed to tell me what is and isn't my business, especially when it applies to people who are important to me. You cannot expect me to honor that."

I froze. I burned. There were so many feelings inside me I couldn't pin any single one down. Anger at

Dominick. Guilt over how my actions impacted those around me. Rage that he had dared to interfere, to contact Jeanette for help—*help for me*—behind my back. Because that's what he'd done. No, I didn't know the exact words he'd used, but I knew in my gut that he'd told Jeanette I was living in lonely misery mired in the past—to come and save me—or some such nonsense.

I slapped his hands away. "You can associate with whomever you choose, but you don't have the right to solicit someone who has already done so much damage in my life to reenter it. Bad enough that she didn't come on her own sooner, but now I know she didn't even come on her own at all, but at your request.

"How pathetic you must think me. How freaking pathetic you've made me seem to her. We—you and I— were friends too. What you've done? Betrayal, that's what I call it." I stopped because my heart was slamming in my chest and my breath was coming short.

Dominick's face flushed. Hurt showed in his eyes. Twice he opened his mouth as if to speak, but each time he closed it again with no words uttered.

My head was pounding. I felt lightheaded and pressed my fingers against my temples. I wanted to be alone. Better that way, anyway. "Go, Dominick. Just go."

"Meg. Please give this some thought. I wasn't only Arthur's friend. I was—*and am*—your friend too." He reached out and his fingers brushed across my hand before I yanked it away.

He stared at me for a long moment before saying, "As you wish." He sighed and shrugged. "I should speak to Jeanette before I go." He added, "If she's back, that is." He paused to breathe.

Dominick seemed to be having the same problem I was with gathering in and pulling oxygen into his lungs. He touched my arm, then gripped it more tightly as I tried to pull away. "It's my fault she's here. I'll tell her you and I have spoken about me asking her to come . . . and . . . well whatever else."

There was a moment in which I remembered that I'd thought Jeanette might be helpful to me—might have my back. Wow, some lessons took more than once or twice to learn. But then, I'd thought I could trust Dominick too.

"No, she's not back yet. If you run into her, tell her she should go. Tell her that for me." I turned my back to him, now hugging myself, wishing only that he'd finish saying whatever he needed to get said and then leave.

"Meg."

His voice sounded strained. I half-turned to face him. "Dominick?"

"One more thing. This is going to sound . . . not great. But I promise it isn't a big thing. It just sounds . . ."

"Not great? Spit it out, Dominick."

"It's about the finder's fee. It's not unusual to offer a finder's fee to someone who helps to facilitate finding or selling a property. It came up in conversation between Jeanette and me. Not even serious, really. We were just talking. But in case someone mentions it, or it comes up later, I want you to be aware."

CREO

Dominick left Emerald Heart only one quick second before being ordered away forever. I was literally seeing red. But my anger did begin to pass. The tension *had* to ease or I would explode. That, however, didn't mean forgiveness was being offered. In Dominick's case, yes, I would forgive him one day. I felt like I knew his heart. That said, trust might be hard to come by for a while.

I sat on the terrace feeling almost empty. I sat with my ears open to hear the easy rhythm of the water and with eyes wide to follow the seabirds as they skimmed the sound or flew from sandbank to islands or to their roosts along the woods. After a while, I noticed that Galahad had left me. I waited, expecting him to return and then maybe we'd go for a walk, but then I realized someone was on the dock. I looked down from the terrace and sure enough, Galahad was being chummy with someone down there. With Jeanette.

She probably felt the stab of my eyes, my simmering anger, because she looked up. She waved, then she and Galahad began climbing the cliff stairs.

Jeanette must've returned while I was talking with Dominick. Thanks to Dominick's confession, I knew now what I hadn't known before. How she'd come to be here, for one. And what she expected to get out of it.

Money.

The anger inside me felt real—like something

churning inside. An explosion was inevitable. I couldn't even begin to form the words that I wanted to say because, in honesty, I didn't want to talk this out. I wanted to hurt her—and not only with words.

She must go, and she would. In the meantime, I needed to calm down.

No more regret. I already had enough of regrets and what-ifs weighing down my conscience.

Jeanette would leave eventually. Striking out at her, with words or otherwise, would only harm me.

Ignoring her wave, I called to Galahad, and we went into the house.

When she knocked on the connecting door, I refused to hear it and simply turned the volume on the TV up louder.

Chapter Fifteen

The next morning, I drove into town to run errands, but mostly to get away to avoid Jeanette. Hopefully, she'd be gone again by the time I returned to Emerald Heart.

Keeping distance between us was the best way to go.

When I returned from town, the gate was locked and Jeanette's car wasn't parked at the hotel. It was a relief—exactly what I'd hoped for—but even so that lonely, unsettled feeling rose in me again. As I parked in front of my house, I saw another envelope was stuck to my front door.

Thank you, Carolyn, I thought. *I need a friendly diversion.* This time I might join her in whatever her current project or interest was. I needed to redirect this negative energy stirring in me.

But when I reached the door, I saw that this envelope was unmarked and not decorated with Carolyn's lovely, calligraphic handwriting. Plus, instead of wedging the note between the door and the frame, the sender had come prepared with adhesive tape to secure it.

The person must have brought their tape dispenser with them, because how else would the tape be so pristine?

I could easily know who'd left it by claiming and

opening the envelope. Instead, I stood there looking at it. Perhaps admiring it. Like an unscratched lottery ticket . . .

This moment of silliness felt good after so much worry. I'd been in that vortex of tension with Jeanette and even Dominick—and had hit the bottom, or top, depending on how you wanted to look at it. Well, I didn't want to play in that space, and I resolved not to. They could take their games elsewhere.

On the other hand, there was no guarantee that whatever was written inside this note would be welcome or even interesting.

I caught my lip in my teeth, thinking, savoring the possibilities.

What about Dominick? I'd been harsh with him. Justified? Yes. Maybe. But we had a long history, and surely he'd earned better treatment from me.

I'd contributed to the chaos in this vortex.

It would be just like Dominick to leave me a nice note, and it wouldn't surprise me a bit if he walked through life armed with handy things like a roll of tape in his glovebox. This card could open the door to a fresh conversation and make an apology easier for both of us.

Mid-reach, I paused. Maybe Carolyn had upped her note-leaving game. *Hmm.* No, I was pretty sure that if she'd taped a note to my door she would've used her super cute, specialty tapes.

The tape pulled away from the door as I took the envelope. I pressed the loose ends of tape neatly around to the back side of the envelope, enjoying myself.

Or Jeanette might've left me a note. But even as I thought it, I was certain she hadn't. This wasn't from her. I shook my head, agreeing with myself.

"Aren't you going to open that?"

I jumped, but kept a tight hold on the envelope, pressing it to my heart and feeling utterly foolish.

"Sorry." Blake gestured toward the wicker chair beside the porch table. "I forgot the roll of tape. It belongs to the Holmans. It's the only tape I've found at their house. I'd hate to lose it."

"Oh." I frowned and held up the envelope. "Did you leave the note?"

He stayed on the flagstone walk. There was indeed a roll of tape on the chair seat. I retrieved it and walked to the porch railing, leaning over to pass the dispenser to him.

I said, "I don't understand."

"Hopefully, the enclosed card will make sense."

"But . . . you're here. Why leave a note card?"

He gave a quick shrug. "In case you weren't here . . . and you weren't. Our earlier chat was slightly awkward. Thought it would be better to let you find this, read it privately, not wanting to put you on the spot or anything. Brought the tape just in case, and then I forgot it."

As I stood there, saying nothing, and making no move to open the envelope, he said, "I'll leave. Let me know about the note. This has nothing to do with whether you do or don't decide to sell. This isn't about that. It's just an invitation."

"Okay," I managed to say, amazed by the strange man and his borrowed tape dispenser. He was no longer a total stranger, maybe. But he seemed rather a mystery.

He stepped away with a smile and a wave and walked around the house, obviously heading toward the trail. Just at that moment, Galahad started barking inside the house. I hurried to open the door, still carrying the unopened invitation.

An invitation.

Inside, I closed the door behind me and leaned back against it. Galahad trotted into the kitchen, stopped at his food dish, and looked back at me, puzzled. I was still in the living room, standing there with my back against the door.

I said softly, "It's an invitation, Galahad. Should I open it?"

As if I might not? That was unlikely. After all, the man had brought a borrowed tape dispenser with him to make sure the note didn't blow away before I found it.

Galahad sat on the kitchen floor, still watching me, waiting, perhaps sensing a change, and questioning what that meant.

A change in the usual habits ... Is that why an unopened envelope, declared by its sender to be an invitation, felt so delicious? I ran my finger over the paper. I could simply open it. I was relatively certain that Blake wasn't inviting me to an investment seminar or a cookware party. True, he'd expressed an interest in the Emerald Heart property, but his manner and tone just now had conveyed something different. If, however, this smacked of business, I would alert Dominick immediately.

And if it didn't? What would I do then?

I unsealed the flap and pulled out what was truly a note, handwritten on a blank piece of writing paper. I was invited to join him for dinner at Wheeler's Grill in town that evening. Casual, he noted.

This evening?

Staring at his handwriting, I wished I could decipher his motives in the loops and whorls.

Manipulation? Seeking to circumvent the usual real estate processes to get a leg up on other bidders? He'd be disappointed if that was his goal. Perhaps it was my charming, winning personality that interested him? I laughed, and Galahad gave me a more hopeful look.

To be honest, Blake did have a certain charm. Attractive too.

I touched my hair. It was dark and long with a few gray strands. I hadn't visited a hair salon in a very long time.

It had been an even longer time since I'd gone on a date.

I didn't fool myself that any risk of romance was involved here, but that made it all the more interesting to test my toes again, to share conversation with a man where there was no investment, no promises. It was perhaps a good testing ground if . . . for *when* I decided to venture out into the world and social circles again.

Presumptuous of him to assume I was free this evening.

I called the number he'd written on the invite.

"Oh, hey," he said. "You got my note?"

"You *know* I got your note."

"And? Any chance you're free? If not, we can go whichever day works best for you. Unless—" He paused, then added, "Unless you're involved with someone. I may have made an unwarranted assumption. If so, I'm sorry."

"Seriously, I—" A moment of honesty forced its way out. "No, I'm not seeing anyone, but in truth, I'm not *ready* to be dating anyone either."

"We don't have to call it a date. Think of it as two solitary people sharing a meal?"

"I do need to eat." I shook my head in disbelief, that apparently, I was going to do this. "Casual, right?"

"The more casual the better."

"I'll drive myself and meet you there?"

There was a short silence. "Sure. Whatever works best for you."

We agreed on a time and disconnected. He'd sounded okay. Not weird or stalkerish. And I was allowed to step a toe or two outside of my own customary behavior, right?

I texted Jeanette, *"I won't be home for supper."* I didn't ask her plans. She could fend for herself and either drive into town or use her microwave.

She responded within seconds, *"Okay."* Then added another bit: *"Going out?"*

I let that question go unanswered. Not her business.

ॐ

What should I wear? I may have brushed and repinned my long, untrimmed hair a dozen times, unsatisfied with it however it looked.

At least Galahad visited a vet and a groomer as needed and appropriate. I should do the same for myself. Well, not a groomer, but an occasional hair trim at the local salon would be a good start.

Finally, I reminded myself that this was a neighbor meeting a neighbor for a meal, and thus as long as I was clean and decently clothed, it didn't matter, so with a last twist and pin, I called it done.

I stared at myself again, wondering how I looked—not necessarily to him, my temporary neighbor-stranger—but to the people I'd known for so long, as well as to the strangers who showed up here either out of curiosity or in hopes of doing business. Suddenly it seemed important that I understand this, and then I was annoyed with myself that it mattered to me. I was still holding the hairbrush, and now I tossed it aside, but my agitation was such that it landed across the room, only to be swiftly retrieved by Galahad. I couldn't help laughing, and that eased some of my tension.

Jeans, a cotton shirt, and a lightweight sweater across my arm in case the evening turned chill, or the restaurant AC was turned up too high, and I was ready.

Chapter Sixteen

It was late afternoon when I parked in the lot beside the restaurant and met Blake on the sidewalk near the entrance. He walked close to me. His hand gently brushed my arm, tentatively, lightly. As if he were checking to see whether I might run? Perhaps I did stiffen a bit—imperceptibly, I hoped—and my breath may have quickened but I had this under control.

For heaven's sake, this wasn't my first date. My last first date had happened almost three decades earlier—which was, in itself, a terrifying thought. So, I pushed it aside and instead I smiled and leaned slightly toward him, saying, "I've always enjoyed Emerald Isle this time of year. September is great because it's still warm and doing business, but a little less crowded with visitors." *Yikes. I sound like a travel agent . . . or a hotel concierge.*

"You okay?" he asked.

I shook my head but said, "Yes. I'm great. Very good restaurant. Have you eaten here before?"

"First time," he said as we paused in front of Wheeler's Grill.

Blake opened and held the door, and we walked in. A hostess was on duty this evening, and she greeted and seated us. So far, so good. I tried to keep up a light, breezy conversation—not brilliant but satisfactory. I hadn't bolted when he'd put his hand on my back as we'd made our way to the table. Nope, I'd handled it casually and confidently. And how sad was it, I thought, that such simple interactions had become major events for me?

Nerves. I was overthinking this.

The server brought utensils and menus to the table and took our drink orders. "Would you care for any appetizers?"

"No," I said. "Not for me."

Blake nodded at the server. "None, thanks."

"I'll get your drinks and then take your food order?"

"Thanks," we said in unison.

As she walked away, I focused on the menu. I couldn't think of any conversation to offer. This had been a mistake.

A tapping noise caught my attention. Blake asked if I was okay. Looking down, I saw it was me, tap-tapping the hilt of my dinner knife on the tabletop. I dropped the utensil, embarrassed and ready to call off my *adventure outside the customary*. I was easing out of my chair, excuses at the ready, when Matt came over from the bar and interrupted my slide into panic. He was grinning, casting looks at me and then at Blake and then back at me again.

"Mignon! Great to see you here. It's been ages."

"Feels like ages and ages. Looks like this place hasn't missed me one little bit." I offered a small laugh and a smile.

"I'm glad to see you here. Now all feels right with the world." He paused, frowned, and added, "Almost all."

I nodded. "This is Blake Stuart. He's renting the Holman house."

"Ah, you're neighbors, then." Matt acknowledged Blake, then turned back to me, asking, "I've been hearing rumors about your plans. Is it true you're thinking of selling Emerald Heart?"

Giving a little groan, I shrugged. "Not sure, but word does get around, doesn't it? I'm still in the thinking stage."

"I always hoped you'd open it back up and get back into business. Arthur talked about expanding and adding on a putting range and all sorts of things." He looked a little embarrassed. "Sorry, Mignon, it's not that I blame you for *not* taking all that on yourself. A hotel is a lot to manage."

"True." I pressed my lips together, determined not to say more—not here, and not with Blake sitting across from me. But then, I thought, why not?

"In fact, I am seriously considering selling. Or not. To keep the hotel open requires funding for updating, repairs, hiring workers, and I don't even *know* what all. To sell it would be easier in a lot of ways, but the prospect of leaving so many years of memories behind is very hard."

He nodded. "Live your best life, Mignon. That's my motto." His look turned serious. "Don't let anyone else tell you what you should do."

"Agreed," I answered, but honestly, I was thinking that this was the oddest, most thoughtful exchange of words I'd ever had with Matt.

He added, "But whatever you decide to do, do it for you, and do it like you mean it."

When I stared, he added, "It's like this, Mignon. Once you've made up your mind—made your decision— you gotta cast the *what-ifs* and *maybes* aside. Don't do it halfway. Go all in like you mean it—and then, one day, you *will* mean it."

೧೪೮

I didn't remark on Matt's words right away. In fact, it seemed to me that Matt might have been speaking to himself as much as to me . . . or perhaps speaking from his own personal experience. Blake didn't pursue it either, not right away. We kind of just looked at each other. Matt, a guy ten-plus years younger than me— someone who'd been good friends with Arthur—had filled up my head with . . . important words? Yeah, I thought so. To Blake, I said something inane, maybe like the surf and turf here is pretty good. Then, somehow, we were talking about potential in people's lives, in business, and even in the Emerald Heart property—the potential that Arthur had seen in it, and somewhere in the midst of all that, we placed our orders and received the food.

Blake said, "I'd like to hear about those plans that Arthur considered."

"Why?"

"Just curious. From all you've said, Arthur was a planner. A builder of sorts, a person who was always thinking. I can relate to that. I'd like to hear more."

"Okay, well, for one thing, Arthur wanted to add another wing that would angle away from the water—still with a slice of water view as he liked to say, but also with a woodland view of the ravine on that side."

"But he didn't get it built."

"Nope. Arthur was in charge of the hotel overall, but I ran the hotel's Department of Practicality, so we didn't add that wing extension, or the tennis court or swimming pool, and certainly not the nine-hole golf course." I sighed.

"Would you have done it differently? In retrospect?"

I shook my head. "You mean, knowing what I know now? That it would just be me? And I'd be caught in this awful place of trying to figure out what to do? No. And even if Arthur had…was still here, it's still a *no*. They were excellent ideas in many ways, but the timing never felt right." I shrugged and looked down at my food. I shook my head as I sank my fork into the salad. "Whether I was correct or not we'll never know, because fate settled the question."

Blake caught sight of Matt across the room, talking to another diner. He nodded toward him. "Seems pretty smart. I like what he said about *do it like you mean it*."

I drew in a quick breath, hesitating. Finally, I agreed that it sounded smart, but added, "Those are catchy words, yes, but *do it like you mean it* doesn't guarantee you've made the right choice."

Blake stared somewhere over my shoulder. He seemed to be thinking again, then he nodded and smiled. "I agree. You can never know whether a choice was the right one because you can never know what would have happened if you'd chosen differently."

"Well, that's annoying. And unsettling."

"Not really. It just means that you make your best choice, make the most of each day, each moment, and then let the rest take care of itself."

"Wow. Well, that's certainly not me either."

He said, "Then do it your way, but don't second-guess yourself. Ever. If it doesn't go as you'd hoped?" He shrugged. "That's what course corrections are for."

I could see his business-oriented, entrepreneurial brain working its gears. Rather than let this chat go further, I focused on finishing the food that was only half-eaten because we'd been that immersed in the conversation. It was kind of nice, actually, talking with him—probably because he hadn't known Arthur. There wasn't any history. It was just me at the table with him. But now I was worrying that I might've invited him into my business unintentionally—because while people like me were still sitting around considering options and pros and cons, people like Arthur and, yes, probably like Blake, were ready to engage and move forward.

Truly, it seemed to me that it was time to *dis*engage

gracefully.

I said, "I'd better get home to Galahad. Heaven knows what he's gotten up to during my absence."

"Interested in a walk on the beach? We have time before sunset."

"Thanks, but not tonight. Galahad isn't accustomed to being on his own for this length of time." Not really true, but as a polite excuse it would do.

"Understood. I'll walk you to your car."

Did he understand? I had no clue, but he escorted me courteously to the small lot where I was parked, and then he stepped back a few feet, clearly waiting for me to drive off. I started my car, gave him a wave, and backed up a bit to get out of my parking space, and as soon as that was accomplished, he turned away. As I drove forward, he rounded the corner, and I understood he was walking over to the beach by himself.

I almost stopped. I almost slipped into an open parking space I was about to pass. But I didn't. I kept going.

It was good to get home. I'd done the right thing in not contributing to mixed messages by lingering on that beach with Blake.

All was well here. The stars were beginning to pop out in a darkening sky, and the seabirds were tucking themselves in for the night and singing out last calls in an otherwise quiet evening. Galahad was happy to see me. I went through my small house turning on the lights. I freshened his water and gave him a treat. It was pretty much the same routine as every other night for a long time now. And yet, something was missing. The lights didn't help with the emptiness—the uneasy unsatisfactory feel of being home tonight. Alone.

Every time I thought I'd made progress in my life, it seemed I only revealed new gaps.

Blake had said something along the lines of *don't second-guess yourself. Just decide and course correct as necessary.* Matt had said *do it like you mean it and one day you will.*

Several years ago, Arthur had said to me, "Don't sweat the small stuff." I didn't recall what we'd been discussing at the time, but it seemed an on-target message for me just now. At the time, I'd pushed back saying, "Small stuff is important too." And he'd answered, "Mignon, I'm sure someone far smarter than I said this or wrote it. I don't know who, but that doesn't matter because it's absolute truth. Life is the war. The events we deal with in our lives are the battles. Fight each battle with the intent to win," he said, "but don't fret over the battles you lose because ultimately it is about the outcome of the war and how you waged it."

He'd said all that while holding aloft a collectible replica sword with a fancy design on the hilt that I thought unlikely any serious swordsman would've willingly been seen with.

I laughed at him, almost stunned, really. "But dear heart, I don't want to fight any battles. I don't want to win *any* war at *any* cost."

He laid the sword gently on the wooden bar of the check-in counter. He moved close to me and took my hands in his, lifting them almost to his lips. Quietly, he said, "That's not what I said. If life is the war, and the goal is to live it well until your last breath, then the battles are fought to support that. Not to harm others—but to fight the enemy within yourself—the enemy that causes a person to fear, holds them back, and makes them doubt themself."

I smiled, possibly coyly, but certainly with sincerity, and said, "I have you for that." I touched his face and whispered, "I'm happy to be here and be part of our life together. I don't know of any battle I wish to fight."

He kissed my hands, then said, "Everyone must fight for something, Mignon."

Shaking my head, I'd said, "Not me, Arthur. I have you. I've already won the war."

I hadn't won anything, of course. The flaw in my pitiable, romantic logic had become overwhelmingly apparent when Arthur got sick.

I was certain that Blake, even Dominick, would agree with Arthur. I was the odd one out.

And tonight, as I lay there in my lonely bed, still unsettled by Matt's advice and the time I'd spent with Blake, I rolled over to touch Arthur's space—his side of the bed. I slid my hand up to his pillow and pulled it close, burying my face in it.

❦

I hadn't cried like this in a while, but I cried a lot that night. The proof was in the marks my tears had left on the pillowcase. I hugged the pillow all the closer for a long moment, but then pushed it away and twisted my way out of the tangled sheets to escape my bed.

The mirror confirmed my tears too. My eyes were red and swollen. They ached.

Was this a new day, or was it only one more day like the endless array of days I'd been struggling through for the past two-plus years? I'd been doing better, hadn't I?

The last few days may have been the best I'd had in a long time, mostly in terms of making progress—despite Jeanette and even Dominick. In honesty, I had to admit Jeanette's arrival had shaken up the mire I was stuck in. Maybe in that shake-up I'd been able to unstick some part of myself. Good might come of that—so long as she left before I blew my stack. But this morning, I felt the effects of the rough night and with a huge surge of annoyance, I knew I'd hit my limit of *hoping* for better.

I wanted something different, and I was willing to do the necessary work. I'd talked to Dominick about selling. I'd spent social time with Blake. What I was afraid of, was backsliding again, straight back into a past that wanted to own me, even my very existence. Of failure that never stopped.

No one could do this for me. I did have something to fight for—*me*. And I needed to do it as though I meant to win.

As if I believed in myself.

Help was fine. But I had to be the prime driver of making the difference. My difference. Of making *my* choices.

Suddenly in pain, I bent over, wrapping my arms across my stomach. *Breathe*, I told myself. *Just breathe.* Gradually, the spasm eased. I understood the cause. I was afraid of making the wrong choices—choices I couldn't walk back. But stasis—making no choices—was also a bad choice. I knew that too, and it might be the worst choice of all.

What I *did* know, what I was learning with each step I took, was that the closer I got to succeeding, the greater the pain. And it was all me. No one was doing this to me. Something inside me was so terrified of moving forward that it seemed determined to stop me by whatever means necessary.

It was up to me to fight it. To prove that I could do this.

Galahad licked my foot. I reached down to touch his head and smiled.

"Good morning to you too." Deep breath. "Ready for breakfast?"

His expression turned hopeful. I stood and sighed, feeling that fleeting moment of determination already draining away.

Funny how things stuck with you, though. Matt's voice kept coming back . . . *Whatever you decide to do, do it like you mean it* . . . Who hadn't heard those words before? They were almost trite. And yet maybe my head and heart hadn't been able to receive them before yesterday.

Whatever you decide—do it like you mean it. *Go all in,* he'd said.

"Okay, Galahad. In case I haven't told you this already, I'm not reopening the hotel. The next question is whether to demolish it and stay here, or . . . leave?" I shrugged, trying to contain the discomfort growing inside me. "Leave and go somewhere else, which means having to sell. But even if I'm willing to pay a fortune to demolish it and continue living here, I'd still have to clear out Arthur's memorabilia."

I sighed. "What will I do with it all?"

I was in my nightshirt, still trying to get my bearings for how to start this day, when suddenly Galahad became agitated, and in that moment, someone was knocking on the front door—not merely knocking but actually pounding their fist and now calling my name. "Mignon!!"

Running to the door, I flipped the locks to open. Jeanette was standing there, her hand raised mid-knock.

"What are you yelling about?" I asked.

"This." She grabbed my arm. "Come see. Did you hear or see anything during the night? Or maybe this morning? I found this a few minutes ago." She pointed to a window a couple of rooms down from hers.

I could hardly believe what I was seeing. "The glass is broken." I looked around us. "What happened?"

She gripped my arm. "Don't go too close. You're barefoot. Looks like most of the glass fell inside, so maybe someone broke the window to get in? Maybe my arrival ran them off before they could do any damage?"

She was speaking fast—as if the words were flooding out of her. Adrenaline, I thought.

"Calm down." I turned my back to the broken window. That's all it was. A broken window. I'd deal with that shortly. "Where have you been?"

Her expression shifted abruptly from excitement to sullenness.

"I went to visit that friend of mine. You're eager to get me out of here, right? Well, I was working out the details with her. She'll be ready for me to move in soon."

"When?"

She made a rude noise. "Soon. If that's not good enough for you, then say the word. I'll find a place to park my car and sleep there until she can take me in."

Coldly, I said, "No need for that."

I walked away. She followed.

"What about the window?" she asked.

"I'm going to get the keys and check the room, but first I'm going to dress and put on shoes. Is that okay?"

"No need to be sarcastic. I'd think you'd be glad that I came along when I did." She added, "You look awful, by the way. Are you sick?"

Yes, I thought. *But just in the heart. Heartsick.*

Not wanting to give her satisfaction, I let her question go unanswered. I walked into my house and shut the door behind me. Within a few minutes, I'd dressed and crossed over to the hotel side with the master key to access the room.

The rock was smooth and rounded, and more than large enough for a well-aimed pitch to smash easily through window glass. It lay on the guestroom carpet near the bed. Maybe about four feet from the window. Glass shards littered the floor in the general area. Nothing else looked out of place.

So a rock had been thrown. Nothing else was damaged. If someone had intended to break in to steal, then it seemed less than well-thought-out. A thrown rock seemed to point to vandalism. Or so it seemed to me. I locked the door again, leaving the scene undisturbed. I'd call the police department and ask them to make a report. This act, whatever the intent had been, had not been random. The rock could only have been thrown by someone trespassing on the property.

I called the authorities first and then Dominick. I gave him a quick summary—rock through the window, glass in the room, no idea who might've done it. I added, "I need to cover the window. Maybe plywood or something?"

"Until you get it fixed, you mean?"

"Actually, does it make sense to fix it?"

A brief pause and then Dominick's voice was slightly tentative, saying, "Because you're thinking of selling? Have you made up your mind, then?"

Another pause, but this time from my side. Finally, I said, "Still not sure. But Dominick, if I'm not reopening the hotel—and I'm not—then I'm reluctant to spend money replacing the window glass. I can't see how intact glass affects the overall value of the property."

"Let's give that some thought. Meanwhile, you said you called the police?"

"Yes. I know it's minor, but I want the incident and damage documented in case we have more issues with vandals or such. It's not as if we don't have that as a history, back when…." I let the sentence trail off.

Dominick picked up the dropped sentence. "True. Better to have it on record. No chance it could've been unintended?"

"How? No one could've hit that window from down by the water, so someone was here on this property. I know they won't test the rock for fingerprints or DNA, but I want it on record in case something big were to happen."

"Reasonable."

"They'll send an officer out sometime today and that'll be it. Hopefully, this was a one-off and I can feel like I overreacted. That would be a good thing."

Dom's voice dropped. "Make the decision, Meg. Be done with it."

"I'll know when it's time."

"Okay. Hey, are *we* okay now?"

I had to think a minute to remember what he was asking about. All that had been superseded by the rock.

"Yes, as far as I'm concerned, Dominick. You?"

"Always. Call me if you need me to do anything else."

I'd known him forever. We were friends. Friendships could get rocky, and I trusted him a little less now, but it never occurred to me that he hadn't meant well and in the end would always have my back.

Jeanette came outside soon after the officer arrived. I was annoyed, but since she was the one who'd brought the broken window to my attention, it made sense that she'd want to contribute to the conversation.

Matt worked two jobs. Part-time police and part-time restaurant owner/manager. Today was the *dry* day, as he liked to joke, because he was on duty. "Someday I'll earn enough on one job to make up for what I lose at the other. Meanwhile, at least I'm moonlighting at my own place."

Today, he said, "The ground is disturbed here below the window."

I grimaced, saying, "Both Jeanette and I stepped there. We weren't thinking."

We walked into the lobby, and I led him to the room.

He took a couple of photos and picked up the rock. "Don't see this kind of rock around here. Do you have them in your garden area?"

"No. I assumed that whoever threw it had found it in the woods."

"Possibly." He studied it again. "But if it was in the woods, it didn't get there naturally. Plus, see the pits and holes with the dirt stuck in 'em? Doesn't look like the dirt we have here. More like it might've come from someone's garden."

I shook my head. "Not from our garden. I don't have anything like that here. So someone brought it with them. That's a lot of effort to go to if you're just wanting to break a window. Windows aren't that complicated to break."

"True. Anyway, it's probably nothing, just something to tuck in the back of your mind. What about your alarm system? It didn't go off?"

"No. The window glass isn't armed. The motion light might well have gone off outside, but if so, I slept through it. It doesn't look like anyone tried to climb in. There was no dirt on the carpet, and the room was still locked."

"What about the camera?" He pointed up at the camera positioned near the awning.

I grimaced. "Sorry. Doesn't work."

He frowned.

"I consider the sight of it to be a deterrent." I shrugged. "It stopped working a while ago. Didn't seem worth the expense to get it fixed as long as the alarms work."

Matt shook his head. "Any recent incidents of people trespassing?"

"Not since Jeanette has been here."

Jeanette said, "Maybe they ran off when I came back this morning."

I'd almost forgotten she was tagging along behind us because she'd been silent. I gave her a look. Matt did too. He asked, "What time was that?"

"About six, maybe. My headlights caught the break."

We both waited for her to explain where she'd been all night, but it wasn't forthcoming. Matt's frown was faint, but I saw it clearly. He was no more satisfied with her account of this than I was.

He asked, "What time, did you say?"

"I returned home about six a.m. Something like that. It was barely light, but anyone who might've been out here and up to no good would easily have heard me coming and vanished before I could see them."

Matt asked, "No other vehicles here?"

This time, Jeanette seemed a bit at a loss. "Well, no."

"So either they ran down the cliff stairs or around the hotel and into the woods?" His frown popped up again. "That means they also arrived that way—in effect walking in?"

"It must." Jeanette looked at me. "What about that guy? The one who keeps coming around?"

Aghast, I said, "You think he'd break my window? Why on earth—" I saw Matt's look. "She's talking about Blake Stuart. The man I had dinner with at your restaurant? That would make no sense at all."

"You keep acting like the world is trying to chase you out of Emerald Heart. Why not him? Maybe he thought rocks and broken glass would scare you out."

For one moment I allowed that possibility to romp through my brain cells, but then I chased it away. "Ridiculous," I said.

Matt asked, "Is he interested in the property?"

I crossed my arms and leveled my gaze right back at his. "As with everyone else who has expressed any interest, I direct them to Dominick. That simple. And no one who knows me at all would believe that such a juvenile act would run me off this place."

Matt nodded. "Okay then. I'll write up the report. Anything else happens, let me know. You gonna get that fixed?"

"Dominick's going to help me with it."

"Anything else?"

"That should do it. Thank you, Matt. Officer, I should say." I held out my hand, and he accepted it and shook it before putting the notebook back into his pocket.

All this fuss over a thrown rock and broken glass— that's what my brain kept saying. But this was nothing like what had happened before. This felt staged. Like maybe staged by someone who had her own agenda. I glanced at Jeanette. She looked up at me. I stared hard to hold her gaze long enough to tell her this wasn't over yet.

As Matt returned to his police vehicle, I turned to Jeanette who was walking away.

"Not so fast."

She stopped and looked back.

I said, "I don't know what you had in mind with that stunt, but it's going to cost you to repair that window."

"What are you talking about?"

"Don't waste my time with denial. I didn't figure it out right away because I was half-asleep, but it's obvious to me now." I moved closer to her, face-to-face, to add, "You should know I've talked to Dominick. He confessed about your finder's fee arrangement with him. But if you think a rock through the window is manipulation enough for me to sell sooner rather than later because you want money, then you are mistaken. Furthermore, it's entirely possible that I'll go with a different agent altogether because this thing between you and Dom stinks to high heaven. Or maybe I'll handle the sale myself. I'll cut you all out of the gravy train." I said the last as mean as I could, complete with pointing fingers. Then I returned to the house and didn't look back. Let her stew.

I cleaned up the glass from the floor—all the pieces I could see—and then ran the vacuum over the carpet. I wouldn't walk in here barefoot, though. Tiny shards could be hiding in the nap waiting to stab the soles of my feet. No thanks. I'd had enough of backstabs. Didn't need any kind of stabs anywhere else on my body, or in my heart.

When Dominick showed up with a plywood square and secured it against the broken glass, our interaction was tense. I thanked him but had little else to say. I walked him out to his car, and as I watched him drive away, I saw what an eyesore it was. If Emerald Heart had looked derelict before, it was much worse now, so with a huge sigh, I called the glass shop and arranged for them to come out and replace the glass. It would be cheaper if I pulled out the sash and drove it to their shop, but then I'd also have to put it back in myself. Nope. Installing anything to do with windows was not in my skill list. Besides, this bill was going on Jeanette's tab—just as I'd told her it would.

The question was whether I could collect. That seemed unlikely, but I could make sure she never forgot she owed it.

⋘⋙

By that afternoon, I'd resumed going through the rooms while trying not to draw Jeanette's attention. Why? To avoid conversation or curiosity or interference? Yes. To avoid her making assumptions that might encourage her in whatever she was up to? Yes. And to keep my temper in check? Definitely.

Had Jeanette broken that window?

I'd been certain of it in that moment, but now I was back to doubting whether she'd actually done it, and thus also doubting my own judgment, so I was avoiding her by staying on the second floor, choosing one room, the one nearest the lobby stairs, for gathering the "keepers" as I'd done on the first floor. I then began the process of going through each room with an eye to items Arthur and/or I had purchased over the years that were worth keeping.

Each time I walked along the hallway with its long wall of glass windows on the garden side, I tried to look away. I didn't know why. Guilt? Once upon a time, I'd loved that garden. I'd planted it and tended the greenery in every shade and shape personally. I'd talked to them too, especially the live oaks, and I didn't care who overheard. The hotel had been Arthur's, but the garden was mine . . . and now I averted my eyes. I'd let it grow out of control and had lost sight of its beauty in the chaos—so I scooted past and into the next room.

That's where Jeanette found me. I was standing on the bed reaching up for a large lithograph of Tintagel—a lovely, moody landscape of craggy rocks and misty ocean beyond. A nice print but not of the quality as the one in the lobby.

"There you are," she said.

I turned too swiftly and nearly lost my balance. Jeanette was leaning against the doorframe of room 202. Slouching, really, and rather arrogantly.

She asked, "Need any help?"

"No," I said, leaving no room for follow-up questions.

But follow up she did.

"Sorry about the Dominick thing. The finder's fee? He and I were just talking, you know. Throwing out silly ideas. Jokes. That particular idea about the finder's fee was just one tiny blip in the conversation. But as it turns out, finder's fees are a real thing." She shrugged.

I looked away quickly. I would not encourage a conversation.

"Who knew?" she added. "It wasn't meant as a serious discussion, though to be honest, I could use an infusion of cash, so if he's willing—and if you are selling—where is the harm? Any payment to me comes out of Dominick's commission, not out of your profit."

Easing the frame down to rest on top of the mattress, I then leaned the whole of it back against the headboard. Then gingerly, I maneuvered my own way off bed and to the floor.

Jeanette said, "It's not like I can influence you one way or the other. I don't have that kind of sway with you, and frankly, I don't want to have that power. I'm always happy to offer my opinion, but to push you to sell . . . and then if you hated the new place and had lots of regrets— I'd feel terrible. So no. As for Dominick acting as your realtor? That's your choice too, but with you and he and Arthur being close friends for so many years, I think it would be pretty lousy to cut him out of a commission if you *do* decide to sell." She pushed away from the doorframe and waved her arms with one definitive motion—like calling a foul in a ball game. "In my opinion—and it's only an opinion—I think that would be truly stinky."

With that, she stepped away, and I heard her soft footfalls gently fading as she walked down the carpeted hallway. When I heard them pause, I knew she was staring out at the garden.

I stood there facing the open doorway, tense, thinking she might come back. She didn't.

She was probably right in most everything she'd just said. And yet she'd fooled me before. I did trust Dominick, perhaps out of habit—though surely with less than the unquestioning trust I'd had in him before.

Chapter Seventeen

Midmorning the next day, I noticed that Jeanette's car was gone again. After taking Galahad for a walk and seeing that her car still wasn't there when we returned, I told him to take a nap and then went through the connecting door into the lobby. I did a quick run through the remaining guest rooms upstairs and cleared out the wall art and objects in the hallways that I wanted to keep. I locked them in the room I'd chosen for storage on the second floor. I'd moved fast to avoid the angsty stuff I'd been swamped by at the beginning of this process. I could do this.

When I reached the lobby stairs to return to the main floor, something about the low-light scene below captured me. The sense of timelessness—or of being out of time—stopped me cold. Soft light filtered in through the front doors, while a greener light from the garden-side doors washed into the ordinary scene. I remembered Arthur remarking on that. How the green garden reflections gave the light a shimmery, watery look.

I repeated in my head, *I can do this*, but the question came back immediately, *Can I do this all the way?*

A deep breath in and a slow release, and then I forced myself to move. The gleaming wooden bar caught my eye as it had a gazillion times over the past two decades, but this time it was as if I was seeing it for the first time, bathed in that odd, ethereal light. Seeing the aged, exquisite wood, but also the items displayed on the wall behind it, reminded me how annoyed I'd been when I discovered how much money Arthur was spending on his collectibles.

By trying so hard to keep what I could of the past—to cling to what was no longer real—I'd been blinded to the obvious. Even now, I was focusing on the guestrooms where the items were mostly generic décor with little monetary value and also little emotional attachment. Yet I was refusing to see the more expensive items on display in the lobby because those items had been *too* special, for Arthur and even for me. To see them with a more appraising eye meant remembering them in a more intimate connection with Arthur.

The more expensive the items were, the more quietly and magically they'd appeared on display. Arthur and I had often *had words* as new acquisitions had appeared.

Like the bronzes … They were just over a foot high. One was of King Arthur astride his horse and holding his sword, but pensive, as if deep in thought or perhaps praying. Another was of Guinevere and Arthur standing close to each other but with only their fingertips touching as their hands held a goblet. No, a chalice.

I'd pitched a fit about the bronzes. The expense. Plus, he'd displayed them, leaving them unprotected in a hotel lobby, and not even in a lockable case. But Arthur had refused to hide them away. The shield. A replica sword. The touristy copies were mixed with originals and Arthur loved them all.

I spun around to look at the Round Table display flanked by bronze candlesticks on the entry table. I'd complained because even though the entry table was high, thus putting the Round Table and its tiny characters out of reach of young children, still I'd seem many adults reach over and touch it. Even pick up and move the figures around. Arthur had said these were much less expensive than the bronzes. To me, they looked like something you'd pick up in a gift shop for a favorite niece or nephew. But some were true collector's items. Oh, Arthur.

I'd been moving the framed prints and other objects from the locked guest rooms to the locked storage rooms to protect them, yes, and because it was part of the sorting process. But it was also because I didn't trust Jeanette. I'd tried to do it when she wasn't around because I didn't want interference, true, but neither did I trust her not to . . . I shook myself.

Did I really believe that? That she'd steal from me? If I did, then what I'd done made no sense.

I'd left the most valuable items in plain sight, within easy reach. Everything in this foyer was only one double-paned insulated glass door away from a smash-and-grab disaster.

Was it about Jeanette or not?

A strange laugh bubbled up in me. It unnerved me. It was my life, my memories, everything that I was trying to change about my current circumstance, that was at risk from Jeanette. Shivers ran up my arms. I hugged myself.

Things. But not *these* things.

If she wanted a bronze statue, she could have it.

But just not my memories. Maybe the brain, or some emotional center in it, couldn't tell the difference?

I was now turning in a slow 360 movement, taking in the lobby walls and furnishings, forcing myself to view the contents of this room objectively.

In the dim light, with only the daylight filtering in shimmery streams through the wide front and back doors, I walked toward the entry table, my arms reaching forward, my hands settling upon the sculpted diorama of the Round Table and Arthur's knights. Not the most expensive item, and easy for me to reach because it wasn't hanging or fastened down—but placed here ages ago by Arthur.

The dust on the Round Table display piece and the tabletop was thick. Thicker than I would've imagined. I didn't think it had been *that* long since I'd dusted. But sometimes our brains tricked us. It let us see what it thought we should see and blanked out acknowledging the rest.

Placing my hands on either side of the round base, I slid it slightly forward for a better grip and then lifted it. It came—not lighter or heavier than I'd expected—I lifted it and then with a shot of horror, I set it back down. Gently. And I snatched my hands away as if I'd been burned. I stared at my palms. Not burned. Not red.

I touched the nearest candlestick. I wrapped my

fingers around the stem of it and then tightened my grip. No burning this time, but still a touch of horror.

It wasn't the objects. It was me. I wasn't going to be able to do this. The guest room objects were one thing. Almost impersonal. These were different. Moving these felt like a . . . dismantling. Of burning down my life and Arthur's, my years here with Arthur. The fewer, but precious years with Sebrina.

My knees went weak. I couldn't breathe. The floor rose up to meet me and I covered my face. I leaned back against the table and brought my legs up to clasp them close. Pressing my face to my knees, I cried. And cried. I may have wailed. Or perhaps that awful sound was coming from Galahad at the connecting door.

There was only me to hear us.

Arthur and Sebrina were gone. Long gone. But to take his treasures and lock them away, much less sell or donate . . .   My hands clenched into fists so hard that I wasn't sure they'd allow me to do what needed to be done.

Empty, depleted, I let myself fall over, still curled up and hands clenched. The floor received me. I don't know how much time passed. On the far side of the adjoining door, Galahad's wails had ceased, but he snuffled and yipped, making noises. Then I heard knocking which was repeated. Had to be the lobby glass doors. If I didn't move, then whoever it was wouldn't spot me. I didn't want to see anyone. Even if I *had* wanted to, I couldn't imagine what they'd think watching me rise from the shadows like a creature from a scary movie, because I must look at least that bad. Nope, better to stay down and still until whoever it was had left.

Galahad began barking again. And then the knocking resumed, but more loudly. Then a voice called out, "Are you okay? I'm calling 911."

A man. Blake? I looked up. I sat up. I called out, "No. Don't do that. I'm fine. You can go away now."

He laughed, but he didn't sound amused. "Seriously? You think I can just walk away? How do I know you aren't ill or having some kind of break with reality?"

I laughed back, my humor equally lacking. "In recent years, my life has been one long, ugly break with reality."

"What's that? I couldn't hear you."

His face was close to the glass, and he looked genuinely concerned.

I stood gingerly, half-expecting my legs to fail me again, but they didn't. I pushed away from the foyer table and moved toward the doors. They were locked but not armed. I flipped the dead bolt to open and stepped quickly back into the dimmer, more concealing light.

"Come in." I gestured as I spoke.

He opened the door partway and peered inside. "You sure?"

I nodded. I don't know whether Galahad could hear the soft thud of the door closing or if it was Blake's voice, low and soft, but my poor dog broke out into barking again—demanding barks.

"Open the door, okay?" I pointed toward the sound

of poor, frenzied Galahad.

"Will do." Blake opened the door, but only a crack—much as he'd done with the front door—and spoke softly, calmly. "Well, hello there, Galahad. You remember me, right?"

I realized the reason for his caution. "He knows you. He won't bite." After a very brief pause, I added, "At least, I don't think he will. He's pretty worked up after . . . all this."

Blake shot me a look.

"It's been a strange day," I said. "A strange few weeks, in fact." *Even longer.*

Galahad's muzzle had worked its way through the open space of the door and the rest of him was trying to follow, but his manner seemed earnest, not threatening. Blake must've agreed, because he opened the door wider. Galahad shot through, gave Blake's shoes the briefest of passing sniffs, and then came straight to me. I knelt to give him a hug because, after all, he'd been worried about me.

I was worried about me too. My hair had straggled across my face and stuck to my cheeks. I clawed it out of the way and fought to pull myself together. I tried to breathe slowly, regaining my control. Maybe Blake wouldn't notice how frazzled I was.

He gave me a long look, then asked, "What was that about?"

"What did you see?" I asked.

"First, just shadows," Blake replied, sounding annoyed, maybe exasperated. "But then either my eyes adjusted to the dimness or maybe the clouds moved and let in more sunlight . . . but it looked like you were lying on the floor. Huddled, maybe? I thought you might be hurt or sick or . . . I don't know what."

"It was nothing. I had a moment, that's all. I'm fine now."

"Mignon."

"Seriously, don't you ever have times when life overwhelms you? I had one of those hitting-the-emotional-wall events."

He tightened his jaw as if holding back his next words. I appreciated that and hoped he'd continue to keep those words to himself. To show him that I was all good now, I reached down to scratch Galahad's head, but my dog was gone. He'd moved away and was now canvassing the foyer, smelling out each nook and cranny and dust bunny. He was calm, but if this continued, I was afraid he'd go into a frenzied hunting mode as he'd done in the early weeks and months after Arthur died. It could take days to calm him down if that happened.

Galahad was older now—more mature—and Arthur had been gone so long, but I couldn't risk letting him go through that again if I could prevent it. Blake's eyes were now following poor Galahad around the room, and the interior must've caught his eye because he swung his gaze here and there, taking in the lobby from end to end, pausing at times, lingering for longer moments on some of Arthur's memorabilia.

Enough.

"I need to get Galahad out of here. I don't allow

him in the hotel area because . . . I guess his nose is too keen and he's still scenting Arthur. Looking for him. He used to get worked up over it, and I don't know if he will now, but I'm going to spare him that, so please excuse us. I'll distract him with treats and then go for a walk." *Ugh.* He was going to think I was hinting for him to join us.

He interrupted my thoughts. "I get it. I know there are dogs that stay beside their owner's . . . with them . . . even after . . ." He stopped. "Never mind. But I do understand." He stepped a little closer to me. "I can stay, for a little while even."

Shaking my head, I said, "No, but thank you. Your arrival interrupted whatever I was lost in and I'm good now. I need to see to Galahad."

"If you're sure that you're okay."

"I am."

"I dropped by hoping to invite you out to supper this evening. If you're interested, the invite is still open."

I did still feel a little shaky, I knew the worst was over. *I hoped.*

"I'll pass this time. I appreciate the invitation."

He scanned the room again. "I'm guessing it has something to do with all this?"

I didn't answer. We were totally in none-of-his-business territory here, even if he *had* been helpful.

"I remember when I had to go through Alyssa's things. Her mother ended up making most of the decisions. I found myself unable to do it alone."

"Truly?"

"Yes. If you need help, let me know." He raised his eyebrows in appreciation as he glanced over the bar and at the wall with the bronze pieces. "Also, don't go taking the quickest path to getting it over with. You've got some interesting things here that should probably be appraised."

I nodded. "I agree."

"I've never been much of a collector, but this looks pretty amazing."

"Well, it was his thing, you know? Not football or golf or building models, but anything related to King Arthur? A huge yes." It felt good to smile.

Snuffling noises got our attention. Galahad was nosing at the locked storage room door. Whining and chuffing, he ran his nose along the base of the door and even up the sides of it.

Randomly, not thinking at all, I mused, "I've been clearing the guest rooms of things I want to keep." *Not again*. I glanced at him. Had he caught my meaning? Yes. He was looking at me directly and his eyebrows were raised, this time in deliberate exaggeration, like a mock villain.

He said, "Good to know."

"No decision yet. Let's keep this talk between the two of us?"

"Yes, ma'am." He smiled. "Call if you change your mind about supper. Meanwhile, I'll get out of your way so you can rescue Galahad from whatever he thinks he may have cornered in there." He grinned. "Need some backup, just in case?"

"Thanks, but I've got it handled." I flashed a grin right back at him.

He nodded and turned toward the door just as we heard the soft swoosh of it closing, and saw Jeanette backlit by the light outside such that I could see the attitude in her posture even if I couldn't see her face all that clearly. When she moved toward us, the light evened out and her smirk became evident. Or twisted. Whatever was in her head came out sounding better than I expected.

"Who's this? Sorry to interrupt."

Blake offered his hand and Jeanette took it. "I'm a neighbor. Blake Stuart."

"I'm Jeanette. Mignon's sister-in-law. Used-to-be sister-in-law, rather."

He gave a nod, acknowledging her introduction. "Pleased to meet you." He cast a quick glance back at me and then to Jeanette again. "I was just on my way out, if you'll excuse me." And he left.

Jeanette's smirk tweaked up a bit. "What is it that you have handled?"

"None of your business." I went to the connecting door. "Galahad. Come."

"Wait, Mignon," Jeanette said. "So this guy . . . He's the one that's been coming around? I get that he's good-looking. He is." She shrugged. "He's got charm. I can tell he's a smooth one. So go out with him. Whatever. But don't try to replace Arthur with him."

Her words were outrageous. Out of nowhere, Jeanette was giving me advice of this nature? Huffy, I said, "You, of all people, have no right to suggest that I would try to replace Arthur—ever."

She squinted at me like her vision was fuzzy or such, then she tilted her head to the side as if confused. "You don't see it, do you." She didn't say it as a question but as a statement that she'd just seen the truth of. I kept my mouth shut. She was dancing into dangerous territory. My heart rate was increasing, and I felt the solid thump of it in my chest.

"You lived your life through Arthur. Since he's been gone, you've been in limbo. Like a zombie waiting for the next impetus to move you forward." She paused, her eyes fixed on my face. "You can't deny that." She moved a couple of steps closer. "Using him—this new guy—like you used Arthur to . . . to take care of you . . . to provide you with a reason to get up every morning is wrong. Wrong on so many levels." She spun on her heel and left. Just like that.

Retorts and arguments were building in my head. My jaw ached and my lips burned with the angry words that cried to be said. But Jeanette had left the room. I would not chase after her. To do so would give some sort of weird credibility to what she'd said. I refused to allow her to get into my head.

Bringing The Emerald Heart Hotel back to the glory he thought the place deserved had been my husband's dream, and he'd enlisted me to help with it. That meant we were partners. A team. I was not a hanger-on to his dream like some sort of parasite or victim.

Had Jeanette been jealous of our relationship? I shook my head. Surely not. I'd never seen anything that even hinted of it. She and I had even been friends, especially in those early days. When things began to fall apart, the dispute was between her and her brother. I was forced into the role of reluctant intermediary, and not by choice. I wanted to stay out of it. I believed they'd work things out. But they seemed determined to pull me into the argument . . . and ultimately, I aligned with my husband because I knew Arthur's heart and Jeanette had become more and more like someone I'd never truly known. And then, after that last argument, she'd left. We'd had no idea that she wouldn't return.

And so today I wouldn't chase her either because if there'd been even a tiny hope that we might somehow mend the break—as she'd said she hoped to do the day she'd shown up on the porch—well, I no longer believed that. I decided Arthur would agree. Jeanette should go. Just go and be done with it.

She'd said her friend was almost ready for her to move in. I'd try to ignore her while keeping a close eye on her.

My dog and I passed back over to our side, the house side. I shut the door firmly between the two of us and Jeanette.

Chapter Eighteen

The next day, I dropped by Wheeler's Grill hoping to catch Matt there. I wanted to ask his objective opinion about what was going on. Jeanette and Dominick, perhaps even Blake, seemed too entwined in my life for me to assess this properly. If, for instance, there were teenagers messing with houses for fun or to steal—if something like that was going on but hadn't made the news, might it be a more reasonable explanation for what was happening around Emerald Heart?

If not for that rock, I would've put the other small annoyances down to imagined troubles. Maybe I'd been too long isolated and too emotionally damaged to see clearly. But the rock . . . that was the outlier. That felt like it must be given attention.

Jeanette—I was suspicious of her with reason. Dominick . . . I no longer trusted him in the blind way I had before, but he didn't throw a rock at my window. I was sure of that. Blake was the one person I *wasn't* suspicious of. Blake was the newest person in my life, and he *had* expressed interest in Emerald Heart, so maybe Blake was *my* blind spot. He'd been kind to me. Maybe he was the person I should trust least of all.

Or was I missing something entirely?

A man I didn't know was behind the bar. He

glanced up as I approached.

"Is Matt here? I was hoping to catch him when it wasn't too busy."

"He's due in, but he's late."

"Well, then, how about a drink? I'll hang around for a few minutes in case he shows up."

"He'd better show. I have plans."

He wasn't looking at me, was speaking more to himself or to the ether, so I didn't bother responding.

I took my drink to a booth over by the window. This time of day—midafternoon—most of the booths and tables were empty. That would change soon. As the minutes passed and I watched the guy behind the bar looking more and more annoyed, I knew I'd wasted a trip here. Even if Matt walked in right now, the situation wouldn't be conducive to an easy chat, especially as other patrons continued to arrive. A twenty-something couple walked in. Shortly after, three men who looked like they were stopping off after work came in and sat at a table.

The street view drew me. I watched vacationers and locals strolling along the sidewalk, but I was thinking about Matt. Anything could've delayed him. Sickness, or maybe he'd been asked to work a longer shift at the police department? I picked up my bag. Time to go.

Just then, I saw Blake and he saw me through the window at the same time. He looked surprised, waved, and came inside quick as a heartbeat. I waited and he joined me, sliding into the booth. Not opposite me, but on *my* side. Perhaps a little too close?

"May I join you?"

A little late for him to ask, but then again, maybe I needed to chill a bit. I reminded myself that Blake had called yesterday evening to check on me after the incident in the lobby. That had been thoughtful. Plus, he'd saved me from falling down the cliff. And he'd been very nice to my dog.

"How are you today?" he asked.

There was an edge of excitement in his tone.

"I'm fine. All better."

He said, "You look wonderful."

What could I say to that? "Thank you."

His smile seemed over-bright, almost too pleased, as he asked, "Am I interrupting?"

"No, I was hoping to meet a friend, but they didn't show."

"Then if you don't mind, and if you have a few minutes . . . I have news," he said. "I'd love to share it with you."

Confused by his sudden appearance, and the impetuous, impromptu feel of the whole—whatever this was—I sat frozen like a deer in the lights . . . caught in the glow of his smile that lit his entire demeanor. Wide-eyed and breathless and waiting, that was me—and not much more than that was in my brain except for thinking that I'd *love* to feel that thrilled about anything. Anything whatsoever.

As I stared, his glow dimmed a fraction. A trace of uncertainty showed in his voice, as he asked, "News.

Want to hear?"

Speak, I told myself.

"Yes?" I forced a small laugh. "I mean, you surprised me." I added, more strongly, "Yes, I'd like to hear your good news."

"It's not settled yet, but I've reached a verbal agreement with the Holmans to buy their house and property."

"Oh." Was this a good thing? Why did he think I'd be overjoyed? Or maybe he was simply excited, and I was the first person he saw that he could share the news with. "I didn't know you were considering buying it. I thought you were taking a break from business while waiting out the do-not-compete."

He smiled at my confusion, but kindly. "I hadn't thought of buying it but seeing Emerald Heart across the ravine day in and day out, I found myself not wanting to leave. The Holmans' acreage is a sizable property, as it turns out. I contacted them and asked if they'd consider selling. They didn't jump at the opportunity right away, but after thinking about it, they changed their minds." The words sounded good, but his smile had dimmed.

Jeanette's words about replacing one for the other instead of living my own life whispered in my head. Though I tried to muster up some enthusiasm, I didn't do so well.

"Blake," I said, "you know that if I sell the hotel and the property that I'm probably not staying, right?

"Sure. Well, that is, you'd have to move, right? But you don't have to move far." He spoke softly, "Frankly, I was hoping for your input about how best to use this property. Combined, the two properties offer amazing development opportunities." He leaned toward me, lowering his voice even more. "You are going to sell. And if you don't, well, then, so be it." He shrugged. "I mean that. But you're still going to have to do something with the hotel and property. The current structure is inadequate in modern terms even aside from the upkeep issue."

Drawing away . . . it was a physical sensation inside me, but it must surely show on the outside too. The coldness I felt . . . Perhaps it radiated out and chilled him because he slid back in his seat, too, moving slightly away from me.

I hated to see his enthusiasm die. I was tempted, drawn to say we could talk about it, that I wasn't sure *yet*, but that yes, I'd probably sell…but I didn't. I held all that in. Blake had been kind and thoughtful, but he'd made a big leap forward and included me in that leap without my permission. Jeanette was wrong in what she'd said about replacing Arthur with someone else who could supply me with dreams, but to keep her wrong, I had to be careful not to encourage Blake. I had to find my own way.

His voice, hesitant at first, grew softer yet surer at the same time. "Hey, I'm sorry. I see we have a disconnect of some kind. My fault, I'm sure. I tend to get enthusiastic about new ideas . . . to see the potential and reach for it, sometimes without looking to see the hazards. I guess they call that having a high tolerance for risk. But please believe me that I didn't intend any disrespect. Sorry for the misunderstanding."

I nodded. "Whatever I choose to do . . . sell or stay . . . whatever—it must work with what I decide to do after. I'm not feeling what that is yet."

Touching his arm, I leaned toward him. "Blake, your imagination is busy creating and planning. Mine is still stuck, but it's getting unstuck, and I don't want to inhibit that by getting swept up into other people's dreams and plans."

Blake reached over and touched my hand. For a moment, I was so strongly reminded of Arthur that I nearly bolted. Instead, I forced myself to stay put and wait.

He said, "Call me when you need me, or even if you just want to talk. When I know more about the plans, I'll let you know—but no expectations, I promise. Just a friendly exchange of information . . . if we're still friends?"

I squeezed his hand and released it. "We are. You keep me informed and I'll do the same for you."

Beyond him, I saw Dominick. When had he arrived? Judging by the look on his face, he'd heard at least part of what I'd said to Blake. Whether he'd correctly understood what he'd overheard was a whole different question. For sure he'd noticed the hand-holding because even post-release, that's where his eyes stayed focused until he looked up.

"Hey, Dominick. You've met Blake? Blake Stuart? I've mentioned him, I'm sure."

Dominick moved the few steps to stand beside our booth. "Of course. I remember." His real-estate-agent smile flashed across his face, but his expression was somber.

Blake offered his hand. Dominick accepted it. The shake was brief.

"You'll represent Mignon if she decides to sell, right?"

"Still waiting to hear what she wants to do. No rush, of course. This isn't a simple decision for her."

"Of course." Blake nodded. "I was asking her to keep me informed. I might want to bid for the property. I hope you'll keep me in mind, should that become a thing."

"Sure. In fact, Mr. Holman called me. Said you'd expressed interest in *his* property too. I saw you earlier out on the street. Figured I'd come over and introduce myself. Apologies if I've interrupted something."

Enough, I thought, but I smiled pleasantly. This was about business.

"No interruption at all. Your timing was excellent," I said, giving them each a look. "In fact, I was just about to leave, so I'll *leave* you two to discuss possibilities, if that's what you want to do." I shook my head as I tapped Blake's arm, indicating that I wanted out. *Boy, did I want out.*

Now Blake and Dominick were both standing there at the end of the booth.

Trying to sound relaxed and only mildly interested, I said, "I'm surprised about the Holmans, but then again, why shouldn't they sell? They love their house up here, but it's huge. Empty nesters and all that. They love being down in Florida." I moved, the exit in my sight, saying, "I'll see you around. Dominick, I'll give you a call later to let you know where my thoughts are about selling just now."

In his most civil, businesslike voice, he said, "Thanks, Meg. I'll look forward to hearing from you whenever it's convenient."

CRLED

I left Blake and Dominick at that booth in the restaurant, feeling as though I'd messed up somehow and was desperately in need of an escape. I'd slipped out as gracefully as possible, but he looked . . . I don't know. Maybe confused. Disappointed, probably.

Why did it all have to be so hard? Arthur had been good with people. He could talk folks into almost anything whether it was cajoling them into a better mood when they were sad, or charming a toddler into eating his veggies, or convincing otherwise disinterested people to discuss his King Arthur stuff. Arthur had been a people person. I'd always just stood next to him looking pleasant while he did the heavy lifting of sociability.

A distance down the block, I stopped and stepped back into a recessed doorway. An empty storefront. Quiet and dark. I remembered it having been a T-shirt/souvenir shop—one of several in this block of stores. This one hadn't made it. For me, at this moment, it was a shady private spot to stand and think. To gather my wits before stepping back out into easy view.

Dominick and Blake were likely now sitting in the booth talking business. Jeanette was at the hotel. Me? I was hiding in this doorway.

What about Galahad? I was sure he was eager for a walk and a treat.

Everyone in my life seemed to be revolving around me, waiting for me to choose my path.

Pressing my back against the plate-glass door behind me, I felt the gritty layer of old dirt coating it, then turned to look inside. The windows were murky with lots of dark shadows beyond them. A big *CLOSED* sign was taped inside the door facing out, facing me. The large room was empty except for some stray racks and shelving.

I was reminded of the thoughts I'd had about how time moved on with or without you.

There wasn't a rule book for everything. What did one do when a child never came home? When no matter how long one waited—the truth would not change, and you knew that. But that reality was at war with what was imprinted in your brain.

And if I couldn't forgive—truly forgive—Jeanette for her treatment of Arthur when he was ill and dying, then how much more impossible was it to forgive her for her part in taking Sebrina from us?

I'd made peace with it, I'd thought. Had I been lying to myself, burying the uglier side of grief deep until the time came that it rose again within me? Like a fire? Like a slashing knife?

Arthur and I had grieved together over the loss of our daughter. Everyone agreed that no one had done anything wrong, that tragedy happened sometimes, empty of rhyme or reason. After the fire of grief and disbelief had consumed itself, it left emptiness inside me, too. Or so I'd thought.

Arthur had counseled forgiveness. He prayed. I tried. Arthur suggested all sorts of things. Some of his suggestions may have worked for him, helped him, but did nothing for me. I simply trudged through each day until eventually I realized I'd resumed living and must find my comfort in my memories. But not in the memory of Sebrina holding her auntie Jeanette's hand as they descended the steps down to the dock, and of how one moment of carelessness, a turned back and a child's inattention, could cause her to trip, bump her head, and topple into the water like a limp doll. Jeanette had heard the splash and spun around, I saw that—I saw it all—and she probably heard my screams from all the way from the terrace above.

Jeanette went into the water immediately, and I was screaming Sebrina's name and stumbling down the cliff steps and ran straight off the side of the dock into the water too.

And the question in my head time and again like a revolving door was, How do you grieve a lost child— One who should climb out of the water, up the ladder onto the dock, and then up the steps and to our home? I would grab one of the heavy, thick-pile bath towels from the laundry basket, meet her at the door, and toss the towel over her head, rubbing her hair as she giggled, and then, still snug in her towel, I'd pick her up in a big bear hug as she laughed all the more.

Still waiting. I was. Despite there being no reason—no logic—in the wait.

How did one accept it? How did one grieve it? And how did one contemplate leaving the house you'd shared with her, and the dock and the cliff stairs that would lead her back home?

People did. Parents. Grandparents. Siblings. But not me.

My hands were pressed against the dirty glass. That realization of it came to me as a surprise. I'd forgotten I was here, still hiding in this recessed doorway.

"Mignon?"

I opened my eyes slowly, and in the glass, dim and distorted, was Dominick's reflection.

"Are you okay?" he asked softly.

Closing my eyes again, I leaned forward, away from him, bowing my head until my forehead touched the glass.

He rested his hands on my shoulders and squeezed ever so slightly.

"What can I do?" he asked.

"Nothing," I whispered.

"This isn't about Arthur, is it?"

"No."

Did he turn me toward him, or did I initiate the

move? Either way, I was suddenly facing Dominick with my forehead pressed against his shirt instead of the shop glass. It wasn't the first time he'd consoled me, offering comfort in a hug—but it had been a long time.

I added, "No, at least not entirely."

"That's what I thought." He paused, then added, "I wondered if that was the root of your problem with Jeanette. Her coming back here triggered this, didn't it?" He pressed his cheek against my hair. "I'm sorry, Meg. I meant well. I truly didn't consider that seeing her would bring all this back for you . . . what happened with Sebrina."

"She'd be twenty-one now. Can you imagine how that would be?" I couldn't help the wistful tone of my voice.

"Meg."

"Probably graduating from college. Finding a job or planning a wedding. Maybe already married with my grandchild on the way." I gulped, but it sounded like a groan. I kept going anyway. "It's as if my life split that day. In some part of my brain, all the good things continued to exist as they'd been, but frozen. Like an old TV show that keeps coming back in reruns. But in the other timeline—the one we're in now—it continued forward . . . without her. I'm functional. Just functional. And only doing that well thanks to Arthur, who put his own grief aside to help me manage mine." I pushed back against him and looked him in the face.

"How do I fix that, Dominick? Arthur kept me going. Arthur was worth living for, and now I don't even have *him*." Loudly, I asked, "How do I fix that?"

His eyes were red and wet. He pressed his lips tightly together and pulled me back in close. He didn't speak, but I felt his cheek brush against my hair as he moved his head gently back and forth in a silent *no*.

After a few moments, he said, "I don't have those answers, Meg, but at some point someone is going to accuse us—the two of us—of inappropriate conduct, like maybe necking and such in a shady, barely private location on a public street." He laughed gently. "Shady behavior in a shady place. Is that like a pun?" He was asking, forcing me to react.

"I don't think so."

"*Humph*. Regardless, I'm fairly well known around here," he said in a false-pompous voice. "I don't want to have to explain what's actually happening here." He gave a quick laugh. "What do you say to moving on? Take a walk with me. Maybe breathe some fresh air and clear your head?"

I nodded as I stepped away, but he slipped his arm through mine. "Not so fast. Walk with me . . ." He tucked my arm into his so closely that we were arm to arm. He pressed his free hand over mine on his forearm. "We'll go down to the water and breathe. I could use some fresh air. How does that sound?"

My legs felt odd, weak, and I was glad to have Dominick to lean against. I appreciated his caring. His gallantry. I smiled, thinking of Arthur. And even Galahad.

Hopefully, Galahad would forgive me for the

delay. I wasn't ready to return home just yet.

As for Matt, I'd catch up with him some other time. Truly, my interest in discussing petty crimes around the area had passed. I'd rather take a stroll along the ocean with a friend.

We removed our shoes and resumed holding hands as we walked out into the sand and toward the ocean. We settled in the dry sand. Neither of us spoke until Dominick said, "You did that grief counseling years ago, right? I remember. Seemed like it helped."

"Yes," I nodded, then I shrugged. "It helped me learn how to manage, but all that *yuck* was still stuck inside me." The counselor had wanted me to work on giving up mementos, donating clothing, all sorts of things that sounded good but were unthinkable. "She wanted me to give it all up—all that I had of who Sebrina had been."

"*Hmm*. Well, I'm guessing that wasn't exactly what she was asking you to do. People hold onto keepsakes in memory of people they've lost, like souvenirs from vacation trips, family events, and so on. Nothing wrong with that . . . so long as they don't interfere with you living your life. You deserve better than to be stuck in the past." He shook his head and tightened his grip on my hand. "Don't get angry. I would've said all this sooner if I'd realized you were still cherishing what no longer existed." He shook his head again. "*Listen to me, Meg, please*. You deserve a life—a life you can't have if the better part of you is trapped in something that ended years ago."

I struggled to pull my hand from his grasp, but he wouldn't let go. He put his arm behind my back.

"Thanks for letting me have my say."

I made a rude noise.

"Tell me this, Meg. Sebrina didn't get a chance to grow up and do all the things you mentioned. If she'd lived and you'd been the one who wasn't here—had left her to grow up without you—how would you feel if you could somehow look down and see that she was still trapped in the past? It would break your heart. The waste of a life with so much opportunity—just stuck. Treading water. Marking time. Through all these years."

"I want to go home."

He sighed.

"Galahad is stuck in the house. He needs to eat. To go out."

He dropped his arm from behind me, but never releasing my hand, he rose to his feet.

"I'm not going to run away."

"I'm not so sure. Besides, it's nice to just hold your hand." He pulled me to my feet. "We've been friends for a long time, haven't we?"

"Yes."

"I've let you down in recent times." He touched my chin. "If I'd realized how deep the problem was, I would've understood your isolation better." He turned us away from the ocean, and suddenly my arm was again tucked into the crook of his as we plowed back through the dry sand. "I thought you were trying to distance yourself from me without hurting my feelings. I guess I took it personally. But now I'm going to be a pest. A nuisance. If I annoy you, then so be it. If you don't like it, you'll have to come right out and tell me." He laughed as we reached the pavement. "Remember, our friendship is separate from any business we might do. Friends first."

He walked me to my car. "You okay to drive?"

"I'm fine now." *Or getting there.*

"Good to hear. You seem okay. I hope you're free tomorrow, because I'm coming over and we are going to talk about Sebrina and Arthur. I have a few memories I'd like to air out."

My stomach clenched. "No."

"Well, then, I'll be talking to myself. Out there on your porch. With Galahad confused, probably whining and barking like he does. *Or* we can chat like real people, real adults, who've known each other for a couple of decades plus." He opened the car door. "I never told you, did I, that Arthur and I argued over who was going to ask you out first?"

"Please," I said with my best disdain.

Dominick laughed it off, saying, "I'll bring lunch. How about pizza? High noon."

When I didn't respond, he said, "You don't have to say anything you don't want to, now or anytime. But you know what, Meg? You've kept it all inside too long. Time to share it with me. Remember, I loved Sebrina too. And Arthur. I'd like to find closure. You can help me with that." He pressed a soft kiss to my forehead. "See you tomorrow."

I snapped my seat belt into place and as I started

the car, I looked up automatically into the rearview mirror, checking behind me. A short distance away, about midway between the diner and the vacant store, stood Blake. He was just standing there, and his posture looked odd.

Obviously, he'd felt awkward about the whole Holman house news and my reaction to it. Should I hop out of the car and go speak with him? Maybe offer a small apology for leaving the restaurant so abruptly, so oddly? But then I saw that Dominick had reached him and they were talking. No need, then.

"Okay, Galahad, I'm on my way."

Chapter Nineteen

Before noon the next day, I unlocked the gate. Jeanette had locked it behind her when she'd left earlier in the morning. Good on her. I'd leave it unlocked until after Dominick came and went. He had a key, but there was no need to make him stop. He'd have pizza, after all. Besides, he wouldn't be staying all that long. Dominick wanted to talk about old times, about Sebrina. I suspected that conversation would be short. Today didn't feel like a day for idle chatter about painful things close to my heart. No day did.

Dominick arrived ten minutes late.

"Sorry. Had to wait for the pizza."

"No problem. Soda, water, or tea?"

"Tea."

"Got it. Be right back." I looked down. "Galahad, please keep Dominick company while I fetch the drinks."

⋙⋘

Dominick tried. He brought up memories of Arthur and Sebrina which made me uncomfortable, and I kept changing the flow of the conversation. Finally, we gave up and switched to the subject of Emerald Heart. That was much safer and less painful than the other topics.

When he left, I rode down to the gate with him and gave him a wave goodbye. I locked the gate and walked back. Galahad had gone in the car with us, but now, my best buddy showed me the dust as he suddenly dashed ahead, apparently in a huge hurry to get home.

As I rounded the curve, I saw him ahead. He was on the cliff terrace, sitting and panting at Blake's feet.

A quick pause, a minor stumble, and then I was walking again, my pace increasing. Surprised, yes, but I was glad to see him.

"Hi, Blake. I didn't know you were here."

"Sorry to just show up," he said.

"No problem."

He looked at me and started to speak, but then he stopped. He cleared his throat and finally said, "Looks like I owe you an apology."

"What's that? An apology? Why?" I smiled. Couldn't help myself. Was he talking about the Holman property thing?

He gave me a long look. "Sorry I misunderstood."

"No wonder." I was confused, though. "With me going back and forth like that . . . sell/don't sell . . . I inflicted my indecision on everyone."

He frowned, but not in a threatening way. A thinking way.

I continued, "But I've got it sorted out now. At least, I hope so."

"Looked that way to me. I didn't realize that you and Dominick Monahan were more than friends."

I stood silent, trying to decipher this. "I *did* tell you that he was my real estate agent."

He crossed his arms and his voice dropped low. "Aside from business, I mean." He pushed away from the railing, gave Galahad a scratch on the head, then said to me, "I wouldn't have been hanging around and seeking you out. It must've been annoying for you." He shook his head. "I apologize for that too. I'll go directly to Monahan from now on if there is any business to discuss."

My spine stiffened. I crossed my arms this time. I truly wanted to know why this guy who'd gone out of his way to be charming, pretty much from the moment we met on the beach, was suddenly behaving like a jerk.

I said, "I'm also certain I told you that any business or sale issues related to Emerald Heart *should* be addressed with him. So what's the deal, Blake? What's going on here?"

"No need to be defensive, Mignon. You aren't at fault. I'm a stranger who came out of nowhere and made assumptions. I saw you and Dominick in that doorway yesterday. Then later I wondered if I was mistaken in what I saw. Thought I'd come over today and ask you about it, but then here he is again and . . . So, my error. Though I *did* ask before if you were . . ." He shook his head. "Never mind. Sorry. I'll be on my way."

What the heck? He, himself, had said *friends* yesterday, right?

I tried to speak reasonably. "Blake, I'd think we'd have to be a lot more personally involved for me to owe you an explanation about other people who might be in my life." I heard the words I was saying, and they were true…but maybe also *not true* depending on one's perspective. And just now, without meaning to, I'd spoken throwing-down-the-gauntlet words. He could've pushed back, but Blake chose not to pick up the word-gauntlet. Instead, he simply nodded and walked away, heading around the end of my house and vanishing from view.

Well, crap.

He'd seen Dominick comforting me and had totally misread the friendly hug as an embrace. I reran today's visit with Dominick and how we might've looked to someone was watching. Like friends? Yes, unless you were thinking that hugging and laughing meant more. How might it have looked to someone who cared that it *might* mean more. As maybe Blake felt.

But I didn't feel the way he did—*if* he did. It was pretty obvious that we were just two people who'd lost our spouses and had jobs and futures in flux and were just floundering around unsure about pretty much everything.

Maybe he wanted it to lead to more.

Not me. I didn't need more. My plate was full, and Jeanette was right about one thing—I didn't need a man to help me find my way. Friends? Yes. Friends were welcome. Apparently, Blake wanted to be more than friends. Maybe a small part of me was interested in that, too, but we were lucky to have discovered I wasn't ready for that before it got … stupid, with unintended damage.

And maybe it was for the best. Maybe he had been getting too close and I'd allowed it. Perhaps it had become part of my confusion when I most needed a clear head.

CRSO

After sharing pizza with Dominick, subsequently *topped* by Blake's strange and confusing complaints, I couldn't settle. Too much of the day was still ahead for me to stay in this agitated state. I needed normalcy—sweetness, kindness—not supercharged emotion. My life seemed to be spinning out of control.

A walk in the woods would help, but *not* toward the Holmans' house. I would visit Carolyn. She was like the aunt I'd never had. She baked me cookies and fudge and offered advice and invited me to church. She was always pleasant, and recently, I'd neglected her.

In the woods, I let Galahad off his leash. He knew the way to Carolyn's house. As Mrs. Holman had done, Carolyn usually kept special treats for him, so he was on board with the visit.

As I went to the back door to knock, Galahad broke off and did a quick sniff-around of her garden and the picnic table and birdbath—all the fascinating things. I knocked softly. No one answered, so I walked around to the front of the house. A car was parked beside some bushes, half-obscured, but it looked familiar. As I moved closer, I saw the token hanging from the rearview mirror, identical to the one I'd seen in Jeanette's car. Stunned by disbelief, I checked the license plate.

Jeanette's.

Why?

I shook my head, trying to clear it. This made no sense. Why would she be parking here? Was she here at this very moment? Visiting Carolyn? She knew Carolyn from way back, but . . .

No other cars were here. I couldn't see in the garage, of course, but I sensed no one was home. I went to the door, and this time I rang the doorbell, waited, and then I knocked. Gripping the knob, I tested it. Locked.

What was going on here? This made no sense. I returned to the backyard and stared at the yard and the woods, my mind empty, hoping for an innocent explanation.

Galahad was still rummaging around in Carolyn's backyard. He was investigating a small garden with plastic twirly things amid some annuals and a few weeds. Carolyn was a great cook and decorator, but not as particular about keeping up the flower plot. I walked over to Galahad, suddenly feeling awkward at a place where I'd never felt unwelcome, until now. I called him to me. It was time to hike back to Emerald Heart. He was busy and ignored me, and in that moment, I was reluctant to raise my voice, so I went to where he was sniffing. A squirrel was nearby and leaving a trail that Galahad couldn't resist—not to chase after, but simply curious— and I saw the rocks. They formed a rock border for the garden. Rounded, smooth river-tumbled rocks, just right to fit within a person's grasp, with enough weight and mass to shatter window glass.

If I'd had paper and a pencil, I would've left a note on Jeanette's windshield.

I had my tote bag with me because I'd planned to give Carolyn a gift—one of Arthur's small collectibles. She'd admired them in the past. Also, I had my small cosmetics bag in my tote. I walked back to the front yard and went straight to Jeanette's car. By leaning across and reaching from one side and then moving to the other side, I was able to write across the windshield in huge red lipstick letters—*I'm waiting. Come see me.*

And about two hours later, she did.

Chapter Twenty

When Galahad scratched at the door, wanting out, I knew Jeanette was back. I stepped out onto the porch, ready for the confrontation. Her car was there now, yes, but no Jeanette.

Galahad had dashed out the door ahead of me, so I went to the terrace. He was already below, having joined her on the dock. I took my time going down the cliff stairs. If the dock was where she wanted to discuss this, I would be happy to oblige.

She stood there and watched me descend. She, too, was red-faced, angry, and ready to blow up.

When I reached the dock and we were on the same level, with only a couple of yards between us, Jeanette said, "You've lost your mind."

"I guess you'd know about irrational behavior."

"Seriously? What was that about, anyway? That message? Lipstick. Really nice touch, Mignon. Truly classy. Carolyn called me, terrified. Thought it was meant for her. Thought someone was threatening *her*."

She spread her arms wide. "*I'm waiting?* No explanation? Seriously? You're lucky she called me first instead of calling the police, or her son, who surely would've called them."

"I know where the rock came from."

She frowned and squinted as if she wasn't hearing me correctly.

I insisted, "Don't give me that look. You know what you did."

"What I did? *You* have finally gone over the edge. You are insane."

"You are a liar. You are a narcissist. You think only of yourself, and whatever it takes to satisfy the flavor of chaos that motivates you. All you did was bring pain into our lives, and that's what you're still doing."

She nodded. "You hate me. I know that. You blame me. Oh, it's about Arthur, yes, and our disagreement, for sure, and how I was such a bad sister and all that. Fine." She waved her arms. "I get it."

"Am I wrong? I'm not, am I?"

"You—" She waved her hand at me, her index finger stabbing the air. "You are the liar. All this talk about me doing . . . heaven knows what? I certainly do not know. I'm not perfect, true, but that's not what's driving this, is it? You blame me for what happened to Sebrina, and that's not fair. Understandable, at least in terms of misplaced anger born of grief, but still not fair. It's unfair *and* it's pure cowardice—nursing your pain and anger and then putting it off on everything and everyone else. And guess what? I don't blame *you* for *that*."

When she spoke again, her voice was hoarse. "You blaming me . . . it set the tone for everything else, didn't it? Arthur and I had our differences, but he devoted his life to protecting you from facing the facts."

"That's not true." I shook my head. "This isn't about Sebrina. No one blamed you for what happened to her. Not even me." I stopped short because my voice was getting louder and harsher. After drawing in a deep breath, I released it with a rough, shuddering sound.

I said, "Did it hurt to see you? I'll be honest—yes. Because it was hard to look at you and not remember that day and what happened. What we then had to live with. There was no going back from that. No do-overs. But *that* wasn't your fault. I knew it—everyone did—and I went out of my way to make sure you didn't feel it from me." My throat seemed to be closing. It was harder to speak.

Pushing through, I said, "Sebrina loved you. I know you loved her. So no, this isn't about what happened the day we lost Sebrina. This is about Arthur and how when you two should've been working together to help your parents, instead you accused him of not caring and letting your mom die and not doing right by you. After the funeral, you took off in a huff and never came back, not even to say goodbye to him before *he* died."

"I wanted to be there, both before he died and after."

"What stopped you?"

"You! *You you you*! You and your freaky, blindly obsessive . . . You. I hated what you were doing to Arthur. To everyone. Your refusal to let go of the past was destroying everyone around you." She fisted her hands. "The last thing I wanted to do was to go where I wasn't welcome, to risk a confrontation. I carry enough guilt around with me. Justified or not, I feel it, and I couldn't bear the thought of having any part in making it worse."

"Go away," I said.

"On cue, right?"

"Go."

"*None of my business, right?* You're like a broken record. Look at this dock. No boat. No one uses it. Not even you. And decorated with No Trespassing signs the size of turkey platters to warn off boaters. I *insist* you look at it." She waved her hands at the entirety of the dock. "Oh yes, it's perfect. It's pristine. You got rid of the offending dock and put in this small one to hold your signs, and you keep it maintained to a T." She pointed up at the hotel. "But that? Look at the building and grounds. You've barely maintained it. You are letting it rot. Holding it hostage maybe, until it's too far gone for anyone to save it? It's a hostage to the past—that's what we all are when we're around you."

"You aren't a hostage to anything. You are trespassing. You aren't wanted here."

She ignored me and kept speaking. "But if the hotel is being held hostage to the past, then what does this dock represent to you?" Her voice dropped to a low tone. "It's scary to think about. It's sick, Mignon." She whispered, "Is it a memorial to Sebrina? Or are you waiting here, keeping it ready, thinking she might come back?" She glared at me. "Come climbing back—?"

That's when I broke. No thought to it. Just action.

Pure, thoughtless intent. I rushed forward and threw out my arms, my hands leading the way. The force as I hit Jeanette's shoulders threw her backward, stumbling, toward the edge. With a wide-eyed look of surprise, she fell. Seeing her fly backward . . . arms wide and her eyes round in shock and disbelief . . . paralyzed me. The sound of the water splashing below—and no Jeanette in sight—brought me to my senses with a heavy dose of horror.

I ran to the edge. Jeanette surfaced, her hands flailing above the water as she struggled to find her footing, then brushing the water, hair, and grasses from her eyes.

She was okay. Irate, yes. But okay. With that thought, something released in my chest, and I was able to breathe.

I stepped down onto the ladder and waved my hand. "Over here, Jeanette. Here." I leaned toward the water and held out my hand as far as my arm allowed. "Come to the ladder. Right here."

Now she was wading through the water. She hit an unexpected low spot, disappeared, and then was back up, waving her arms until she was steady. She rubbed the water from her eyes yet again and pushed the wet hair straggling across her face out of the way.

"I'm so sorry, Jeanette. I didn't mean that . . . I mean, I didn't intend to do that." But I had, so I was lying. "I just lost it . . . my cool. Here, let me help you out."

Jeanette grabbed the side rail of the ladder. "Get

away. Stand back. Don't touch me."

Embarrassed, I did as she demanded, but I moved only a few steps to the side. She came up the ladder slowly, gasping, her eyes fixed on me. Her hair hung in ropy strands framing her face, along with other pieces of questionable-looking bits of debris from the sound water. Her clothing was drenched and dripping.

"Let's get you up to the house. You're wet . . ." *Stupid.* I couldn't believe I'd done this.

"Cold. It's so cold and disgusting. Get out of my way." She got her own shove in as she pushed past me to the stairs, heading straight up to the terrace. "Don't touch me!"

I pulled my hand back. I let her go. I was stunned, shocked at myself. I wanted to feel at least a bit of satisfaction, justification even, but I couldn't dredge it up out of the shame that seemed to have draped itself around me. I wished for a do-over, but there wasn't one. Not for this. There was no way to excuse this or to escape the blame for my reaction—for the physical violence and in that same place where . . .

Yes, Jeanette carried guilt over what had happened so long ago. How could she not? She'd pressed me to let Sebrina go out in the boat with her. The two of them begging like they were both children. *Please, Mama, please. Please Mignon, we'll be fine. Don't be a spoilsport.* Jeanette had taken charge of Sebrina and had then been distracted—had turned her back—and then Sebrina had . . . Honestly, though, turning her back to the partially untied boat to grab the bag of life jackets wasn't being careless. Sebrina had been six and familiar with the dock and the boats—old enough to watch her step and to have been careful.

The grudge I held was born of my broken heart.

And now I owed Jeanette an apology. A genuine apology. And that grated.

Forcing myself to climb the stairs to the upper level while trying to frame the right words, I nearly tripped, but caught myself. I would almost have preferred to fall and require first aid—anything that would delay me having to humble myself before Jeanette.

As I neared the top, I heard a motor idling, and saw Matt's vehicle. He was standing, facing the hotel lobby doors, speaking with Jeanette. I approached slowly.

"Is there a problem?" I asked.

He turned toward me. "Is there?"

Jeanette and I had had our tiff, but she wouldn't have had time to call him, and if she'd somehow managed to call him instantly, even so he would never have been able to get here so quickly. "Okay. What's up?"

"Jeanette said you two had an argument. That you pushed her into Bogue Sound."

I frowned. "So, Matt, you're telepathic now?"

"What?"

"How'd you get here so quickly? You must've come for something else."

"Did you push her off the dock and into the water?"

"Not on purpose . . . although in years past I recall

a few people here and there being pushed off docks. Of course, that was attributed to high spirits. This wasn't done in *that* spirit, but other than a drenching, Jeanette looks like she survived it."

"Mignon . . . Don't presume on our friendship. If your sister-in-law—"

I interrupted. "*Not* my sister-in-law. Used to be, and she wasn't a very good one back when she was."

"Still mad, I see."

He deserved respect. I tried to give it by pushing aside my pride and embarrassment.

"I did shove her. It was impulsive. No forethought. No intent to harm her. Unfortunately, she was standing close to the edge and went over. I would've jumped in to help her, but she told me not to. She climbed out, and I was trying to figure out how to apologize when I saw her up here complaining to you."

"She wasn't complaining. I asked her how she came to be wet, and she told me. If she wants to file a complaint, I'll have to take it and pursue it."

"Fine. She can make her official complaint on her way off my property. I've been asking her to leave since she arrived and she always has an excuse, but we're done now." I looked at Jeanette. "Sorry I pushed you. Didn't mean to hurt you . . . or to get you wet, even."

Taking a deep breath, I made sure I was speaking loudly enough for Matt to hear me clearly as I said to Jeanette, "You should not have said all that stuff about Sebrina. She's my daughter. Not *was*. She will *always* be my daughter, whether she's physically here beside me or not. Any baggage you carry around about that is on you. Your problem. Say whatever you want to Matt or anyone else, but pack your bags and get out of here."

To Matt, I said, "I'm sorry you found yourself in the middle of this. I get that it's your job and you gotta do what you gotta do. Let me know if you need me to sign something or turn myself in or whatever. I'll be in the garden for a little while cooling off." I walked away.

I'd said all the wrong things. All the stuff that made me look guilty. Well, I was guilty. If she wanted to press charges against me? Fine. That was her right. I'd tell the judge the same thing. I might be pigheaded sometimes, and even occasionally mistaken, but...I'd also lied. To smooth things over? Or had I shifted the facts and shaded the meanings, to make what I'd done seem less awful? No excuse for that.

The iron bench was cool and hard beneath my legs. I leaned forward, my elbows on my thighs and my face in my hands.

Matt asked, "You okay, Mignon?"

He'd followed. I wasn't surprised. I nodded, but kept my hands up, still hiding my face, deeply embarrassed. This was surely my lowest point. I uttered a silent prayer that this particular screwup wouldn't get any worse. I'd done enough damage today. No more.

"She isn't filing a report. Not making any complaint. She could, though. A friendly push, Mignon? Not so much." He shook his head. "She could claim battery." He made a noise. "But she wasn't injured, just angry. She wants to let it go."

I dropped my hands from my face, but continued staring at the ground, not wanting to meet his eyes. "I was in the wrong, Matt. I know that. I lost it with her. I've been asking her to leave since she showed up a few weeks ago—I told you that, right? I tried to make it work. She's been stringing me along, saying she has a friend she's going to be staying with. Soon. *Soon and soon.* At one point, I thought she might even be a help to me—me being alone here and all—but that didn't last long. She was uninvited and unwelcome, and now she just needs to go."

"Uninvited? You said that before. I admit I was surprised when I saw her in town. I'd thought that the break between her and Arthur and you was unfixable."

"As they say . . . stuff happens in families."

"True, but if no one is trying to fix it, then it won't be fixed."

"I think it's gone on too long to be mended. Maybe if she'd reached out before Arthur died . . . But since then? Each day has made the break more permanent. Matt, at this point, I can't see what value she could possibly bring to my life. Only aggravation and bad memories."

"Yet she did reach out, right? She's here."

"She's only here because Dominick contacted her."

"Oh."

In a sudden resurgence of anger, I said, "Yeah, he thought I needed rescue and that maybe Jeanette could help. As for Jeanette, she was just wanting a finder's fee."

He frowned. "Finder's fee?"

Finally, I looked him square in the face. "For persuading me—*if* she could persuade me—to sell this property."

"Well," he said, but those four letters in one short syllable seemed full of interest. He added, "You think that has anything to do with that rock through the window? You haven't had any other scares, right? No other vandalism?" He handed me an envelope. "The report I wrote up . . . I brought it for you to review. That's why I came today. If I missed anything we discussed or if there's any new info, let me know."

I was about to say I'd found those same rocks in Carolyn's garden, along with Jeanette's car parked very discreetly . . . but I didn't. I bit my lip to keep it in. I took a deep breath, and this time I lied by omission. "A couple of things happened right after she came—noises but no damage, probably nothing, and developers dropped by without invitation—but all that stopped until the broken window." I was staring at him now. He was sharing some of the same suspicions I'd been harboring. Maybe I should've told him what I suspected about Jeanette, but he'd have to put that into my broken window report, naming her specifically. I couldn't do it.

"If you don't mind me asking? Are you going to sell? Is that even a possibility? I ask because if you *are,* then why put up with this craziness? Why not just move on? If you aren't, then figure out what you *do* want to do so that you can live your life. Remember what I said to you in the restaurant the other day."

I nodded, but didn't respond otherwise. I resumed staring at my clasped hands and the ground at my feet.

"If you want me to amend the report, let me know. If you need to vent, to just spitball it or talk it out, you know you are welcome to call me. You have friends, Mignon. Make use of us."

He was right. I'd shut so many people out, but some of those friends were still there. Even going by the Grill, as I had . . . had been a half-hearted effort at reaching out. With consequences. I sighed.

"And if you're serious about Jeanette leaving—and judging by what you've told me and what happened today, maybe it's a good idea—then if she doesn't leave as requested, let me know. I'll have a word with her. Might help, might not. But at least it will be on the record in case you have to go the legal route to evict her."

He patted my shoulder awkwardly, then stood and walked away. At some point, Galahad had returned to me and settled under the bench. Overhead the breeze swayed the boughs of the trees and nearer my level, the understory plants were growing, or not, with no regard whatsoever for what was happening in my life. Yet I cared about them. I'd planted and sweated over them when I was creating this garden. If I sold this place, then in the space of minutes a backhoe could destroy their world to make way for whatever amenities the new owner preferred.

Would the plants care? Were they self-aware? On some level, they must be. After all, plants had strategies for dealing with certain pests or climate stressors, right? Sap to heal a wound or trap a pest. Thorns as defensive armor, or even poisons. Not a thinking response, but a . . . well, maybe I could call it an autonomic response. People did that too sometimes. When people wanted to avoid a pest, they might surprise themselves by being rude or brusque to that person . . . or by pushing a person off a dock and into the water with no more intelligent thought than a plant giving someone a bad case of poison ivy.

Humph. I had more in common with these plants than I knew.

I'd read that there was even a fungus that helped root systems between plants communicate underground, which was just another take on ecosystems being dependent or interdependent. Everybody needed a friend, right? Especially in a pinch. I'd done my best to cut mine out of my life because they were inconvenient . . . *Ouch.* Inconvenient because they interfered with my enjoyment of being lost in those memories? Of *living* in them. Because my friends and neighbors lived in the here and now and not in vanished yesterdays.

Embarrassing, really.

Thinking of Arthur, I touched my cheek and smiled. He would've said something like that, perhaps even asking which plant kingdom I hailed from, making a weak joke to comfort me and to make me feel more reasonable and engaged and to try for a light laugh before *planting* a loving kiss on my cheek.

Okay, so I wasn't perfect. Hopefully, I had a little

more sentience and self-will than the flora around me, and a higher, more directed sense of purpose to use whatever power was in me for the better. When my phone rang, I jumped, having forgotten it was in my pocket. I fished it out.

Blake.

So this day's events weren't done with me.

Should I answer his call?

Chapter Twenty-One

"Hello, Blake."

"Hey, Mignon, I was hoping to speak with you again."

"Really? Okay then. Did you overlook any complaints you'd like to add to what you said to me earlier today? If it's unpleasant, then this is the day to get it said." I cleared my throat. "Because I'm not going to be doing *unpleasant* tomorrow. No unpleasant stuff at all. Today is the day to get it said or to forget it altogether."

"Mignon . . . you sound . . . I don't know." He sighed. "And I added to whatever the problem is. I'm sorry about that. I called because earlier . . . when I was there at your house? That wasn't my best moment."

"No, maybe it wasn't. That said, I know a little bit about having moments we'd rather redo and even totally avoid on the second go-round."

"Yeah." He cleared his throat. "I should never have said those words aloud. It was what I was thinking in the moment and before I could stop them, out they came—loud and embarrassing. But it wasn't your fault. I had assumptions happening in the background of my brain. You didn't do anything wrong. I was just seeing what I wanted to. Or didn't want to."

I made a strangled noise. I almost laughed. *Wanted* to laugh. This emotional mix felt almost like the edge of hysteria, except I was too tired. Drained. So my eyes burned and my cheeks got wet, but I didn't fall apart. Galahad joined me up on the bench and sniffed at the tears. His muzzle was so gentle that it tickled. I ran my hand down the silky curls of his neck and back.

"Are you okay?" Blake asked softly.

I nodded. Of course, he couldn't hear that over the phone, so I cleared my throat as he'd done and said, "I'll be fine."

"Mignon, whatever is going on between you and Monahan is your business. My common sense may have had a glitch, but that's done, and my ears still work. I'm a good listener. I'm available to listen to anything you might want to talk about. Friends do that, right?"

I nodded again and looked Galahad in the eyes as I answered, "Okay."

"Okay *what*?" He sounded puzzled.

"I'd like to talk."

"Just say when and where."

"Here. Now."

"Oh. Well, I'm not at home but on my way. It'll be a few minutes? I stopped at the grocery, so if it's not an emergency, I should drop this stuff off at the house first and then I'll walk over?"

"Perfect," I said. "I'll be here taking care of a few things myself."

"*Ooookayyyy*. You sound a little mysterious. Maybe even ominous."

"Nope, just waking up. Like from a long nap."

"Okay. Still mysterious. But I'm not scared. I'll be there in maybe thirty minutes? Might be a little longer, but I'll get there as soon as I can."

"Thanks, Blake. I'll probably be over in the hotel lobby area, so look for me there."

☙❧

I went into the house to wash up. It was still afternoon—late afternoon—but the day had been chock-full of almost every conceivable emotion. Friendly pizza with Dominick. Being accused of . . . *what*? Of *something* by Blake. Assaulting Jeanette. Showdown with law enforcement. Yep, I nodded, it was pretty darn full of stuff I never wanted to experience again. Except the pizza.

I ran a brush through my hair and then pinned it up with a clip. My eyes looked okay—no telltale signs of crying—not bad, considering. I flipped off the light switch and went out to the hallway and stepped into the office space.

Trying not to think about it too deeply, I grabbed the hotel keys, and pausing to tell Galahad to *stay*, I went through the doors into the lobby. Quiet. No one. No sign of Jeanette. I looked through the lobby doors and saw her car parked out front.

In the storage room, the prints and paintings were neatly grouped, leaning against the wall as I'd left them.

Knickknacks and other objects were arranged on a shelving unit, and the overflow items were organized on the floor. I left the door open and went back to the lobby to take down the bronze sculptures and other objects and move them into this room too. Each one—clasped in my hands or cradled in my arms—felt like I was carrying pieces of Arthur . . . removing him bit by bit from the hotel he'd loved and tucking those pieces away into a dark room where things that were no longer current or useful—but still treasured—were stashed.

And it took remarkably little time.

I made a quick stop in a nearby room to check my face again. No dust or dirt smears. Tired, though. The fine lines around my eyes gave away my age. And yet as difficult as today had been, I felt less worn than most mornings even after a good night's sleep. If nothing else, the day's events had given me extra shots of adrenaline or endorphins. There was a bittersweet satisfaction in accomplishing the tasks that had floored me, literally, only two days before.

Progress.

◌◌◌

In case my earlier visitors had neglected to lock the gate, I walked down the road to check it. Mostly though, it was an excuse for a walk. I was simply in need of healthy activity to clear the tension still hanging around me. Blake would be arriving on foot through the woods, so I had a little time yet.

I walked back, not rushing. For the first time in a long time, I was really hearing the birdsong and the brush of leaves as the breeze shifted the boughs overhead. As always, as I neared the hotel area, the forest fell away. The view was totally open from the buildings to the cliff, and highlighted the water view. And the sky. And the far shore. That view drew me to the terrace, and I stood there, feeling an odd, but lovely sense of peace.

Blake would see me here, waiting, when he arrived.

No more guilt, I thought. I'd lost my self-control and had done things I should not have. Frankly, Jeanette was correct that I kept the dock well-maintained, but she was wrong about why. It wasn't as some sort of shrine to grief or even due to madness, but rather, it was because I couldn't afford to maintain everything to the same degree. The original big dock was no longer in use in the same way it had been when the hotel was operational, and thus way too expensive to repair and keep attractive if it brought no value, thus I had it taken down. The smaller dock was just sort of filling in because The Emerald Heart Hotel *should* have a dock even if it *was* small.

We didn't need fancy now. I focused on upkeep for the dock and cliff stairs because that's what people noticed first and might be tempted to use despite the warning signs. It was both an expense and a liability issue. What was the alternative? Pull it all down? Give up on the hotel entirely?

Part of me found the idea of giving up unthinkable, but if I made the move to sell while the market was good and the hotel was still in reasonable condition, perhaps I could have more choice in the matter of its fate, more sway in what became of it.

Still waiting for Blake to arrive, I brought out a pitcher of iced tea and two tall glasses of ice and set them on the low stone wall by the Adirondack chairs. He came around the end of the house and joined me on the terrace. I poured our tea and handed him one of the glasses, saying, "Let's talk."

He nodded.

I said, "I wanted to talk to you about what happened earlier today, and maybe about some other stuff too."

"I'm all ears." He half-smiled. "That's a strange expression, isn't it?"

"The tea is unsweet. Are you good with that?"

"Avoiding sugar?"

I shrugged. "Some tea holds its own without added sweetener." I paused. "But if you'd like sugar or lemon, I can go grab some from the kitchen."

He took a sip. "No, it's good."

The tea chat was a delaying tactic on my part. I could see he knew it and was humoring me. We shared an odd sense of humor. Of being amused by unexpected things. Knowing that, I squared my shoulders. I could do this.

I said, "Dominick Monahan was my husband's lifelong friend. He became my friend when Arthur introduced us long, long ago. I know I can depend on him."

Blake nodded but didn't speak.

"We have been friends forever," I said. "We're not *just* friends. Being in each other's lives for more than two decades . . . that means something more than *just*."

"I saw you two down by that storefront. It looked like more than friendship."

"He was consoling me. As friends do. Over an old, but still very tender wound."

A shadow of impatience showed itself in a frown—swiftly gone but unmistakable. "Mignon, we were sitting in the restaurant and talking and then he came along and you practically ran away, and he followed right after you. I stepped out onto the sidewalk, saw him at that storefront, and when I walked closer, saw the two of you in a . . . an *involved* embrace."

He shook his head as if regretting his words, and added, "But that's your business. You don't owe me or anyone an explanation that you don't want to give. What I said earlier today was unwarranted, and that's why I called to apologize." He raised his glass. "And then you invited me over. I came here promising to be a good listener, but I'm not doing that as well as advertised."

I smiled, but it was no more than a polite effort. I was feeling heaviness, reasonably so, considering what I was about to say out loud.

"You know how things from the past don't always stay there? They pop up when you least expect them— even though you *should* expect them—but that would require thinking of them . . . and that's a whole other thing, so let's not go there. Give me a sec, right?" I waved my hands at the dock below. "You probably don't know this, but Arthur and I lost our daughter, Sebrina, fifteen years ago. She was only six." My hands had stayed out there, but motionless as if framing a movie scene. "Here."

He shook his head. "I'm sorry. Here? I don't understand." He asked in a softer voice, "Do you mean specifically here?"

I nodded. "Down there." I drew in a deep breath, hoping it would see me through. "Sebrina and her aunt, Arthur's sister, Jeanette—whom you met briefly the other day—wanted to go out on the boat, and after they persuaded me, I said Sebrina could go. I was watching from up here, anxious. No reason. Just an off-feeling kind of day. I wanted to call her back, but I hesitated, and in that moment, Sebrina tripped over a rope. She stumbled over the side. The boat had been partially untied and had drifted a foot or so away. Sebrina . . . she went down in that gap between the boat and the dock. She must've hit her head on one or the other. It was hard to tell from where I was, and by that point I was already running down the stairs.

"Jeanette went into the water after her. Me . . ." I grabbed the side of my head, my fingers tangled in my hair. "I knew my girl would be climbing back up the ladder with maybe a knot on her head and crying and maybe needing stitches . . . but she knew how to swim. A good swimmer. She hadn't put on her life jacket. That's what Jeanette had turned away for—to grab the net bag with the jackets. As soon as I reached the dock, I jumped in too."

"She couldn't find her. I couldn't find her. The bottom was murky and stirred up." I sipped my tea and ever so carefully set it back on the wall. "Except that's not precisely true."

"I don't understand."

"I know." I sighed. "So, I don't remember exactly what happened after we jumped in the water. I guess I lost it?" I grimaced. "Hysteria? Someone at some point medicated me." I shook my head. "Sedated, I guess. At any rate, I don't dispute that it was probably necessary. Arthur handled things. He wanted to protect me. I know that. Except that they *did* recover her body. Someone told me I was still on the scene, but I have no recollection of it. The interment . . . happened while I was elsewhere."

"I didn't know." His hand touched my arm.

"It's long ago now. By the time I was myself again, the formal traditions for saying goodbye were over. The grieving continued but everyone was trying to move on. In my head, I was stuck at the time of the incident, certain she'd be climbing that ladder back up to the dock within moments." With my elbows on the armrests, I rested my forehead against my hands. "I could not get far enough past that certainty to accept that it was never going to happen, not even after Arthur took me to the cemetery. I could never . . . process that she was there. In that place." I whispered, "I had no sense of her being there." I shrugged. "Just emptiness."

I nodded. I'd gotten the words said and the world hadn't ended. "Arthur decided to be cremated." My throat hurt. My chest ached.

We just breathed. Blake waited.

Finally, I said, "I'm not totally deluded. I know she's gone, but . . ." I touched my temple. "But in my head—in some small, stubborn part of my brain, in a fold of my brain that's tenacious and protective and wants what it wants and refuses to accept the truth—her loss is like a line of demarcation that can't be crossed. I understand that it sounds stupid after all this time."

Blake said, "You never stopped waiting?"

"Not exactly." I looked down at my fingers, white and strained, gripping the chair arm. I tried but couldn't relax them. Finally, I said, "The waiting, despite reality, went on for a long time, but now it's more that I *can't* let her go."

He didn't offer platitudes. We just sat there silently. After a minute or two, he reached over and placed his hand on mine—the one nearest him—and simply kept it there until my fingers relaxed. That apparently signaled to my other hand that it was okay to relax. I turned my hand to clasp his.

Very quietly, he said, "Alyssa was on her way home and never arrived. Car accident. I was waiting for her. We had an anniversary celebration planned."

He understood what I was trying to say. My heart tried to break all over again for both of us. I wanted to say something light and clever to signal an end to this . . . whatever it was. This emotional angst? But the words wouldn't come.

Blake spoke. "What about your husband? As far as letting go, I mean?"

"You mean, me letting *him* go?"

"Okay."

"It's been a struggle learning how to manage living without him. He was quite a guy. A fine man. A super husband. Everyone loved him. I wish you could've known him. He did his best to protect me from . . . hard things." I nodded. "I miss him." After a pause, I asked, "What about you? Your wife?"

"Same."

I asked, "You said you had trouble going through her things?"

"Yes. My mother-in-law helped. Did you have that trouble with Arthur?"

I shook my head. "As he lost weight and stopped being as active, he, himself, began donating his clothing. Ticked me off at first. Frustrated me. As if he was giving in. Surrendering hope. But hope was already gone—I knew that. He was doing it because he wanted to spare me...or didn't trust me to do it. That's what he did with Sebrina's items. A few things disappeared here and there, and then one day—poof. Almost all her things were gone. I raged about it and cried for weeks. I'm sure that proved to him that he was right." I paused. "I would've done it myself, though, but in my own time." I felt like I was running out of breath. This was all too hard to say aloud, to share it like it wasn't painful when it truly, truly was. I fell silent.

A long minute passed, and he asked, "Is there anything I can do to help?"

"No, though maybe you already have. I spoke of this and didn't die. Didn't faint. *And* before you got here, I managed to clear Arthur's collection from the lobby today without needing rescue or a doctor's care."

"I don't think I can take credit for any of that."

"A person earns credit. They can't simply take it."

"Deep. I'll have to think about that."

I gave a short laugh. "Not that deep. In fact, they *can* take credit or claim credit, but if it's unearned, then it's just a sham."

His voice soft, "What credit are you trying to earn?"

A few trite words bloomed in my head like expected, approved responses. I pushed those away and offered what was left in my mind. "Self-reliance. Self-determination. Knowing that wrongly or rightly, I made a decision separate and apart from anyone else—not seeking or needing their approval or setting them up to take the blame if it goes way wrong. That I made the choice and continued moving forward regardless of success or failure."

This time Blake drew in a long breath. He held it for a moment and then offered, "Autonomy?"

I barked a light, undignified, but genuine laugh. "Yes. One word. And it's a good word. Autonomy."

He smiled. "One of the building blocks of autonomy is having financial independence."

Just that quickly, my defenses rose. We were back

to his particular interest—my property. Sometimes I forgot and thought that his interest was in me too, but even if that was true, I wasn't the end goal for him. That was the property. I almost cursed at him. I stopped myself from engaging in the same kind of out-loud embarrassment that he'd committed earlier. Instead, I said, "So we are back to the discussion about selling Emerald Heart?" My voice sounded wooden.

He shook his head. "Only if you want to be."

"A lot of people have an interest in that."

"Not me. I've changed my plans."

"Oh." After a long moment, I asked, "Seriously?"

He nodded. "Yes, ma'am."

There was an inviting look in his eyes. He wanted me to ask about the new plans. I wouldn't. No distractions. No temptations. I had to stay the course. I envied the certainty in his tone. I needed to find some of that for myself. I sighed. "I always thought I'd know what to do when the time came."

"That's what we tell ourselves when we don't want to make the decision."

"Jerk," I said, then added, "Sorry."

He grinned and sipped his tea, then said, "As a matter of fact, you've put up with me popping into your life uninvited, so you're entitled to say what you will. I was invited today, of course, and we did go on that date, which was fun, right?"

I nodded.

"I'd like to know if I can continue to invite you out? Is there an opportunity there? Or does that complicate your relationship with Monahan?"

Quite the shift in topic. Kind of threw me, but I rallied with a deep breath and a physical shift that turned me toward him and removed the dock from my direct line of sight.

"We are not in a romantic relationship."

He gave me a funny look. "Who is *we*?"

After a tiny pause, I said, "You were asking about Dominick."

He nodded. "Just making sure."

Another tiny pause, and I decided not to pursue that further for now. I said, "I hope I haven't overwhelmed you with all this honesty."

"I'm glad you told me. Loss, grief, big changes in our lives—those are tough things to go through. When people share those events with other people, special bonds are formed."

His words came out sounding like a motivational speech. Too canned. I couldn't help it, but I laughed. It was not a happy sound. "Yeah? Like with Jeanette?"

"Well, yes. Seems to me like there's an undeniable bond. Bonds aren't necessarily easy or pleasant. Just bonds."

I grunted in disagreement. Not my best sound.

He laughed and touched my arm again. "That's why people often prefer fresh starts. Shaking off those bonds from the past and letting go of all the baggage that comes along with a shared history can be freeing."

Letting go of all the baggage? Code word for memories? I didn't want them to own me, but to shake them off like they didn't matter?

"No thanks," I said. "The past may not be perfect, and can hurt even, but I won't be *shaking* off the memories." I shook my head.

Blake said, "Not quite what I was suggesting."

I waved my hand as if to brush away the crux of the matter with a gesture. I said, "No, I get it. Memories. Let them go, right? Grief. Move on? That's what everyone says." I shrugged, but sharply, suddenly feeling done with this. *Done.*

"Anyway, I just wanted you to understand the backstory." I stopped there, but then the cutoff felt too abrupt. I added, "So now you know."

"Why does it matter to you that I understand? What do you want me to take away from this?"

"Pardon?"

"Like should I back off? Leave you to work out your life without distracting you? You can be blunt with me. I want to be helpful, even if that means making myself scarce. On the other hand, if there's something I can do, anything, to help, I want to do that." He touched my hand. "Just tell me, Mignon."

"You make it sound so either/or. So simple. I've been living in a fog for two years. Maybe longer. How do I suddenly see sense and become a decision maker? I surely do not know. All I know is that today I cleared Arthur's treasures out of the lobby. That was a big win for me. And I've told you—a man who is still a relative stranger—the truth about my daughter and the humiliating reality that I'm mired in the past, lost with my memories."

"Trapped with your memories. They've got a hold on you."

"No." The reverse was true. "Nope, I have a hold on them, and I'm clutching them to my heart as tightly as I can."

"But you'd like to be free of them."

He said it so simply and low-key, as if it were obvious and easy. My temper flared. "It *isn't* that easy to move past such . . . such . . ."

"Traumas? I agree. It isn't easy at all. Some people never make it past them, but most of us make it at least part of the way and find a way to reconcile what we lost with what we have now—with what we can make of the lives we still have."

His tone was gentle, but his words, though rational, were unsympathetic. It felt as though he'd slapped me with his words. Rude things like, *You think you're so smart, but you don't know much because you're here with me, whining and awash in self-pity . . .* The words wanted to be said, but I gave myself some credit for learning a small lesson today, and I went silent.

No more, I thought. That could be my *autonomous* decision for the day.

I was drawing in breath to say exactly that when Blake added, "Remember, Mignon, I learned the hard way. Grief groups. Therapy. I'm hardheaded and determined. Some say single-minded. Takes a lot to get emotional truths through this skull."

He frowned as he turned more fully toward the

hotel to look at something beyond me. As for me, I was deflated. It felt as if someone had stolen the words right out of my mouth and had then returned them to me in a much more gracious, more worthy tone.

His frown became a squint as he said, "So Jeanette is leaving?"

"What?" I looked over at the hotel. Jeanette was carrying her bags to her car. *"About time."*

"Are you sure?"

"Yes, I'm sure. Of course, I am. Admittedly, I also wish things were in some measure resolved between us before she goes . . . but then it will be best for the both of us never to run into each other ever again."

"Well, here's the moment, right?"

"Me? Stop her when she's finally getting out of here?"

"Autonomy. No, you don't have to go after her, but nothing and no one is stopping you except yourself."

I was tempted to slap him. We do all sorts of unacceptable behaviors to protect the most vulnerable part of ourselves—but I read the intent in his carefully schooled, almost blank expression and knew the truth of it.

Without a word, I left him there on the terrace and crossed the narrow road and parking area to where Jeanette was getting into the driver's seat of her car.

Chapter Twenty-Two

I knocked on the car window.

Jeanette gave me a look, long and hard, before lowering the window glass.

I asked, "You're leaving?"

Immediately, she reached for the button to raise the window back up into place. Without thinking, I put my fingers on the beveled top edge of the glass. Jeanette moved quickly to stop the closing of the window and to reverse the direction, choosing to spare my fingers.

"I thought maybe we could have a civil chat before you leave. If you have time?"

She said, "Haven't we tried that already? It hasn't gotten us anywhere."

"But if you're leaving . . . I'd like to try again, Jeanette. This may be our last opportunity."

Her expression hardened, but then she sighed.

"Okay. Porch?"

"Why don't we sit in the garden? You can go through the lobby if you like, and I'll cut through the kitchen and grab us each a glass of tea."

"What about your . . . visitor?"

I glanced back toward the deck. Blake was gone.

"Just us," I said.

"All right," she said.

She sounded wary. I could hardly blame her.

As I walked toward the house, I thought, *"More tea. Good thing I made extra."*

∝∾

She wasn't sitting on the bench. She was standing—leaning against the low, arching branch of a live oak with her arms crossed. That branch was as big around as many tree trunks. This was a mature tree and much of the leaf growth was well above her head. The shade was delicious. The huge iron decorative circle bench had already been in place around the trunk when Arthur and I moved here. The tree had filled in noticeably over the twenty years we'd been here, but there was room still to grow.

I handed Jeanette the tall glass of tea, and then I sat on my usual bench. Jeanette slowly sat on the bench ring, perhaps not yet trusting my motives.

She said, "I don't know what you hope to accomplish with this, unless you have a weapon out here that I haven't yet noticed."

"I have already apologized several times for pushing you into the water."

"I tried several times to discuss our differences, remember?"

I blew out, making an ugly noise with my lips. "A long time after the fact."

"Okay then," she said. "Have it your way. This is

your party. Go for it. It's your turn, but get it said now."

Deep breath. Sip of tea. Wiping wet fingertips on my jeans and clearing my throat. Jeanette watched, looking bored as she waited.

"We can't fix anything. Stuff can't just be forgiven and forgotten. I'm not even sure we understand all that went wrong. Frankly, I'm tired of wondering. Of going through it over and over, trying to figure it out. Finally, I put it aside. You were gone and apparently not coming back. But then you did return, bringing all that misery up again, and frankly it ticked me off. I have no intention of going over it again. I'd rather say that no one's perfect. People do stuff they regret. Feelings get hurt. My question is this: Where did the kindness of giving a loved one the benefit of the doubt go? To having other people's backs when hard times hit?"

She rolled her eyes at me. "No joke."

"Truly? That's all you have to say?"

I stood. She moved slightly in response. I tried to relax my posture at least a little.

"What happened, Jeanette? If I was psychic, maybe I'd already know, but since I'm not, I need you to tell me."

"I *told* you already."

"Don't bring Sebrina into this. We've already gone over that."

"No," Jeanette said. "I *told* you when I first arrived. Things were heated. Emotional. We were all going through a lot when Mom got sick, and the treatment went on and on. Tough decisions had to be made. It was awful. We got into the big argument—"

"Not *we*. You and Arthur."

She shook her head. "Not quite how I remember it."

"Because you were busy trying to make me your ally against Arthur."

"Again, not how I remember it."

"*Exactly* how *I* remember it."

I nodded. She did too. We'd reached an impasse.

"So you left and that was that," I said. "We never heard from you again. Why? I need to know. And don't put it off on guilt or embarrassment. You tried to do that before."

"That was part of it. Pride, too. On both sides."

"I know Arthur tried to reach out to you after. I did too. You ignored us."

"Not exactly." She stopped speaking, but didn't break eye contact, so I waited. Finally, she continued, "I'll say this. Don't try to override me or tell me I'm wrong. I'll just throw it out here and then I'm done. That last year before Mom died, I came home because I'd lost everything. My marriage. My job. My savings. I was living with Mom and when she passed, Arthur sold the house, and I lost even *that* roof. Her last expenses . . . they ate up all the profit from the sale of the house. Yes, that grated.

"Seeing you and Arthur here together, with assets and with each other, was hard. Assets you and he would never have had if Dad hadn't poured his own savings into this place. *That's* what I was arguing with Arthur about. You can say it isn't pertinent, that it's old news in the King family and maybe bad choices or bad luck on my part. But yes, I couldn't help being angry and feeling like I'd come out on the short end." She pulled in a ragged breath. "I don't want to discuss the right and wrong of it. I don't want to weigh the relative merits of who did what. I'm tired and I'm done with it, Mignon." She shook her head. "As to why I didn't come back during Arthur's sickness . . ." She shivered. "I ran into some trouble."

I waited.

"I had a job. Lost a job. Had a roof over my head. Lost the home. It goes on and on and begins to feel pathetic—and I'm done with *pathetic,* so I won't talk about it. I will say that I left here in anger and resentment. Guilt, yes, and pride, too, which kept me from returning home a failure. My address was . . . unreliable for a while."

"I'm sorry."

"It's in the past. I'm not about fault any longer. I was doing better when Dominick called. He told me about your situation, and it gave me a destination. A reason to go somewhere. To continue moving forward." She nodded as if to herself. "That's what I'm doing now. I'm moving forward—not to outrun trouble or run away from it—but to live in the present. So I came here to Emerald Heart first, but my friend has the room cleared for me now so I can move over to Morehead and get out of your way."

She sat on the circle bench again and slumped just

a bit. "I'm glad we're talking. I'd given up the effort. I'm glad you decided to try one more time."

I said, "I do have one question, if you'll do me the favor of answering it?"

That wary look had returned to her face. I could hardly blame her.

"Why did you park your car at Carolyn's? You did that more than once, didn't you? Those times when you kept leaving?" I shook my head. "But there were other times you left the car here and disappeared. Where were you then?"

She pressed her lips together, her expression clearly uncomfortable.

"Jeanette," I said softly. "Never mind. If it's something I don't need to know, then it's all good. I'm going to assume you've been hanging out with Carolyn." And about the rock? Nope, I was going to let that go too. I could hardly expect forgiveness if I wasn't willing to extend it, even if she hadn't admitted guilt or asked for that forgiveness. "So never mind."

"I appreciate that, Mignon."

Did it hurt? Those old wounds that were still not truly resolved? Yes, but less. Down to a dull ache, perhaps. I was with Jeanette in not wanting to deal with who was at fault for what. I had no wish to wallow in my regrets and mistakes either, to look back to when those wounds felt as if they might rip me apart. So I understood. Those wounds had been dulled for a while, sort of, but only waited to flare again and bring it all back and worse, but now they were healing. Tender flesh still, but knitting. I wanted that healing almost more than anything.

I said, "I'm not angry now. Trust me, believe me, when I say I don't blame you. And I don't want to blame myself. You don't have to leave. At least not yet. Unless you actually want a change of scene. I'm not sure what I'll decide to do about selling, and I wouldn't want you to lose the place with your friend by not taking advantage of it while it's available. It's up to you."

Her expression shifted from surprised, to annoyed, to thoughtful. She looked aside before speaking. "She's expecting me. Put a lot of effort into making room for me in her home. I should go. But it would be nice to know I have somewhere to come back to if it doesn't work out."

"As long as The Emerald Heart Hotel is standing—and has water and power —you are welcome. Arthur would want that. And so do I."

We each left our respective benches and met in the middle and hugged. An awkward, brief hug, but it qualified. As she walked away, I stayed in the garden, half-hidden by the graceful, immense swirling branches of the live oaks as my eyes stung, welling with tears. But these felt healing, too. I suspected it was the same for Jeanette, but neither of us was ready to display that vulnerability to the other quite yet. If we continued in each other's lives, I believed we might get there.

I pressed the backs of my hands to my eyes and sniffled, and then suddenly I was moving, running as I hurried from the garden and around to the front of the hotel.

Jeanette saw me. She paused just as she was getting into her car. With her hand poised on the top of the car door, she waited for me to speak.

"Stay in touch this time, okay?"

She bit her lip and looked away, then met my eyes with a steady gaze. She said, "I don't know whether I should say this. You might not believe me or might think I'm being manipulative, but I'm not. I promise. This is the simple truth. I want you to know because maybe some of what I've done over the past weeks might make more sense. May I?"

I fought the frown that formed on my face, but form it did. "Go ahead."

"When Dominick called, I'd been stuck in a state of mind without purpose. His call gave me direction. I think I've already said that much to you." She squinched up her face for no more than a second, then shook her head and said, "I had some idea that I was coming to the rescue, that I would make up for the past by helping you . . . not because you wouldn't eventually figure the grief and stuff out on your own, but with the hotel. If you decided to reopen, I wanted to be part of what you and Arthur built here."

She cleared her throat. "I knew you couldn't do it alone—it would be too much for any one person—but I thought I could bring value to you and to Emerald Heart." She shrugged. "I guess that won't happen after all, but over the course of my stay here, I found value myself—in myself. Not sure what I'll choose to do, but if you need me, need my help . . ." She nodded. "Just give me a call and I'll come immediately."

Jeanette climbed into her car. My eyes burned, again, but I kept from dabbing at my lashes until she'd driven away.

Then I remembered the gate key. She'd kept her copy.

I smiled. Of course, she'd kept it. How else would she unlock and relock the gate on her way out? And that meant she could always unlock it again, at least for as long as Emerald Heart remained in my control.

Chapter Twenty-Three

Doubling down—that's what I did. I went toe to toe with the closets, the dresser drawers, the cabinets, and faced them down. Even though Arthur had dealt with both his and Sebrina's items long ago, there were still traces. Odd items that had been dropped into a drawer or tucked into unexpected closets—and I'd seen a lot of them over the past two years, despite that willful blindness that wanted to protect me from pain. But then or now, it would not have been mine or Arthur's wish to erase every keepsake. I'd take the pain to have the memories. And that's exactly how it felt when faced with a broken shoelace.

Somehow, that shoelace had been pushed around in a junk drawer for many, many years. I remembered it now, holding it in my hand like a talisman that could make or break me. Sebrina had graduated from training wheels to riding her two-wheeler without assistance. She'd managed it and had come to a stop safely to the cheers of her two adoring parents and had then come running back to us—and the lace broke. She'd fallen and scratched her knee. She'd survived the bike ride to be felled by a shoelace.

Arthur hugged her and consoled her, gaining wet blotches on his shirt. I went into the house to pull out the first aid kit for an antibiotic ointment and a bandage, while

he carried her inside. In no time, we'd had Sebrina sitting on the kitchen stool, happily chomping on a cookie while I washed the wound.

A simple story, and surely one repeated around the world innumerable times since the invention of shoelaces and scraped knees.

Yet to me, in that moment, it felt overwhelming. I held the shoelace in my hands and cried. Alone.

When I stopped crying, the shoelace went back into the drawer.

A day or two later, I opened the small storage closet in the lobby behind the bar/check-in desk. It was lost in a corner, very narrow and easily overlooked. Arthur had stored cleaning supplies there that he wanted within easy reach of the lobby desk.

I removed the broom and mop. They were leaning against a box of old rags used for dusting and polishing. In so doing, I dislodged an old bottle of glass cleaner that toppled to the floor. Luckily, it was all but empty. There were odd things stocked in the far back. I was almost derailed by a jacket of Arthur's that he must've shoved on top of the stacked stuff and then forgotten. Beneath it was a sweater and a cap. I held them to me, remembering when he'd worn them. Autumn. Yes. Arthur had loved the fall because he could bring out the sweaters.

I hugged them to me. They smelled of dust and old furniture polish. With a last squeeze, I set them on top of the bar.

There was a knock at Arthur's etched glass double doors. I saw Blake and waved to him to come in.

He looked surprised. When he pushed the door open, he said, "I assumed they were locked."

Still a little choked up over Arthur's sweater and cap, I shrugged. Blake saw the clothing items and noted the open closet door, the cleaning supplies.

"Ah," he said.

"Indeed."

He gave a pointed look at the sweater and jacket. "You're doing okay?"

"Better than I expected."

He nodded. "Need any help?"

"Well, actually, since you're offering, there are some boxes in there. It's an awkward reach in that narrow closet but you can probably manage it." I made the biceps muscle move that every kid knew.

"Got it," he said.

Blake maneuvered into the closet, going in practically sideways to get a grip on the first box, but he made it out. "Where to?"

I gestured toward the sweater on the bar.

He set the first box there on the bar and went back for the second one which was on the floor. Again, he had to do some fancy maneuvering to get the box unwedged, then slid it around so that he could grab it and exit the closet. He set it beside the first box, then brushed his hands together, as in, *Job done.*

"Thanks."

"So you're really serious about this?"

"I am. It's tough at times. So many memories. Attachments. I wasn't happy about it at the time, but now I am grateful that Arthur took care of so much of it, donating and such, and didn't leave it all for me." I sighed. "He knew me well."

"Shall I grab those last items in there? There's some stuff up on a shelf too."

"Please. That would be great. Very useful."

He smiled. "That's me. Useful."

"Sorry. Did that seem . . . I don't know. Condescending?"

"No ma'am. If I'm going to invite myself over then the least I can be is useful. Makes me feel good to be useful."

I squinted. Was he being flirty again? Didn't think so. Lonely? In the mood for company? And I was a short walk away? Yeah, probably.

"Please know that I appreciate your help."

He nodded.

The last items were more cleaning stuff, a few odd tools, a roll of duct tape, and a can of WD-40. I left Blake to that task, touched the sweaters, then opened a box.

And froze. Literally. My arms were stuck in midair with the box top in my hands.

I couldn't think. Couldn't breathe. Might've made a noise. I tried to speak, but the pain in my chest was so extreme, I was breaking in two.

"Mignon?"

Still, I couldn't breathe, couldn't move.

Blake put his hands on my arms. Gently, he eased my fingers away from the cardboard and put the box top off to the side. He held my wrists, one in each of his hands, so gently, so carefully, but I still couldn't move, and so he slid his hands, his arms around me, again with a touch so light that I hardly felt it, but I did feel his warmth. My face near his chest, his throat, his heartbeat. The warmth of a human I trusted. I sagged into his arms. I began to feel real again. Alive. But it hurt. I cried, and he continued to hold me silently and with care.

"Her things. The two boxes that Arthur said he'd kept for me. For whenever I was ready." I butted my forehead against Blake's chest. "Ready? No. Never ready."

Blake leaned his head forward so that his cheek was near my ear. He spoke softly. "Not ready today. Someday maybe. There's no timeline for this, Mignon."

I shook my head against him, feeling the slight roughness of the shirt fabric. He was going to have wet splotches on his shirt just as Arthur had after consoling Sebrina. And, ironically, or perhaps like a madwoman, I smiled ever so slightly, remembering that scene for the second time within such a short time, and yet, this time . . . the memory held me up. It lifted me from that dark, frozen place that wanted to capture me again.

I grasped Blake's arms, those biceps that he'd used to empty the closet, yet had then offered comfort as gently and kindly as was possible for one human being to freely give another. I pushed back, also gently. Grateful, too. Sorry to give up the warmth, the matching rhythm of his beating heart.

"Thank you yet again. I'm sorry I keep breaking down like this. I should be in a better place with it all by now. Everyone is tired of me doing this. So am I."

He shook his head. "No. I've been there, remember? Still go there from time to time. You will too. People mean well. They don't know what to say. Accept that they mean well, and that they want to offer comfort, to say something comforting."

"I'm tired of platitudes. I'm tired of feeling like I'm not measuring up. *Moving on? Aargh.* If I hear that I need to move on one more time, I'll . . . I don't know what I'll do."

"I felt the same as you, but finally I realized that I had to give them credit for trying to offer me comfort, even if it landed wide of the mark. A lot of those folks not only want to show compassion but are afraid of going through loss themselves, so either they already know there are no right words and these are simply the best they have, or they hope to control their own fear of future loss by telling you that grief will pass. But again, *I say* that there's no timeline for it. Respect the person you lost by respecting the grief and giving the grief process room to work itself out when you need to."

Impulsively, I hugged him again, then I stepped away but kept my eyes on his, trying to think of the right thing to say, the best way to express my gratitude, when he asked, "So does this mean that you're going to sell?"

Shocked, I stepped back still another step, but then I saw a certain twinkle in his gray eyes and slowly, my smile grew.

"Seriously?" I asked.

"Curious, maybe. Mostly I'm just asking for effect."

"What effect?"

"Your smile." He cleared his throat. "So, is there anything else you need lifted down, or lifted up today?"

"I think I've done enough ups and downs for one day. I'll take Galahad for a walk. A brisk one. It will do us both good."

He gestured toward Sebrina's boxes. "Anywhere you'd like me to put these for now? To make sure they're safe and ready when *you're* ready?"

"Will I ever be ready?" I said it as a throwaway line, a question with no answer.

"Arthur believed you'd be ready one day."

That silenced the cynic in me.

Blake asked, "Want company on the walk?" He sounded hopeful.

"I think I'd be lousy company, but if you'll put those boxes in the storage room over there, Galahad and I will walk you home."

"It's a deal, Mignon. Those treats the Holmans left aren't getting any fresher."

"Galahad won't mind. Trust me."

"I do," he said, adding, "Can you get that door for me?" He picked up both boxes together, stacked and ready to store with the other keepers.

∞

The next morning, I woke, resolved to be done with cryptic conversations. If anyone overhead discussions about Emerald Heart over lunch, or elsewhere, so be it. This morning, I rose, washed, dressed—made sure Galahad was set—and drove into town. I marched straight up to the front door of Dominick's realty office. I stood there on the sidewalk so I could be seen, this time not wanting to blend into the background.

The door opened behind me. Marion looked out at me and asked, "Something wrong, Mignon? Are you coming in?"

"I'm fine, and yes, I am." As she held the door open, I said, "Thank you very much."

Dominick saw me enter and rose from behind his desk. He smiled and reached out to hug me before ushering me to a chair and closing the office door.

With his hand still on the doorknob, he said, "I can tell by your face that you've reached a decision."

"Have a seat, Dominick." I waited. As he settled in his chair, I said, "I want to thank you for being a wonderful friend for so many years."

"Uh oh, you've got me worried."

I laughed softly. "That I won't sell?"

"No, not that. But that you might leave the area."

He looked serious. His eyes were darker. His voice was tense.

"But, Dominick, that was always a possibility, right? It doesn't mean that I'd never come back to visit."

"But, Meg . . ."

In that moment, in Dominick's eyes, I saw a flash of pain. Had Blake seen something I'd missed? Could it be that Dominick was more than *just* a close friend after all—at least in Dominick's mind? My heart hurt a little for him, but not much. If his feelings for me were truly deep, they surely would've been more obvious, or he would've been more persistent during these two long years. Still, I didn't want to hurt him—just in case—so I chose my words carefully, keeping the tone unemotional and not inviting him into my planning for my future.

"Dominick, my friend. Among the memories I treasure are those of our long history entwined with Arthur, Sebrina, and others who've come and gone in our lives. You know I'm grateful to you for everything you've done . . . for Arthur, of course, and for me, too. Well, almost everything. Contacting Jeanette was rather outside of what was . . . But even that has worked out. In fact, one might say she accomplished your intent in inviting her here, right? I don't mean encouraging me to sell, but rather shaking me out of my mire. So thank you for that. She and I have finally come to terms—a meeting of the minds and an agreement to disagree about certain things—none of which are important enough to derail us from moving forward."

"I'm glad."

"Me too."

"But what about you? What are you planning?"

"I'm working that out now. I haven't officially decided all the details."

He sat back in his chair and gave me a long look. "Then why do you look . . . I don't know. Relieved? Relaxed?"

"Let's just say I've moved all decisions to a mental checklist of things undone. I'm busy checking things off metaphorically. Is that the right word? Well, regardless, you get the idea."

"Isn't that just another way of procrastinating?"

"Nope. It's a methodical, process-oriented approach to problem resolution."

"Okay. So . . ." He shrugged and grimaced. "I'm not sure what to say except that that sounds like a load of—"

I interrupted. "*And* I'm planning a trip. That's the last item on the list." Sort of, though not exactly the last, truly ultimate item. There was something else, but I wasn't ready to explain that to him.

"When and to where?"

"Still working out the details."

He stared at me and then grinned. "Does it involve promontories, by any chance?"

I smiled back and gave a one-shouldered shrug. "Looking that way."

Dominick stood and offered his hand. "Take a beach walk with me?"

"With pleasure."

As we were walking along the strand, Dominick said, "I've been wanting to tell you something." He shrugged. "Not a huge deal, but it's pretty new and I've been hesitant." He took my arm in his as he sometimes did. "But I don't like the feeling of secrecy, especially between us."

"Okay, you've got my curiosity up." I forced a smile to hide my sudden tension. Please, no declarations, no complications . . .

"Jeanette told me you'd asked her why she disappeared at times and why she left her car at Carolyn's house."

"Yes, I did."

"Since the answer involved me, she was reluctant to tell you. You two had been on tricky footing for so long. We were trying to be discreet. I picked her up down there. Sometimes she walked down to Carolyn's house, sometimes she drove down and left her car there. We've been spending time together."

A quick, sideways glance showed me he was smiling—*big smiling* complete with flushed cheeks.

I wanted to be annoyed, maybe even angry. It was my immediate response, but then the whole thing made absolutely perfect sense. "That's why you contacted her to begin with."

"Yeah, I guess so. Not that I admitted it to myself at the time. I did think she might be helpful to you, and I hoped you two would make things good between you. After she returned, we struck up the relationship, but I didn't want to lose my friend over my girlfriend. I don't know if you remember, but I always had a thing for Jeanette. But she was Arthur's older sister and she didn't have any interest in me, the kid brother's friend. There's only two years between us, but when you're young that can feel like a lot, you know . . ." And he rattled on for a while about how he'd never quite lost that feeling for Jeanette and I made all the right noises, even though I felt a tiny bit like wanting to cry—but in a good way.

I interrupted once to ask, "So are you the friend she's been waiting to move in with?"

"Me? No. It's a woman she used to work with. Jeanette and I are still figuring how this works between us."

"Do you want it to work out?"

His voice softened. "We've both been disappointed in our relationships. Does that sound too archaic? Sorry." He shrugged but kept his arm in mine.

All the usual remarks wanted to roll off my tongue—like taking a chance on happiness *or whatever, whatever*. Hadn't I heard all the standard platitudes from everyone else about how I'd experienced a loss but at least I'd had all those happy years? So very many well-meant words that still made me cringe? Instead, I squeezed his arm back and said, "Whatever you two do, be kind to each other and enjoy yourselves along the way. Life is short."

"Thanks, Meg."

I nodded. I was happy for them. At least, for now. Only heaven knew what the future would bring them. But I wished for happiness for them.

And still hoped to find it for *me*.

CRSO

When I returned home, there was a note on my door. Not taped. This one was from Carolyn, and she was asking me to call her when I got home.

That's when I remembered that first note—the one I'd never opened because Jeanette had shown up.

I found the envelope on the end table. I picked it up, revealing an outline of dust marking where it had been dropped and forgotten. For goodness sake. Shame on me for being such a poor housekeeper. I opened the flap. She'd written in her careful script:

Mignon, Please give me a call when it's convenient? I'd like to chat with you about Nathan. He's back to live with me for a while.

Oh, dear. Never mind the dusting failure. I was a lousy friend and neighbor. I owed her an apology, in-person. A phone call wouldn't do.

I walked myself down the path, with Galahad along for the stroll and prepared to humble myself in person.

Carolyn answered my knock on her door. She pressed her hand to her cheek.

"Oh, my goodness, Mignon. Didn't I say to call? I had every intention of walking up to see you. I hate that I've inconvenienced you."

"I owe you an apology, Carolyn. First off, the note you left me ages ago about your grandson coming back to stay with you . . . I laid it on the table and then got sidetracked. I totally forgot it and didn't open it until today. As for what was going on between Jeanette and I, I should've handled it without disturbing you."

"Oh, goodness," she said again. "You mean the red lipstick message? Well, that was something, for sure. Like one of those thriller books I like to read. I was just that scared once my imagination got going, you know." She took my arm and practically dragged me over the threshold into the house as she continued speaking.

"Jeanette explained it was a joke the two of you had going between you." She shook her head. "Sure was good to see her when she came back to town. Been so long. I was just that pleased to hear it was a prank. I know there's been some difficult feelings between you two for years, it seems like. More glad than I can say that it's in the past." She chuckled. "Quite a joke, though. I'm going to keep that in mind myself. Never know when I might want to get someone's attention."

That remark set me back a bit. I offered, "Well, probably not. Certainly you should *not* follow my example when it comes to family disputes or to pranks. I have a pretty poor track record with that. What about Nathan, is he okay?"

Carolyn said, "Have a seat, Mignon. Right there." She pointed to the kitchen table. A dish covered in foil was there. "That's for you. I was going to bring it up to you."

I moved one end of the foil and peeked. Chocolate covered nuts. "Walnut or pecan?"

"Some of each," she said, with a grin.

"You shouldn't have, but I'm glad you did."

"In truth, my dear, it's an apology. I want to know how much it will cost to replace that glass."

"Pardon? What about the glass?"

"No, no indeed. I insist."

"I'm sorry. Please tell me what this is about."

"The window glass that my grandson broke." She watched my face and saw I was stunned. She nodded. "Oh, he did it all right, and then got scared and ran off. He confessed to me. I made it clear to him that I would tell you and pay for it but that he'd have to apologize and work off the cost to repay me." She looked sad. "Nathan's not a bad boy, but sometimes he's so careless that it amazes me. That's not to say that I totally believe it was an accident, but I *do* believe he's very sorry. I think it was due to all that grief he was carrying. You know how he took to your dear husband. Arthur was like a mentor to him. A second father almost. You won't believe what Nathan's reading now. One of those King Arthur books. He goes around saying Old English stuff—that's what he calls it, anyway. Sounds pretty strange, I must say."

I had to pause before responding, and to cover for that I gave Carolyn a hug. When I stepped back, I said, "Give me a heads-up when he's coming to apologize to make sure I'm home. He can meet me at Emerald Heart."

☙❧

When Nathan showed up in front of Emerald

Heart, I was sitting on the terrace in an Adirondack chair. Carolyn had called to let me know, and Nathan must've come directly up as soon as she hung up the phone. His dark hair looked longer and shaggier, and he'd grown several inches taller, and lankier too. The difference between a twelve-year-old boy and one who was now fifteen was vast, at least physically, but I searched face as he made his apology, and he just looked shy and lost.

I had questions, admonitions, all sorts of things I'd planned to say, but there was so much going on in his expression, so many different emotions I couldn't read, that instead of launching into all that, I simply asked, "Why?"

"I'm sorry."

He tried to meet my eyes, but they kept sort of sliding away.

"Your grandmother already told me you regret what you did. But I don't understand *why* you did it? Weren't we always friends to you? My husband and I certainly thought so."

"I'm sorry he died." Nathan shrugged and looked away. "I'd gone back to live with my parents. When they broke up again and I came back . . . I knew he was gone. It didn't feel right. I hung around here some. Tried hard not to disturb you." He looked down at his feet, scuffing his sneakers in the dirt. "Then I heard you were selling it. I didn't mean to be angry about it. I was tossing the rock around, almost like it was a baseball, except . . . not a baseball. I didn't plan on . . . but then I saw the doors . . . Mr. King loved those doors, and I knew he'd never walk back through them, and even if he did, his Camelot would be gone anyway . . . And then it just happened."

"What did you call it?"

"A baseball?" he offered, sounding uncertain.

"No. Camelot. Why did you call it that?"

"The castle, you know? Mr. King said that thing people say? That a man's home is his castle? And then he'd add that *his* was called Camelot. And then he'd start singing something, from a show or movie, I think, and"—Nathan's mouth kind of quirked up in a half grin—"and he sounded all goofy."

"Yeah, I know how that went."

We nodded at each other.

"So anyway, he said he'd grown up seeing the castle up on the hill, except he called it a promontory, and—"

I interrupted, couldn't help myself. "A castle? Seriously?"

"Sure. I mean, yes, ma'am. I couldn't see it myself at first, but then we went out in the kayaks during that . . . What do they call it? I saw the kayaks are all gone now." He paused, then resumed, "He said it was the hour when the light was just right." Nathan shrugged again.

"I understand. The golden hour."

"Yeah, and then I saw it. The light from the west hit those walls that look so plain usually, but when that light hit them, they had that . . . Sounds stupid to say. That fairy-tale look? Like the place was glowing. Maybe from a whole different time ago." He scratched his head.

"Sounds stupid, I guess."

"No." I shook my head, unable to speak properly. My tears were going to erupt at any moment, possibly drowning us both and bringing up the level of Bogue Sound by at least a foot. I breathed, trying to rein it all in. If I broke down, it would be embarrassing for me and probably terrifying for Nathan to witness.

"Ms. King, I know what I did wasn't right. I was just mad. Had no good reason to take it out on the Heart." The grin had vanished. His eyes were sad and red-rimmed now. He looked down again. "If you have any work I can do around here to cover the bill, I'd like to work off what the repair costs. Grandma said she was paying you, but I need to pay her back, or work it off directly, if that's possible."

I stood. "Yes, Nathan." I got it said with only a minimal catch in my voice. I was able to add, "You'll be around for a while?"

"Yes, ma'am. Looks like it."

"Then I'll let you know. Tell your grandma that you and I will handle the cost of the repair between ourselves."

Sadness and relief seemed to wash across his face. "Thank you."

Slowly, I stood. "Meanwhile, I have something for you."

"I don't understand."

"Come with me." I walked toward the lobby. When I pushed the glass door open, I saw him hesitate. "I'm glad you didn't break these."

"Yes, ma'am."

I pointed toward the bar where a box waited. "Take a look."

He peeked in and said, "Mr. King's Round Table?"

"Complete with knights. They are yours now. I know Mr. King—Arthur—would want you to have this."

He looked downcast.

"What's wrong?"

"So, it's true." He glanced around the room, his eyes lighting on the empty shelves and bare walls, confirming that everything King Arthur–related was gone.

"The sale? It hasn't happened yet, but yes, it probably will. I can't manage this place on my own. Not without Arthur."

Nathan nodded. "Yes, ma'am."

His grandma must've really drilled the *yes, ma'am, no, ma'am* into him. Did him good, I thought. Or maybe he found comfort in the structure or tradition. Couldn't fault him for that. I was much the same.

"Take the box out to my car and I'll drive you down to the house."

"Are you sure? I broke your window."

"I'm sure. And no worries. If someone buys this place before you work off the debt . . . of course, I can't promise they'll leave the place *as is*, but I'll let them know you're available for any jobs they need to have done, that you're familiar with the garden and can cut the grass too."

"Thank you." He picked up the box and with a last

look at the nearly empty lobby, he pushed through the glass doors and went out to the car. If he seemed to pause and trace a section of etching with his finger, I didn't choose to remark on it.

He'd been coming up here, trying not to bother me. How many of those sounds, those noises in the early morning or late evening, had been this kid trying to recapture a few good memories and hold them close?

I wish I'd known. I would've loved to have shared those times, those memories with him.

Emerald Heart. A fairy tale Camelot castle. *The Heart*, per Nathan. Who knew?

I smiled. Apparently, Arthur had. And then Nathan. And now, I did.

"Nathan, one more thing?"

"Yes, ma'am?"

"There are two kayaks in the storage shed. The two Mr. King and I used. I'm okay if you want to give them a workout—if your grandmother approves, of course."

Chapter Twenty-Four

The end of September was near. It had been a strange month. One that had been unimaginable in August, but it had happened. And I was grateful.

I invited Blake out to dine. After our meal, I said, "We never did take that beach walk. Seems a shame to miss the chance again."

"I agree, Mignon. It would be my pleasure."

We left our shoes at the end of the public access crossover, then traversed the soft, warm mounds of sand between there and the smoother, damp area of beach. The waning afternoon sun set the golden lights in the sand aglow and brushed the swelling waves with an iridescent, greenish cast as they curled and broke. The tide had turned. It was working its way back up to and beyond where we were currently walking. The water was still warm this time of year thanks to the Gulf Stream, and I took Blake's hand in mine, drawing him with me to walk closer to the water. I wanted to feel the wavelets running over my feet and around my toes. I held his hand firmly but briefly, giving it a squeeze before letting it go.

I said, "Blake, I owe you my sincere thanks. I appreciate your attention, your encouragement, especially about grief. Others tried to help, but I guess I wasn't ready to hear it from them. You showed up at the right time and helped me risk this big step back into the world, so I'm going to pay you the respect of being honest with you."

"Mignon—"

"Please. Allow me to speak?"

He nodded. "All right. I'm listening."

"You came here knowing no one and having left a job, probably something high-pressure and consuming, and suddenly here you were in Emerald Isle. A beach town. It didn't take long for running and swimming to fall short of fascinating activities."

"True, but—"

"Please?"

He nodded.

"It was my good fortune to meet you. I enjoy your company and I think you enjoy mine—but because I was a novelty. New. The damsel trapped in the tower—a.k.a. the mysterious hotel. You're the kind of man who loves a challenge and who'll jump into rescue mode—the riskier, the better—especially when you're between ventures. *But* I'm not risky. I'm not even very interesting. I have only the faintest idea of who I really am." I touched his arm because I could see he was about to interrupt again, but he didn't. He held back.

"What really brought us together, Blake? Was it that we'd each experienced loss? Grief?" I shook my head. "It's not enough. This can't work between us. It's good we found out before anyone's heart was too deeply involved."

"Mignon. Do I get a turn to speak?"

"No, Blake." I smiled, but softly. "No, because you are so very persuasive. I would listen and would fall in line with whatever you propose because it sounds compelling and exciting. Been there, done that with Arthur. I don't blame him. Those were the choices I made, and it was good. But I lost myself. This time, Blake, I'm gonna do what's calling to me, however incomplete or uncertain that siren call is. I want to see where it leads."

This time I put my finger to his lips, before adding, "I want to focus on that. I don't want to lose sight of finding that path because I'm afraid of being alone or of screwing it up."

He took my hand and touched his lips to my wrist before releasing me.

"I get it," he said. "I've seen people get caught up in other people's lives and forget their own. People do that for all sorts of reasons. Chasing love, or because someone else's life looks more interesting . . . whatever. It also happens when people are lonely—not *alone*, but *lonely*. I know about lonely." He grimaced. "It makes people vulnerable."

He was speaking of himself? I thought maybe so.

He said, "You showed me that I didn't have to rush into the next project. I've never been good at just having fun. When Alyssa died, I lost control of my life, my time. I ran hard and worked even harder to avoid the grief. I filled every second of my life so that I wouldn't have the space to remember. You did the opposite.

"We both dedicated equal persistence and energy

to it, totally missing the obvious. You and I, Mignon, could just have fun. We don't have to build new lives or take on new projects and ventures. We don't have to hide from anything. We can simply be ourselves and see where it goes, instead of being so focused on achieving goals—or shutting out the pain—that we miss the whole point of living."

Blake's voice grew softer, and he leaned closer. "Will you do me a favor? And maybe even yourself too? There's no obligation to agree. Only listen?"

"What?"

He whispered, "I hear the wall going up."

I refused to respond to that. He was right, but still . . .

Blake sighed. He put his hands on my arms and leaned his head forward and down until his forehead touched mine. But that was it. We simply stood like that for a few moments. The ocean raced up and tickled our feet, then swept the sand out from around and under our toes and then did it again a few more times, until he stood tall again, stepped back, and released my arms. I felt almost cheated.

He said, "Okay. Change of subject? Dominick wants to get your thoughts on something. Me too. I'll be there to listen in. Again, it's totally up to you. It's only an option, and an opportunity to . . ." he smiled. "To have it your way—whichever way you want it."

"Dominick and you?"

"No need to worry. We've talked. We're good."

"Okay. So, what's this about then?"

"I won't say. This is his idea and I'll let him do the honors." He shrugged. "Could be a good thing, Mignon. Hear him out? Don't say no too quickly." He grinned. "I don't know if you realize this, but you can be intimidating."

"Ha ha. That's funny." I couldn't help but laugh.

"Tomorrow afternoon at Dominick's office?"

I nodded.

Blake slid his arms around me, so gently, so swiftly that I had no time to object before he took them away again. Swift like a hug, but more than a hug.

He asked, "Can we walk a little longer? Worried about Galahad?"

"I told him I'd be home later than usual today because I had that big speech planned."

"And he approved?"

I nodded, trying to keep a serious expression on my face. "Yes, when he heard I was going out with you, he was good with it. He likes you."

He took my hand. This time he kept it as we walked toward the sun setting over The Point.

CRSO

Blake had said the meeting was planned for the next afternoon at the realty office. "Meet us there," he'd said. "Listen to what they propose." And so here I was, one day later, parking in the nearby lot.

Dominick tucked his arm through mine and held it

snugly. I looked up and he met my eyes. This was the Dominick I'd always trusted . . . with a few minor blips along the way. We walked into the realty office together, and as we approached his office, through the large window, I saw someone—no, *two* someones already there. Jeanette and Blake. Blake was smiling at me in greeting, in a friendly but reserved way. Jeanette looked apprehensive and ready to bolt.

Dominick whispered, "Give this a listen, Mignon?"

"I'm here. Listening. For now."

"Good enough." He offered me a seat near the desk where I'd have a view of everyone. He seated himself at the desk, then leaned forward, his forearms on the desktop, his fingers clasped together, and his eyes fastened on me.

He said, "You've been struggling with deciding whether to sell Emerald Heart or reopen it, or even demolish the building. I don't recommend the last option for reasons we've already discussed. The first two options? We"—he nodded toward the other two—"have a proposition."

Dominick continued, "In full disclosure, this was my idea. Jeanette liked the idea, and so I approached Blake to see if he'd come in as a partner. We have a variety of skills and resources between us. Blake has the financial wherewithal and a business interest, but no interest in the day to day running of a hotel. Jeanette has the time and interest to work on-site. She'll live on the premises while the renovation is in progress. For business as usual, we'll have to hire employees to support her, just as you'd have to do if you chose to reopen it yourself. As for me, I have the business acumen, some financial resources, and a strong interest in supporting the running of the hotel."

He settled his gaze back on me. "We can purchase Emerald Heart outright as a group. That would free you to move on with your life in whatever way you choose." He paused. "Or if you prefer, you can keep an interest in the property, but in a lesser way, selling the majority interest to us, thus retaining an interest while still allowing you to afford a fresh start."

This had come out of nowhere. Jeanette managing the hotel? Blake throwing cash at an enterprise that had barely turned a profit during the last years it was in operation? And what about Dominick? Had he suddenly gotten sentimental over physical assets and was now embracing risky investments?

I half-expected the Mad Hatter to come strolling through the office door at any moment.

Dominick continued, "Ultimately, if we can't make this work, and it becomes necessary to sell, we'll do that, but this will give Emerald Heart a second chance. A new chance. We'll enhance the property, add amenities, and upgrade the facility."

"Wow." I shook my head. "I had no idea any of you were thinking in these terms."

Jeanette said, "If you'd rather I wasn't part of it, it's okay to say so. I told Dominick what I'd said to you about initially coming here, wanting to help. He told me he'd already been thinking about how he could pull the monies together to purchase Emerald Heart, and he and Blake talked—not to exclude you, but to have a firm idea of how this business arrangement would work before presenting it to you."

Blake said, "It's up to you. No hard feelings either way. It's more about what *you* see for the future—for yourself and for Emerald Heart."

I nodded.

Dominick said, "These are rough numbers based upon the options. We need to move quickly, though, to catch the market while the financials are in our favor." He handed me a sheet of paper with numbers. "Take a look and let me know."

I accepted the paper from him but was almost afraid to look at it.

Blake stood. "I think you're done with me, right?"

Dominick walked Blake out. Jeanette stayed back with me.

"What do you think about all this, Jeanette? Are you really up to managing a hotel?"

"I couldn't do it alone, but with the right help? Yes. I think this is not only a fresh start for Emerald Heart but also for me—and you too, Mignon."

I shook my head. "Truly, I'm not at all sure that this is a good idea for anyone." I focused on the floor, avoiding her eyes. "If this does go forward, what happens if you find yourself in over your head? Can you handle the pressure this will put on you, Jeanette?"

The fact was I still didn't know the details of her former troubles. But what if her troubles weren't former, after all, and this pressure could send her into some sort of emotional spiral or breakdown?

"Don't worry about that. I'm good," she said. "If there's anything I need support or guidance in, well, Dominick is nearby."

I stood. "I'm inclined to agree to the offer with a few conditions. I'll share those with Dominick, and he can discuss them with you and Blake." I started to walk away, but then turned back to her, saying, "If this does come to fruition, I can recommend someone to help with grass-cutting and garden work."

Was that hope I saw on her face?

"There's something else, Jeanette. I'm planning a trip. I was wondering if, while I'm gone, you'd be willing to watch Galahad? Assuming The Emerald Heart Hotel is still available when that time comes, maybe you could stay at the house? It would be good for Galahad, I think. I'm guessing you'll be moving in there anyway when the deal is done, right?"

"Mignon . . . what about you? What will you do?"

Her soft voice, her question, surprised me. Was that kindness I'd heard?

Maybe I would've heard it sooner if I'd truly been listening.

"No worries," I said. "I'm not sure, but I think this may be a good thing." I nodded. "Options. It's always good to have them."

CR&ED

When I returned to Emerald Heart, I went straight to Arthur's office. Because I'd already sorted through the papers in and around the desk and bureau, it was easy to put my hands on the information we'd collected when we were researching our dream trip. I unfolded the huge map of the United Kingdom and taped it back up on the wall—almost three years after we'd taken it down, having given in to reality and accepted that the map no longer symbolized plans for the future, but rather, something that wasn't going to happen.

Now it *would*, though not quite as planned.

Chapter Twenty-Five

We had agreed on terms for The Emerald Heart Hotel and property. My plate was now cleared of future responsibilities in what had begun as Arthur's dream and then became our life. My payout would be more than enough to keep me solvent for quite some time while I figured out what the years ahead would look like for me.

I was still here wrapping things up at my end, wanting to get the last things sorted and cleared ahead of the quick closing date.

This morning when I rolled out of bed, the air was fresh, and I knew the breeze would be as sweet as it had ever been. There was much that I'd miss. I'd worked so hard getting all the things sorted out and disposed of or put into storage by a set date—a date I'd etched in stone (virtually) by taking the plunge and purchasing the airline tickets for my trip and making hotel and tour reservations.

When I'd asked Jeanette how confident she was about taking charge of the hotel, I'd had to face that same question about me. Committing to firm dates was a vote of confidence in myself.

Setting the date also ensured that I'd been too busy to fret much over whether I was making the right choices or not. I couldn't retreat into the old habit of hiding in my memories when things got hard because this now involved other people and commitments, including a jet to Heathrow that wouldn't wait for me to be ready. I'd come so far that I felt safe from losing my focus now, and I opened the windows for the breeze not guessing how much that simple act might cost me.

There were always a thousand little traps ready to trip the unwary or derail those who were too certain they'd overcome the darker things that haunted them.

I froze in place, fixated, my mind blank as I watched the curtains capture the air and that beautiful, familiar shade of blue billowed into the room knocking a small knickknack off a nearby end table. The sound of a ceramic bird hitting the floor and shattering dented the spell just enough that I stumbled backward, but then the hem of the curtain brushed my cheek, and my breath caught.

My chest hurt. I tried to breathe.

So close. I was so close to breaking free. My eyes stung.

At my feet, Galahad whined. Any moment now, Sebrina would dance gracefully out from behind the curtains. Arthur would be near to me, and I—

Galahad nipped my leg. I yelped, more in shock than pain.

"Bad boy," I shouted, checking to see if he'd broken the skin. He hung his head.

I looked at the curtains. My curtains. Chosen long ago because Sebrina had loved the color blue. They were worn and faded now—hardly any blue left in them—and of no value to anyone but me.

Not even to me. To me, they were a trap. Maybe a trigger.

Grabbing the fabric, handfuls of it in both my hands, I yanked. The hardware gave partway, and I pulled again, harder. One panel came off entirely, taking the rod and bits of wallboard with it. The other hung at an angle, the rod and hardware fixture not completely detached from the wall. It looked crazy. Only a crazy woman would do this . . . but heaven help me, it felt good.

Emotion filled me, warming me inside. My eyes burned. This act felt good in a way that dunking Jeanette hadn't. Galahad barked. I laughed and dropped to my knees to hug him, feeling joy that I hadn't felt since . . . I didn't even know. It had been far too long.

Beyond Galahad, I caught sight of Arthur's urn on the mantel. My gaze stopped there. I stared, holding him so tightly that he squirmed. I lost my balance and sat full-out on the floor.

First moving to my hands and knees, then to my feet, I backed away from the mantel. I knew what must be done. I headed straight to the office. I slammed open the closet door in a hurry lest I lose momentum, then fumbled behind the big, dusty garment bag until I found her dress—her blue twirly dress covered only in thin dry cleaner plastic. I snatched it from the closet, hanger, and all, and ripped away the bag. I pressed the dress to my heart and buried my face in the satiny fabric. My baby. My girl. Gone, but not entirely. Forever in my heart. But it was different now.

Different because I knew what to do next—and was frantic to reach that next step before I derailed again.

Hugging the dress, I ran back to the living room. This dress would go in one of the two boxes Blake had pulled from the storage closet, but first I was going to take a pair of scissors to it. I took Arthur's urn from the mantel and with both the urn and the dress held securely in my arms, I went to the kitchen for the shears.

Chapter Twenty-Six

I'd never flown by myself and had rarely packed for more than a long weekend trip. People who ran small, family-owned hotels often didn't have the luxury of taking extended vacation-style trips . . . at least, that had been my personal experience. As renovations were about to commence at The Emerald Heart Hotel, Jeanette would have the chance to learn that herself. Of course, she'd have Dominick's help.

What kind of team would they make, especially when it came to hotel management? Was I smiling? Maybe even laughing softly? I was glad I'd be out of town for a while. Heck, I would soon be out of the country.

What they did would *not* be my business.

I stood in the lobby, lights off and alone. The larger furniture items like the massive chest by the front doors and the mahogany bar were still here. Otherwise, it was empty. Most of my keepers, including Arthur's collection, were safely stowed in a storage unit. Dominick had suggested that they might like to either purchase or lease some of the lithographs and bronzes for the hotel décor after the renovations were complete.

Yeah, I thought Arthur would like that.

The trip that Arthur and I had talked about, had

planned for years, and that we had finally come close to taking, had been structured so that we each had our special interests included. Arthur had called it a *legendary adventure in-the-making*.

His diagnosis had ended the planning as our focus shifted to more mortal concerns. When it came to legendary, I figured Arthur and I had had a pretty great run, even with the heartaches. No one would be writing histories and poetry about our love story, and that was probably good. People should find their own stories, their unique and shared experiences, and live their own, deliberate lives.

That was my current plan for myself.

I went to the adjoining door, paused for one last look, then returned to the house side to finish packing.

As I was reviewing my packing list, the doorbell rang. Galahad barked. I knew it was Blake. For just an instant, I was thrown back to that strange day only weeks ago when a man had emerged from Bogue Sound onto my dock and had appeared at the top of the cliff stairs.

Now he was knocking on my door. And he wasn't a stranger. And Galahad beat me there.

I went to answer the door, muttering, "He's here to see me, boy." I had to all but push him aside to open it.

Blake said, "You're really going."

"I am."

"Alone."

"Yes. This is something I must do for myself." *For Arthur too*, I added silently. I planned to give him a personal, proper goodbye that I hadn't been able to manage at the end of his illness.

"I respect your wishes, but if at any time you change your mind, call or text and I'll join you. I haven't toured the UK in years." He took my hand. "It's going to seem odd over there alone. Are you sure?"

"I'm sure."

"Okay then." He gave in. "Can I drive you to the airport?"

"Nope, I have that handled." I gave him a hug. "I have to do this, Blake."

He nodded. "And you'll do fine."

"I will." *I hope.*

"What time are you leaving? Need anything carried to your car?"

I didn't answer. I touched his cheek. His gray eyes were concerned.

"Mignon. I want to tell you to have a good trip, to say the right kind of goodbye, but"—he frowned—"I don't know what those words are. Instead, may I say to please return safely, and soon? This place won't be the same without you." He added, "Nor will I."

Our arms moved in unison, encompassing each other, and Blake kissed me. I kissed him back. And that was exactly the right goodbye and didn't require words at all.

☙❧

I was nervous about the flight, about understanding

what I could take through security or what must go into my checked bag, the weight of the bag, how early to arrive at the airport. I experienced a moment of panic in the security line where I was certain a uniformed official was going to yank me out because I'd violated some rule. On board the plane, I had a window seat and was fascinated by the view around and below me until, hardly knowing it was happening, I fell asleep.

With the arrival, there was a whole new kind of craziness getting through Heathrow and surviving the cab ride—or *black cab,* as they called them—as my driver navigated the streets of London and got me to the hotel. It wasn't until after I'd checked into the hotel, had entered my room, looked at my suitcase and around the room again, that I realized the problem. I was alone.

Yeah. Okay. Nice furnishings. The bed looked good, neat and clean. Towels were nicely folded in the bathroom. The windows overlooked the street three floors below. Great city view. When I turned back to the room's interior, I wanted to remark on the view or on the attractive color scheme in the room or debrief the journey in a cozy chat, but no one was with me. Not even Galahad. For a moment, my mind went blank. *What next?*

I fixed my attention on my suitcase, nodded at it, and said, "Nice view out there."

Silly, but it was enough. My eyes were heavy and gritty and jet lag or not, I took a quick shower and then crawled into bed.

Nice bed.

I was out in a flash.

In the morning, as I was getting clothing from my suitcase, I found the journal.

Black leather. It was a little the worse for wear. I'd written in it from time to time over the years and had then forgotten it entirely for many more years.

I thumbed through the pages, seeing rough sketches in both pen and pencil as well as passages of commentary, penned mostly when I was much, much younger, and when I'd had something on my mind. Inconsistently used, and it was very surprising to find this old journal here now.

I hadn't packed this.

Last I recalled, this journal had been on the bookshelf in the living room squeezed between some of Arthur's thick historical or archeological tomes.

That was Jeanette's living room now. She was the onsite manager of The Emerald Heart Hotel, which was still closed but undergoing renovations as well as planning for improvements, like a new wing . . . overlooking the ravine with a narrow view of the water. Yes, just as Arthur had envisioned. Someone . . . maybe Dominick . . . had even mentioned a putting green. *Sigh.*

Only Jeanette could've put this journal in my suitcase. But why?

She'd stood at Arthur's bookcase in the living room. Had asked if she could borrow a book. She must've grabbed the journal at the same time. Accidentally, I was sure. There wasn't anything that interesting written in it.

I let the pages flip and then I closed it, intending to return it to the suitcase, but there, nestled next to a pair of shoes, was a thin package of pencils and a couple of pens. I fished them out and found a tiny sharpener and an eraser stashed there, too.

Okay. This felt like a message . . . or maybe a suggestion?

Well, then, wasn't I open to following new paths now? Maybe reviving a few forgotten ones?

I took the journal and writing implements and dropped them into my tote bag alongside a few other items. One never knew what one might encounter when on an adventure, right?

For this first full day here, I'd get my bearings before starting the official sightseeing tomorrow. Today, I would wander the streets of London with my map, a digital guidebook on my cell phone, and now a journal in my tote bag. I would sit in a pub or somewhere else iconic and sip whatever the locals sipped.

I'd keep an eye open for a special gift for Jeanette. Not because of the journal, but because she was watching Galahad while I was traveling. She was also holding a room for me at the Emerald Heart for when I returned, a place to stay while I figured out what to do next.

In fact, she'd given me an excellent rate for the room stay—with an open-ended departure date.

⊱⊰

For the second day of my trip, I did one of those on/off bus tours around London. I saw a lot and my sore feet testified to that fact.

Early on the third day, I was ready and waiting in the lobby with my luggage when the cab arrived to deliver me to Paddington Station, where I would take the train to Liskeard in Cornwall. I intended to stroll the streets of Liskeard for the remainder of the day, stay there tonight, and in the morning a hired car would take me to Arthur's special destination, Tintagel. I had plans there. After my mission was complete, the hired car would bear me north toward the Cotswolds and I'd join a small bus tour for a couple of days in Wales before heading into Scotland.

For this trip, much of what Arthur and I had researched and planned still held true. It helped. If I got nervous about making connections or talking to strangers, I whispered to the tote instead. It wasn't the same as sharing my thoughts with Arthur in person, but it worked.

At Tintagel, the driver interrupted my thoughts, asking, "Shall I walk through the site with you? I can give you a tour. I know a bit about it and more."

"No, thank you. I have a personal mission."

"Thought so," he said. "You have that look . . . have had the whole way here. Seen it before. Well, take your time then." He opened my car door and I exited, but simply stood there. "That way, ma'am. Up that long walk there. You'll be looking for the Arthur statue on the promontory. The statue is called Gallos. *Representative,* you know? Lots of places have a claim on King Arthur, and other lords and leaders have claims on this place. You want any color about that just let me know. Not the first time I've been here."

I looked the man in the eyes and said, "Thank you."

"Sure you're good on your own for this?"

"I've worked hard to be good on my own." I nodded. "Maybe this is my test."

Walking past the shop and toward the goal, it felt almost like the very edge of the earth. No one was near as I pulled the tote bag closer, yet a whisper felt appropriate. "I wish you could see this, Arthur. There's the bridge and there's the statue. Somewhere below us is the cave. Merlin's Cave, right? How often did we talk about this, sweetheart?"

I looked around, taking in the landscape, then I focused on the water—beautiful in its rhythm, its sound and smell, but so different from home. "Arthur, this is the Celtic Sea. I wish you could see it, but it looks so very cold."

At the actual edge of this world, at this ancient spot in Cornwall, the wind blew in off the sea just as it had done since land, water, and air had come into being, and the continents had separated. I'd read that the Cornish word, Gallos, meant power. I felt like I was getting a taste of that power as the windborne mist washed my face, whipped the loose strands of my long hair across my cheeks and mouth, and urged me to close my eyes. Despite the chill coming in from the sea, and wishing I'd brought a jacket or a heavier sweater, I tried to hold my position there and take in all the feels and scents as my Arthur would've done.

Hoping no one was close enough to hear, I recited a few lines that Arthur had particularly liked in *Idylls of the King*, and knew I was making a mess of it. I stopped short. This was pointless.

And it felt empty.

What had I thought would happen after this . . . ceremony? Not this.

This was for Arthur. My gift to Arthur. But Arthur was gone.

I thought, *God, I've come all this way and now I feel . . . I'm lost. Still lost.*

My eyes burned now, not from tears, but from the wind. That same wind caught the tote bag on my arm and pulled hard at it, nearly overbalancing me. I grabbed it with my free hand and hugged it to me tightly.

This was to be my parting gift to Arthur—the dream he'd carried so long—where he'd put so much of his heart. Now I was here and . . .

And whatever I was hoping to find . . . wasn't.

Arthur and I had had twenty-plus good years. More than two decades, most of it spent at the hotel in Emerald Isle.

The wind whipped around me again. I stumbled backward, prepared to fall away from the cliff rather than risk falling forward.

The sky was darkening as clouds moved in, doubtless bringing rain showers. I had been forewarned about the weather here and had a small umbrella in my bag, but if I was going to do this—fulfill my mission here—then I needed to get on with it.

I found the blue-wrapped package down near the bottom of the tote. It was small and tied up with a bit of lace. Some of Arthur's ashes were secured inside the fabric from Sebrina's dress. I would toss this precious package into the Celtic Sea far below. A fitting tribute. Arthur would've approved. I'd been sure of it.

But would he have cared? Truly?

This was earthbound . . . treasures I could touch. Like the mementos I'd held so dear. They meant nothing to Arthur now.

Pressing the small package against my cheek and then to my heart, I knew. Perhaps I'd always known, but hadn't understood.

I'd been lost, but not Arthur. Arthur could've made this trip during the years before his sickness took over, but he hadn't. Because while the trip, like my supposedly grand gesture here, had been fun to think about, and even to plan, he'd already been right where he wanted to be.

Where his heart was.

My eyes watered. Maybe crying, maybe simply from being bludgeoned by the wind. My tears wet the blue satin fabric and I held it so tightly that I felt the contents *give* beneath my fingers.

Enough of this. I turned away from the edge of the promontory—a truly impressive promontory very different from our much smaller, but friendlier bluff. I gave a nod to the lonely statue atop the rock and made my way back to the shops. Away from the wind, I returned my package to my tote and went in to shop for a gift for Jeanette. Carolyn too. Maybe even something for Nathan.

The next morning, I awoke at the hotel in Liskeard. The tourism literature said it was the gateway to the moors. Nice. I stretched and reached across my hugging pillow to the space next to me. I let my hand rest there on the cool sheet for a long moment and thought about the day ahead, and of Arthur. There was a trace of melancholy in the thought, but not despair.

I could look forward to this day.

What had Blake said about loss? That the grief might ease over time, but it never went away. Never stopped being a real thing in one's life and that sometimes it needed to breathe as if it had a life of its own. That when it did, it demanded respect—grief demanded, deserved respect because of the loss it represented. And one's ability to love even in the face of loss. Equally important, respect meant appreciating your own life and living it—not being lost in it, past or present—and, to that end, I pushed the covers aside and stepped quietly over to the window and opened the curtains wide to greet the morning.

That small package I'd crafted in my kitchen? It stayed in my tote for the remainder of the trip, snug and handy, as I went from attractions to gardens to museums, and if I sometimes talked to my tote bag and people gave me odd looks—so what? When I returned home, I'd settle this package where it belonged . . . where Arthur's heart had been for most of his life. Where he'd lived his best life.

⚭

The day before my flight back to North Carolina, Blake texted asking where I'd be coming home to. He wanted to be there to greet me.

Home. What a lovely word. I texted back, "Emerald Heart parking lot."

He replied, "I'll be there."

Blake had given me my space. I looked forward to seeing him, but I warned myself about expectations. Until this text, I hadn't heard from him at all. As the days had passed, I'd told myself that he was respecting my wishes, but was that reality? He might well have already refocused his attention elsewhere. Maybe he wanted to meet me to explain that, and apologize, in person?

Or was that fear whispering in my head?

Either way, even if I was disappointed, I would be fine. I knew that now.

Settled on the homebound flight, I pulled out my journal and took a stroll through the pages. The earliest entries were from when I met Arthur in high school as a new kid in a new place, and from our college years in Wake Forest, and from when he proposed, and we married. The entries were infrequent, only marking important events. Some events were even more poignantly highlighted by the absence of entries, like the loss of Sebrina and Arthur's struggle with illness.

Thank goodness for my notes about the trip and the sights I'd seen. Without those—neatly dated and property identified—this trip would all be a blur.

I put the journal on the tray table, pressed along the bound edge of the pages to help them stay open, then chose a pencil from the little holder. Biting my lip, I leaned forward, the top of my head brushing the seatback in front of me, ignoring the person beside me as I focused. I needed to write out these few thoughts before meeting Blake again, greeting Jeanette and Galahad, and Dominick, too. Returning to the familiarity of home would make it all too easy to allow old habits to reclaim me. I would not let that happen. This would be my message to my future self. I started with this:

One healthy thing each day was the promise I made to myself to break the stranglehold of the past—to allow me to move forward. I'd kept a list, at least in my head, because I was lost and trying to find an anchor, or a signpost, but those weren't real things. They were limited solutions—temporal and without substance. Illusory. But somewhere along the way I lost track of the list. I'd forgotten about it—in a good way. Because I was busy. Busy actually living my life. Even while doing the difficult things.

I paused with my pencil suspended over the journal. Those had been easy words to write, but getting free hadn't been easy, had it? Likewise, it was probably unwise to declare victory. I smiled and resumed writing.

There were more than a few bumps along the way, and some painful backslides, but each forward progress moved the needle—a needle that measured my progress between dependency and what? Autonomy? Blake's word. Until one day I found myself on a cliff—a cliff far from home—only to discover, like Dorothy, that she'd never needed to go anywhere for rescue. Her rescue was always there with her, inside her—waiting to comfort and guide her regardless of where she was. She had only to ask. And now...well, as Matt advised, "I'll do it like I mean it...until I <u>do truly</u> mean it."

A prayer on a cliff. Understanding that the trappings of our lives are less real, less valuable and less essential than the substance of our hearts and hopes. Today, I am exhausted but triumphant despite my aching feet because I made this trip on my own. Yet my satisfaction, my heart, isn't back at the hotel or in any particular place. My goal is to refuse chaos and seek light, to live mindfully in the present and treasure that which can't be held, yet will withstand the trials of earthly limits. To find faith and hold to it.

I am writing this now to help me remember what I've learned. Tonight, I'll be home. Tomorrow I'll rise bright and early, ready to live my life whatever the future brings to me. Or brings me to.

Also, and <u>never forget</u>—mornings (and all the hours from one sunrise to the next) should always be the best time of day.

❦

Blake was waiting there in the semidarkness beneath the parking lot lights of the hotel. I parked and climbed out, grabbing my tote which was considerably heavier now than when I'd started this adventure. In hardly more than a heartbeat, Blake was there beside me.

Gallantly, he reached for the tote bag and gratefully, I released it to him but instead of carrying it, he set it gently on the pavement at our feet, then wrapped me in his arms. His hug was the best welcome possible.

It felt like home.

Epilogue

Two days home, my bags are unpacked, my laundry is done, and Galahad and I are settled into our guest room at The Emerald Heart Hotel. It's lovely, like a suite, and someone has stocked the cabinets with food and there's even a mini fridge in place. Jeanette apologized for giving me Room 205, at the far end of the wing. She thought we'd be more comfortable a bit out of the way as the work to update The Heart was beginning.

Galahad has been confused since my return and keeps trying to return to the residence. Ironic, in that now that he has access to the hotel side, it seems to have lost its fascination for him. I'm not sure what that means, but there's probably meaning in it. In any event, our stay is temporary, and we are managing.

"Come with me," I say, gesturing to him. I'm due to meet up with Jeanette and Nathan at the live oaks garden and it feels unfair to leave Galahad shut up in the room alone, so I invite him to come along. He is happy to oblige.

I've arranged a surprise for him.

Blake is waiting there in the garden for us. He calls to Galahad, mentioning the T word and waving a stick, and the two set off down the trail to the Holman house. Galahad's tail is about to wag right off him and I'm quite certain my sweet dog is grinning.

Jeanette and I have chosen a spot in the garden for the blue package of ashes. Also, she found a small metal box in one of the closets. She hands it to me, suggesting we use it to secure the package.

"Good idea, Jeanette."

With Nathan's help, we dig a hole in the garden where the roots allow it, after all, these live oaks *are* the heart of the garden. Together we handle this duty, one that I'm sure seems as strange to them as it does to me. When the earth has been refilled, and the top has been smoothed, I say a small prayer and then Nathan adds to it, and Jeanette says, "Amen."

After a long moment of silence, she adds, "We'd better set a big flowerpot or something heavy on top of this or Galahad will dig the whole works up," and then, in a totally unseemly reaction, one of us giggles and then we all laugh, hugging each other as we cry.

Satisfactory? Yes, and more. The moment, the hugs, the laughter and tears—they are perfect.

I know what should be set on top. Not a huge flowerpot, but a statue I've ordered that should be here in a few days—a replica of Arthur on the promontory. Gallos, that is. It's not full-size, but pretty big so it won't get lost amid the winding arms of the oaks. It's a surprise, a house-warming gift (maybe a hotel-warming gift?) for Jeanette and Dominick and I'm pretty sure they won't object.

The Emerald Heart Hotel Department of Practicality—under the administration of Mignon King—is now officially closed. I am moving on to new pursuits and looking forward to seeing what the future brings. At the moment, the options are wide open.

Sir Galahad is kicking up leaves as he dashes out of the beautiful Emerald Heart forest in a rush to rejoin us, and Blake comes into view soon after. He stands beneath a nearby live oak, in the dappled shade, resting a hand on one of the strong, twisting branches. He watches as we three rise to our feet, and he smiles.

I smile back as he asks, "All done?"

"For now," I say.

"Where to next, Mignon?"

I shake my head slowly, half-teasing as I say, "Anything is possible, but why don't we start with lunch and a walk on the beach?"

Actually, there is a certain vacant storefront available for lease down by the oceanfront that attracted my attention recently, but I'm not quite ready to open that topic up for discussion. Instead, I look at Blake and repeat what I'd said moments before, this time with more emphasis, *"Anything is possible."*

The End

Thank you for reading Emerald Heart.
I hope you enjoyed it.

Author's Note

Emerald Heart is the story of Arthur and Mignon King—their love story—and of Mignon's struggle to find her life again after losing him. It is a story about family and friends, and estrangements and working things out. But I struggled with the setting. How do I write a book set in Emerald Isle, NC, but also have forests and lots of acreage for a hotel and even room for the live oak garden—all of which seemed important to the story I was envisioning?

Regarding the grove of live oaks in the garden at Emerald Heart . . .   Twelve years ago, when Beach Rental (the first of the Emerald Isle, NC novels) was published, two of the main characters (Ben and Juli) met over grilled cheese sandwiches at the Cox Family Restaurant in Morehead City. After that meeting, they walked along the sidewalk and ended up in a vacant lot filled with beautiful live oaks. I, myself, had eaten at that restaurant, had walked on that sidewalk and had happened upon the grove of live oaks in that vacant lot. I'd stood in that lot on the low cliff looking across Bogue Sound and had seen the coastline of Emerald Isle. I knew that lot was the perfect location for Ben and Juli to have the conversation that changed both their lives—and so that's what happened. I always wanted to feature that lot and its beautiful trees in another story, so, as is possible in a fictional world, I borrowed the live oaks and put them in the also-borrowed setting of Emerald Isle Woods Park.

Despite my many trips to Emerald Isle over the years, I had never seen Emerald Isle Woods Park. I'm sure we must have driven past the park sign countless times—especially on the way to The Point, but I was always focused on the oceanfront. Wow, was I missing out!

Earlier this year, I visited my cousin and his family in Emerald Isle and was explaining my problem with finding the right setting for Emerald Heart—and that's when I learned about Emerald Isle Woods Park. I went to see it for myself and as I walked the trails and enjoyed the views, I knew it would be the perfect setting for The Emerald Heart Hotel, as well as a fun setting to simply write about.

One last note: In many of my books I use actual restaurants. The two restaurants named in this book, the Beach Diner and Wheeler's Grill, are totally fictional, so no need to go looking for them. Instead, there are many other wonderful restaurants to enjoy.

~ Thank you for reading Emerald Heart!!   November 2023 ~ Grace Greene

Discussion Questions

1. Grief and loss come in many forms. The loss of a spouse, a child, a parent, a beloved friend and so on, are among the most difficult we can face, but those losses may also alter other relationships, and the loss of cherished traditions. What other losses can bring us grief? Does acknowledging the loss help? Or discussing it with trusted friends or family? There are options for more persistent grief, including therapy. Grief and mourning are very individual, yet so very common in our lives. Mignon had multiple griefs piled on top of each other. How might that have made her ability to deal with the grief more difficult?

2. Blake tells Mignon that special bonds are formed when people go through events like big changes or tough times together, *"that those bonds aren't necessarily easy or pleasant," but are still bonds*. Mignon believed that her estrangement from Jeanette had absolved her of those bonds, yet her actions seem to prove otherwise. Do you agree? Do bonds exist whether they are wanted or not, and even if they aren't healthy? How do you handle them?

3. Ultimately, Mignon wanted autonomy – the freedom to choose without being constrained by the past, or by the opinions and expectations of others, however well-meaning. Does embracing autonomy give Mignon the freedom she needs to build her confidence? Does that confidence then allow her to plan for a new future and stop second-guessing herself and getting mired in *what-ifs*?

4. The symbology of Jeanette keeping the key and thus keeping the door open to returning to the *heart* of their shared history at Emerald Heart was actually unintended by the author, but given that Jeanette was hoping to find a home there, it makes sense. Mignon sees Jeanette keeping the key as hopeful, and proof that the two women are moving toward a true reconciliation. How does that mesh with the final decision about the future of The Emerald Heart Hotel?

5. What are your thoughts about Mignon's decision to bring Arthur's ashes home with her and bury the small blue package in the live oak grove? About her realizations on the cliff?

About the Author

Photo © 2018 Amy G Photography

Grace Greene is an award-winning and USA Today bestselling author of women's fiction and contemporary romance with suspense set in the countryside of her native Virginia *(The Happiness In Between, The Memory of Butterflies, the Cub Creek Series, and The Wildflower House Series)* and on the breezy beaches of Emerald Isle, North Carolina *(The Emerald Isle, NC Stories Series, and Barefoot Tides Series). A Barefoot Tide*, represented the merging of two worlds—that of Cub Creek and Emerald Isle, through the eyes of a new character, and continues in the sequel, *A Dancing Tide. Wildflower Wedding* joined *The Wildflower House Series* lineup in February 2022, and *Beach Heart* was released in June of that year.

Grace's newest release, Emerald Heart (Dec. 2023), is a single title set in Emerald Isle, but this time from the amazing vantage point of the forested area overlooking the beautiful marshes and islands and waters of Bogue Sound.

Visit www.gracegreene.com for more information, and to connect with Grace.

BOOKS BY GRACE GREENE

Emerald Isle, North Carolina Series
Beach Rental *(Book 1)*
Beach Winds *(Book 2)*
Beach Wedding *(Book 3)*
Beach Walk *(Christmas Novella)*

Barefoot Tides Two-Book Series
A Barefoot Tide *(Book 1)*
A Dancing Tide *(Book 2)*

Emerald Isle, NC Single-Title Novels and Novellas
Emerald Heart
Beach Heart
"Beach Towel" (A Short Story)
Beach Christmas *(Christmas Novella)*
Clair *(Beach Brides Novella Series)*

Cub Creek Novels ~ Series and Single Titles
Cub Creek *(Cub Creek Series, Book 1)*
Leaving Cub Creek *(Cub Creek Series, Book 2)*
The Happiness In Between
The Memory of Butterflies
A Light Last Seen

The Wildflower House Novels
Wildflower Heart *(Book 1)*
Wildflower Hope *(Book 2)*
Wildflower Christmas *(A Wildflower House Novella) (Book 3)*
Wildflower Wedding *(A Wildflower House Novella) (Book 4)*

Virginia Country Roads
Kincaid's Hope
A Stranger in Wynnedower

www.GraceGreene.com